'Til Death

CUTTER SLAGLE

Second edition

ISBN: 9798877338753

Cover art by Steve Smith
Book design by KH Koehler Design

Contents

Also by Cutter Slagle

Novels

The Next Victim

Short Works

A Motive for Murder

Another Motive for Murder

A Final Motive for Murder

Author's Note

To date, writing *'Til Death* has been one of my favorite life experiences. A week before my debut novel, *The Next Victim*, was released in 2015, I was laid off from my full-time job. This meant I got to collect unemployment and focus entirely on writing my second book. This was the first time in my life I felt like a true writer. I got to eat, sleep, and breathe this project. Although it was the first and last time—again, to date—that I've been blessed enough to be in this position, it's one that will be etched in my memory forever.

Personally and professionally, I had a lot of goals I wanted to accomplish with *TD*. And while many of them didn't come to fruition, creating this story did allow me to use the art of writing in a way I'd never done before: I used it as a healing tool. When I sat down to draft *TD*, I was still experiencing some mild heartbreak from a failed relationship. To help me get over my pain, I created Orlin Joshua Abbott, or, as he's known throughout the novel, O.J. You see, the guy I was trying to get over had been nicknamed "O.J." by yours truly. As such, I made the character a mean, awful person, a real-life monster. Of course, *TD* is one hundred percent fiction. The only thing the actual O.J. and the character O.J. have in common is a nickname.

One final note on this matter: The process worked like a charm. Looking back now, this has to be when I discovered that writing could be used as a form of therapy.

Like *The Next Victim*, *'Til Death* was published by Dolce Blant Publishing. It came out in 2016, and I got to celebrate this release in Los Angeles, with multiple book signings and events with other authors from the publishing house. This was yet another first for me, followed by a feeling of never wanting the excitement and fulfillment of "writing life" to end.

Unfortunately, life is full of surprises. *TD* didn't sell well, my unemployment ran out, and I was forced to go back to work fulltime at a marketing firm. I found it too challenging to balance a nine-to-five job, social life (I was only 29 at the time), and active pursuit of a fiction writing career. So, when my contract for *TD* expired, the novel joined *The Next Victim* on my hard drive, where it has stayed until now.

I've had the privilege to learn many things in life, including that timing is everything, and that, with age, comes wisdom and perspective. Thank God! I know that now is definitely the right time to re-release *'Til Death—Cutter's Version*. Sorry to all of you Taylor Swift fans. I just couldn't help myself.

Anyway, if you're reading this, you've chosen my second published novel as your next read, and I'm extremely grateful. Again, like *The Next Victim*, *'Til Death* has been edited and cleaned up, but the original story remains present. I hope you enjoy reading it as much as I enjoyed writing it.

To Amanda –
You're my 'til death.

1

"I think Joshua murdered those women." She made the statement without blinking. Her voice was completely flat as if she hadn't just accused her husband of being a cold-blooded killer.

"You can't be serious," he said.

"Why not?" she argued.

"You may hate the man, Cate, but that doesn't make him a monster."

"Oh, my God." She brought her trembling hand up to cover her mouth. Still, she knew the damage was already done.

She let the silence creep in slowly and linger. She wanted a minute to carefully choose her next words, but nothing came to mind.

For the first time that night, Cate became aware of the cool air sneaking in through the open kitchen window. With her cell phone in the crook of her right shoulder, she reached over the bleached white sink with both hands and pulled the glass windowpanes shut. She'd never gotten used to the fact that Southern California did get cold, especially in the evening, and even in June.

Next, Cate turned the small copper lock until she heard a *clicking* sound. She felt her back muscles tense immediately as a cruel, ironic thought washed over her: *Had she just locked a killer inside the house?*

"Cate? Are you still there, Cate?"

She heard him release a deep breath on the other end of the line. He probably even took a moment to pinch the bridge of his nose; Matt always seemed to do that when he was frustrated—and he was *definitely* frustrated. She could more than hear that in his thick tone.

"Cate?" His voice deepened.

"Yes," she answered finally. "I'm still here."

"Good."

"You don't believe me, do you?"

"I never said that I didn't believe you, Cate."

"You didn't have to, Matt. But, you've seen the bruises. You know what Joshua is capable of, his temper."

"And, *you* know the difficult situation I'm currently in," he said. "Besides, I don't think O.J. is capable of strangling two women."

That nickname. She *hated* that nickname. "You're a cop, Matt. *You*, more than anyone, should understand that people are capable of just about anything."

"I'm sorry," he whispered.

She didn't respond; she couldn't. Instead, she grabbed her half-full glass of merlot from the mahogany countertop. Cate didn't bother sipping the remains but finished the vino in one big, greedy gulp.

The liquid burned going down, but she didn't mind. Cate welcomed the sensation—enjoyed it, even. There was something oddly comforting about the way the bitter wine coursed through her small, tender body. And, the buzz. The oncoming buzz was a nice incentive, too.

"You're drinking, aren't you?"

Could Matt smell the smoky scent of the wine through the phone? "Yes," she answered. "I'm a big girl, Matt."

"Are you still taking the Ambien?"

"Only when I want to relax," she admitted. "When I can't sleep."

"Like tonight?"

She knew he couldn't see her, but Cate still rolled her eyes. "No, not tonight. Just the wine."

He sighed again. Cate could almost picture him now.

Matt was most likely outside, sitting in his favorite rocking chair on his back porch, enjoying the late summer night. The sleeves of his crisp, white dress shirt would be rolled up to his elbows, revealing his strong forearms. His black hair would be swept to the side of his face, and his light blue eyes would be focused on his perfectly manicured yard. Matt was so damn proud of that yard.

Cate could even imagine his signature scent: a citrus-type aroma mixed with a hint of sandalwood that she credited to his aftershave.

Yes, Matt often smelled as good as he looked. And, while she routinely found herself imagining life with him instead of Joshua, Cate had to remind herself quite regularly that Matt wasn't her knight in shining armor. Therefore, he wouldn't be rescuing her from this nightmare any time soon.

10

"Are you really scared of O.J., Cate? I mean, I know you two have your differences, and I want to help. Believe me, I've been *trying* to find the right way to help. But, the murders—you don't truly believe he's a part of that, do you?"

"It's probably just the wine talking."

The truth was that Cate didn't know what she actually believed, not anymore. All she knew for certain was that her husband of less than a year wasn't who she'd thought he was. Joshua was a stranger. As a result, maybe she was grasping at straws, looking for any sort of way out, even if that meant branding the man she'd once loved—maybe still loved—a killer.

"Are you sure you're okay?"

"Yes." She sank onto the soft barstool in front of the kitchen counter. Her bare feet barely met the cream-colored carpet. "I shouldn't have called so late on a Sunday. You have work in the morning."

"It's fine, really," he said through a muffled yawn. "You know I don't sleep. I was awake. Kathy's snoring seems to be getting worse."

"Oh," Cate started, but then wished she hadn't. "Kathy's there?" She knew the question was dripping with distaste, but she just couldn't help herself.

"Yeah, she came over earlier. I made dinner and she—"

"I'm going to let you go," Cate cut him off. She didn't know how his evening with Kathy had ended, and she didn't want to know. "Sleep well, Matt. Thanks for the chat."

"Anytime, kid. Get some rest."

Cate set her phone down on the counter and slowly started drumming her chipped fingernails against the hard surface. Her empty wine glass seemed to mock her, but she refused to give into temptation. She'd have to open another bottle, and Joshua would *definitely* have something to say about that.

Suddenly, Cate caught her reflection in the large, square microwave. The image almost caused her to scream.

Her chin-length blonde hair needed to be washed, and probably even highlighted. The dark circles under her eyes proved she hadn't slept in days. She could swim in the gray T-shirt that had once been so formfitting. She hadn't had an appetite in over a week.

Cate didn't recognize herself. She wasn't sure if anyone in her life would at this point.

She wanted to turn and look the other way, but she couldn't. The fact

11

that she appeared to be in her forties versus her actual age—twenty-seven—shocked her in such a way that she couldn't stop staring at herself.

"What are you doing up?"

She jumped rather guiltily at the sound of his voice. She hadn't heard him come down the stairs, but, then again, that was one of Joshua's specialties: moving like the wind. Quickly, quietly, unexpectedly.

"I asked you a question."

Cate looked into his dark eyes; she knew he'd want her full attention. "I-I-I couldn't sleep," she stuttered. "I thought a glass of wine might help."

He inched closer to her. She pivoted her body around so they were face to face. She had to look up at him, but Cate knew Joshua liked that.

He was completely naked except for a pair of blue and white checkered boxers and the gold wedding band on his left hand. His toned body glistened with a thin layer of sweat. Though the overhead light in the kitchen was dull, Cate had no trouble whatsoever noticing the perfection of his frame.

An athlete in high school, Joshua still hit the gym at least five days a week and even clocked around fifteen miles of running on top of that. From his broad biceps and tight, hairless chest all the way down to his flat stomach and infamous "V"-shaped pelvis, he had a physique that most thirty-year-old men would kill for.

One of the traits that had attracted her to Joshua in the first place was his passion. Sure, the way he looked was nice, too. Hell, in the beginning, Cate hadn't been able to keep her hands off of him. But, even more, he had an unbreakable will to take care of himself. Not just for appearances, but also for health reasons. He *wanted* to be in shape. He craved it. It was all about perfection.

"And, who were you talking to?" He arched his left eyebrow. To anyone else, his brown, disheveled hair would have been comical, but Cate knew better than to laugh.

She followed his stiff gaze down to her cell phone. Had he heard her on the phone? Or, had he just put two and two together?

Cate quickly became confused. Should she lie? He knew she and Matt were friends, but would Joshua misunderstand a phone call past midnight? She almost guaranteed it would send him into a fit of rage.

Cate decided to play Russian roulette. "I was talking to my mom. Turns out, she couldn't sleep, either, so . . ."

"You know, Cate," he said, leaning in swiftly so his nose was just an inch from her own. The heavy stench of musk was almost nauseating. "You're not a good liar. And, if I really wanted to know who you were talking to behind my back, I'd take your phone and look for myself. Of course, then I'd probably have to smash it against your pretty little face. And, you don't want that, Catie. Do you?" His tone was steady and still managed to feel as if a glass of ice water had been poured down the back of her neck.

She absolutely hated it when he called her "Catie." It made her feel so helpless like a schoolgirl being reprimanded by her teacher. Or worse, her stepfather.

"Catie, you better answer me. Do you want me to hit you?"

"No, Joshua." Her voice matched his; it was as smooth as butter. If he expected her to cry, she wasn't going to. Her tears were a weakness of the past.

"Good." He straightened his stance. Without warning, his right hand flew out. But, instead of connecting with her face, Joshua used his fist to grip a handful of her hair and give it a slight tug.

Cate never flinched. She knew this game all too well.

"I know we've had some tough times since our marriage, Catie," he started, "but there's something you need to remember."

"What's that?" Cate knew he would expect her to ask.

"You took a vow: 'til death do us part. And, that's one vow I'm going to make sure you keep."

2

Revenge was tricky. He hadn't even started planning his and still somehow knew the thought to be completely true.

On one hand, he had to be careful to not get caught. Three weeks fresh out of the can, and the last thing he wanted to do was go back. He refused to; it wasn't even an option. He'd die first. Or kill, if need be.

But, his upcoming task was about more than just not getting caught. He had to decide how far he wanted to go. How much did he want to make the guilty party suffer?

"As much as fucking possible," he muttered under his breath.

"Excuse me?"

Collins looked up at the female bartender; she'd overheard his outburst. Short, blonde-ish hair, little to no makeup, and a small lizard tattoo creeping out of the left side of her tank top—she was cute in a very white trash, never-take-home-to-mom sort of way.

Still, that didn't mean she was completely useless. Sure, he wasn't going to take her home, but Collins was almost positive the men's room offered the privacy he needed to get what he wanted from the girl. After all, he'd been away for more than a year; he was more than ready to make up for lost time.

"Did you need something else?" Her voice was raspy, and when she spoke, she leaned over the scarred barrier and not so subtly thrust her small tits toward him.

"I'll take another beer." *Yes, she was definitely going to get it.* But, first, back to his revenge plot. He had to figure out this important mission.

There just happened to be one minor snag that was poking its ugly head out: Collins wasn't exactly sure where to target his revenge. He had an idea, but before he made a move, he wanted to be one hundred percent certain.

This had been a long time coming, and he refused to screw it up now. He'd wanted to act for the past fourteen years, ever since he was eighteen and the "accident" took place.

Collins was the one who usually tried to avoid traveling down the rickety path of memory lane. *What was the point?* Especially when he was met continuously with the same burnout feeling: incompleteness—as if he were missing a limb or something.

Collins blamed the alcohol, and maybe that half a joint he'd smoked earlier for the spontaneous weight of his family drama. After all, he was still trying to build up his tolerance after it had decayed while on lockdown.

Or, maybe it was the simple fact that he'd been contemplating his revenge act and the two topics had melded together perfectly, much like gasoline and a lit match.

He picked up the sweating glass the woman had fetched him and took a long, hard swallow. Collins ignored the fact that he'd gotten mostly foam. He'd make the bitch pay later. Maybe he'd be extra rough with her.

As he set the glass of brown ale back on the bar, he purposely ignored the cracked mirror that covered the wall in front of him. Collins didn't need the bluntness of a reflection to be reminded that he was the spitting image of his father.

Collins had the same thinning, light blond hair as his father; the same dark green eyes that seemed to hide even darker secrets; a small gut that proved that no matter how many sit-ups he did, it was permanent; and, finally, an unhealthy obsession with wearing nothing but black clothing—shirts, pants, boots.

He wasn't exactly sure what he feared more, knowing he was becoming his father and that there was no way to stop it, or that he didn't *want* to stop it.

Collins was well aware of the fact that his father hadn't been perfect, but who the hell was, anyway? He'd still been a good man. Collins thought so, and his own opinion was the only one he gave two shits about.

What was that old saying? An opinion was like an asshole, everyone had one. Well, Collins didn't particularly care about anyone else's thoughts regarding his father. Or their assholes.

He took another swig of his beer. This time, he hadn't been quick enough to dodge the mirror and his streaky reflection stared back at him angrily. Collins saw his father. He shuddered.

He knew for a fact that his old man wouldn't be proud of him. Flat-out disappointed was more like it. After all, did most parents embrace a life of drugs and crime for their children?

But, that had been the life Collins had opted for, and he didn't blame anyone else for the sticky outcome except himself. Well, maybe there were a couple of other guilty-adjacent parties involved in his destructive, less-than-desirable life choices. Time would tell.

Then again, he'd just officially entered manhood when his dad suddenly dropped dead. What would have been the proper way to react to such gut-wrenching news? Finish high school? Graduate college? Pursue some pathetic nine-to-fiver while simultaneously searching endlessly for that special someone to settle down with behind a white picket fence, and then produce two-point-five children and clean up dog crap from off the front yard, all the while wearing a sparkling white smile? Was that *really* the American Dream?

Collins had done the complete opposite. Even if his father's fate had turned out differently, he suspected his life would still not have played out like some homage to the fifties—that just wasn't him.

Instead, he'd dropped out of high school, gotten involved with the local drug scene—using before dealing—and then bounced around different jails for different petty crimes for the next decade before becoming a year-long guest of the Arizona Department of Corrections facility in Winslow when he was stopped for running a red light and found with more than five grams of heroin in his possession.

Truth be told, he missed his father terribly, but Collins was grateful the old man wasn't around to see how he'd turned out. Even more, he was glad he was alone, with no family or friends to judge him or make excuses for him.

That was always the worst, the excuses.

Collins hated to hear things like, "He just fell in with the wrong crowd." Or, the even so famous, "He has a sickness." Why was naiveté so damn common when it came to loved ones and the mistakes they made?

It was all about responsibility. He hadn't fallen in with the wrong crowd, and he wasn't sick. He'd chosen his own way in life, and, like a man, he'd dealt with the consequences.

But, that was all over now. Collins might have earned the title "convicted felon," but he wasn't going to let it stop him from getting what he wanted most out of life: revenge.

He grunted into his glass, then choked down what was left of his now

16

warm beer. Collins wanted another one. Hell, he wanted at least three more, but he knew better. It had taken him a while, a lot of wasted time and money, but he had finally learned a thing or two about limits. And, if he was going to set his plan into motion, then he wasn't going to exceed those limits.

Well, for the most part, anyway.

The place was getting packed. Collins checked his gold wristwatch. It was almost noon. The lunch crowd was settling in—construction workers, patrolmen, and anyone who wanted a cheap, quick meal.

His focus stayed on the watch for a moment. He'd acquired the piece when he'd caught a trusted employee skimming off the top. The first time he'd experienced this type of problem, Collins knew he'd have to set an example. So, he'd taken the thief's watch and his hand. He'd disposed of the hand, of course, but kept the piece of jewelry.

"Can I get you anything else?"

She was back. This time, when she leaned over the bar, she winked. Collins knew the bartender wasn't asking to refill his beer. Her combined scent of berry blend and fresh sweat almost had him drooling.

He wanted it all: the beer, her, and maybe even world peace. Still, there was a time and place for everything, and, right now, he needed to be someplace else.

"Another time." He threw down a twenty-dollar bill and noticed her frown. "Don't worry. I'll be back." He added a quick wink of his own.

It was time to get serious.

Collins stood from the bar stool, barely missing an old man with a pool stick, and headed for the front exit.

Yes, revenge was certainly tricky. This was even truer if you planned on accomplishing it the right way. And, Collins planned on getting it done perfectly.

3

"How's Cate?"

"Cate is Cate," O.J. answered. "Why do you ask?"

Matt knew better than to bring up Cate, but like an annoying itch begging to be scratched, he'd gone ahead and clawed at the subject, digging for relief. Matt just couldn't seem to help himself.

Now, he was met with the difficult task of deciding what to say next. If Cate was telling the truth about O.J.'s temper—and why wouldn't she be?—then the absolute last thing he wanted to do was give the other man ammo for another fight.

"Take it from me, partner," O.J. said, "never get married."

Matt attempted to mask his confusion, but the gesture wasn't easy—even for a man who'd been known to win more than his fair share of Texas hold 'em games down at Tammi's Pub on Saturday nights.

Even though he'd managed to escape the dark corner he'd backed himself into moments ago, he couldn't resist the delicious temptation of pressing forward. What did that say about his personal feelings toward Cate?

He was afraid of the answer.

"Why *did* you get married?" Matt tried to make his voice as steady and neutral as possible. He was almost positive he'd failed. "It seems like—"

"You know why I married her, Matt," O.J. interrupted. "I didn't have a choice." The man's strong right hand clasped Matt's shoulder and gave it a slight squeeze.

The signal was loud and clear: The topic of Cate was no longer up for discussion.

Matt looked around, taking in his surroundings. The small room was almost completely full. Crowded on a good day, the space was littered with

18

six desks that all had trouble not wobbling. He couldn't speak for the other deputies, but Matt had personally chosen an old dictionary to help keep the balance at his station.

Straight ahead, a whiteboard had been rolled in and locked into place. The surface was stained with harsh images and crooked handwriting. Then again, this wasn't a mandatory workshop on how to neatly dot your *i*'s and cross your *t*'s; it was a murder investigation.

There were half a dozen men and two women in total occupying the open space. Matt found his tattered leather seat, and his head fell into a back-and-forth bobbing motion. It was as if he were watching an intense tennis match as he tried to nonchalantly study his colleagues.

A mix of race, weight, height, and age, the present taskforce was a real smorgasbord of the finest Perry's Creek had to offer—which wasn't saying much. Then again, in a town that only had one stoplight, it didn't take the biggest or brightest to write a speeding ticket or enforce the pick-up-after-your-dog rule.

Matt knew the others well and had even gone to high school with a couple of them, but he and O.J. were the oldest, had been at the department the longest, and were partners—if the term truly meant anything here.

Simply put, they'd grown up together; went to school together; graduated community college together; trained together; and now worked the same shift together, protecting their hometown. Except that it had never really needed protecting.

Until now.

"Have you heard the rumor?"

Matt turned to O.J., who had taken a seat at his own desk. "No," he answered. "What's happening?"

"The sheriff phoned a friend." O.J. nodded toward the front of the room with his cleft chin. "He doesn't have enough faith in his own team to solve the murders. It's fucking bullshit!"

So, that's who the stranger is.

Matt's boss, Sheriff Shannon Sutton, was short, slightly overweight, and had thinning black hair that he insisted on slicking back with some sort of white wax. The hair on his pear-shaped head was even thinner than the dark hair on his arms. If Hollywood ever decided to buy the film rights to his life, only one actor would fit the part: Danny DeVito.

But, some women were obviously into that look. The sheriff had been happily married for over thirty-five years.

However, the man standing next to Sutton was a stranger to Matt, and, while he appeared to be the same age as the police sheriff, the stranger carried himself with a little more couth. Or maybe he'd just been better blessed by the gene pool gods.

Sutton's guest sported a crisp navy suit tailored to perfection, black dress shoes, and a matching belt. The gray streaks in his blonde hair only added to his distinction, and it was neatly swept away from his face to reveal a handful of wrinkles, proving the man wasn't afraid of his older age. He wore his life proudly. Matt admired that.

"Okay, everyone, quiet down and listen up." Sheriff Sutton's small voice somehow managed to fill the room. "First, thank you all for being here this morning. For some of you, this isn't your shift or even your day to work. I appreciate that you're all here. We may be a small team, but we're still a team, nonetheless."

"Who the hell is he trying to impress?" O.J. whispered.

"As you all know," the sheriff continued, "we have a situation here. A bad one. This is probably one of the worst cases Perry's Creek has ever seen. And to make matters worse, I've got Mayor Jackson on my hide. So…"—Matt watched as Sutton slowly turned and faced the man in the suit.—"…drastic times call for drastic measures."

O.J. leaned toward Matt. "Like this old man is really going to be able to help the department."

Matt shrugged. "I guess we'll see." To him, the stranger's grays, wrinkles, and age only proved one thing: experience.

"This is Beau Reynolds, and he's here in an *unofficial* capacity."

O.J.'s hand shot up into the air. "What does that mean, Sheriff?"

"I'm getting there, Deputy Abbott. Let me finish."

Matt managed to disguise his impromptu fit of laughter as a dry coughing spell. Nothing had changed since high school: O.J. was still getting into trouble with the teacher.

"As I was saying, Beau is here to help us. He's doing me a favor. And, while he's not a man of the law anymore, he will still be treated like a professional, with only the utmost respect. You will be reporting to him.

"Beau is here from about an hour west of us. San Diego. He has plenty of experience with these types of cases. Pardon my language"—the sheriff crossed his arms—"but Beau knows his shit."

Matt decided that that must have been the man's cue, as he and the sheriff did a sloppy two-step: Beau moved forward, and Sutton faded into the background by the whiteboard.

"Good morning, Deputies. As Sheriff Sutton stated, I'm Beau Reynolds. I'm here to help catch the son of a bitch who has strangled two women."

Matt thought it was interesting to hear the man speak. His voice was dry, deep, and, though soft, still made a reasonable impact.

"Once upon a time, I was a detective and solved quite a few cases for the City of San Diego and its surrounding areas. But, just because I've lost my title doesn't mean I've lost my hunger or ability to stop these types of scumbags. Like Shannon said: I know my shit.

"Basically, I'm here to offer a fresh set of eyes. From what I've been told, no one in this room has ever worked a murder investigation. That's fine. We may be able to use that to our advantage.

"Now, it's my job to show you how to work the clues and pick apart what we already have. Because, quite honestly, if we can't solve this case now, with what the killer has already left us, then we're not good cops. And, chances are that we'll never find the person responsible for these murders."

"Is it just me," O.J. said, "or is this guy a fucking joke?"

Matt never got a chance to offer up his own opinion.

"Excuse me." Beau tilted his head toward O.J. "What's your name, Deputy?"

O.J. noisily cleared his throat. "I'm Deputy O.J. Abbott, sir."

"All right," Beau said. "Did you have a question, Deputy O.J. Abbott? Because you seem to be rather chatty this morning."

"No, sir," O.J. answered. "No question."

"Then, can I continue, Deputy?"

"Yes, sir."

"Thank you."

Matt didn't have to look over to confirm O.J.'s anger; he knew his friend's face would be red, his teeth would be firmly pressed into his bottom lip, and his eyes wide. Hell, he'd probably even begun to sweat at the base of his neck. O.J. had never been one to accept public humiliation calmly.

"Now," Beau moved on, "I'd like to start today's briefing by going over the crime scene photos. There's an obvious pattern here, and we need to find out why. What does this pattern mean to the killer?

"Answering this question will lead us to the person responsible for the murders. And, due to the small size of the community, at least one of you in this room knows who that person is—you just haven't realized it yet."

21

Matt could barely catch his breath, and his gaze immediately drifted to O.J. Could Cate's suspicions about her husband be accurate?

4

The first time Joshua hit her was on their honeymoon. The blow had come completely unexpected. Cate wasn't even sure what had originally set her new husband off, but she assumed it had been trivial.

After all, she believed that was how most domestic disturbance stories went. The husband comes home from work to find his dinner cold and beer warm, ultimately pushing him into a fit of rage. Or, was it the simple aggravation of another grueling day at the office that led to the need to beat something or someone?

Either way, now, nearly ten months later, she was getting better at determining what put her husband in his angry place.

Joshua liked to have a clean home. Joshua liked to have dinner waiting for him on the table each night. Joshua liked to have sex at least three times a week.

And, these "main rules" were just the beginning.

Their relationship hadn't always been that way. At one time, Joshua had been sweet, caring, even romantic. Cate had been attracted to the loving side of him, the only side she thought had existed, and she hated to admit that she still was, even though that side rarely made an appearance anymore.

They'd met by fate, if fate truly existed. Cate used to think it did, but now she wondered if she'd met Joshua because of something even worse like karma.

She and her mother had just moved to Perry's Creek. They'd been in Southern California for less than forty-eight hours. Cate had gone in search of lunch, leaving her mom to finish unpacking the three medium-sized cardboard boxes that would eventually make up the dining room. Lost and hungry, Cate ran a stop sign, putting her directly in Deputy Abbott's sights.

However, after a quick back and forth, Joshua hadn't asked for her license and registration, but her phone number. *The beginning of the end* was how Cate now considered that first encounter because exactly two months later, they'd gotten married.

"I must be a masochist," Cate whispered aloud. She looked into the round mirror that hung in the upstairs hallway.

She hated thinking about the dark, uneven path that was her past. After all, what was the point? Especially when the bulk of that journey consisted of heartaches and twisted nightmares?

Sometimes, though, it was as if Cate didn't have a choice. Her past decisions often swam into view with Olympian-like speed, offering no rhyme or reason.

Again, she contributed the self-torture to karma. Because her previous mistakes were frequently too hard to ignore or swat away, she'd usually give in and remember them, allowing the less-than-desirable moments to play out like some poorly written TV movie of the week that only she had been given access to watch—her life sentence, no judge or jury needed.

The sudden knock on the front door made Cate frown. She wasn't used to having visitors on a Wednesday morning at 10:00 a.m. Still, without looking, she knew who her guest was. Only one possibility made any sense.

Cate rounded the corner and started down the hardwood stairs. Directly in front of her was the white front door surrounded on two sides by two tall, skinny windows. Her mother stared back at her from the right side of the entrance, a deeply disappointing look already stretched across her tight face.

The woman was attractive, and, at the age of fifty-one, still very much concerned with her appearance. That much was crystal clear by her over-applied lipstick and mascara, as well as her teased, bleached hair.

Cate's mother often seemed to forget that she was a mom, wearing colorful blouses that were either too tight or too low-cut. The one she sported today was hot pink, sleeveless, and tucked into very form-fitting jeans. Open-toed, leather wedges completed the outfit, adding minimal height to the woman's five-foot-seven, average frame.

"The door is locked, Cate!" she shouted through the window. "Why is the door locked?"

Cate didn't answer the question. Instead, she half-smiled at her mom, turned the deadbolt, and pulled open the door.

"Hi, Mom."

"Why was your door locked?" Her mother bypassed Cate in the foyer and headed directly for the living room off to the left.

"To keep out the unwanted."

"Like your husband?"

"That's not funny, Mom." Cate closed the door and then twisted the deadbolt. "I take it you read the paper? Two women have been murdered, and the killer hasn't been caught."

"You worry too much, Cate. You've always been that way, and I don't know why." Her mom chose to sit on the charcoal couch stationed in the corner of the room—or the "sitting room," as Joshua often called it.

The small room, surrounded by floor-to-ceiling windows, didn't offer a TV, stereo system, or any other form of entertainment—just a skylight, views of the wide, vacant country surroundings, and enough furniture to comfortably seat five people.

Cate chose the matching cloth chair directly opposite her mother. "I'm pretty sure you know why I worry so much."

"Don't be that way, Catie Cat. I didn't come here to fight. I promise."

Cate knew deep down that her mom was most likely telling the truth. The woman wasn't much of a fighter. Still, sometimes it was just so damn easy to start an argument with her. They shared a muddy past, and disagreements were bound to happen.

"I thought we could spend the day together, Catie. Maybe get our nails done or have a girl's lunch?"

"I can't today, Mom. I have to work in an hour." Even at the age of twenty-seven, Cate hated to disappoint her mother. Perhaps it had something to do with the fact that it was a feat that was getting easier to accomplish, or because her mother seemed to wear the look of a victim all too well.

Regardless, intentional or not, Cate's mom had mastered the talent of making others feel guilty.

"Work?" Georgia's voice went up an octave. It was as if the word was foreign to the woman. "I don't understand why you're working. You're married now. The least Orlin could do is ensure that you don't have to have a job."

"I work because I want to. I like having a job," Cate admitted. "It gives me a purpose. And, don't call him Orlin. You know he hates that."

Georgia nodded. "Why else do you think I keep doing it?"

Cate rolled her eyes but couldn't resist cracking a small smile. The woman was a real pain in the ass and the root cause behind a lot of Cate's troubles, but at the end of the day, she was family—Cate's only family besides Joshua. No matter what had happened, Cate still loved her mother.

"Can't you call in sick? We haven't spent the whole day together in a long time."

"No. Jerry's going out of town next week, and he needs to teach me a few things about the new system."

"You manage a coffee shop, Cate. What do you need to learn? The difference between decaf and regular?"

"Most mothers would be happy if their daughter had a thriving career, not ask them to blow the day off to get a manicure."

"Not just a manicure, sweetie," Georgia said. "I was also planning on springing for a pedicure."

"Not funny, Mom."

"Okay, okay." Georgia raised her hands, the gold bracelets on her left wrist colliding with her watch and creating a jingle-jangle sound. "Well, I'm already here. Do you have time to make some coffee? Or, is that cruel to ask since you have to go do that at work soon?"

"No, Mother," Cate said. "I already put on a pot a few moments ago. It should be ready by now."

Cate stood and started for the kitchen with her mom close behind. They passed a similar room that at least offered a TV and a couple of landscape paintings that Joshua had picked out. They dodged the dining room and its glass table for four and settled in the kitchen, with Georgia trading her spot on the couch for a tall bar stool. Cate set out to pour the coffee.

"Cream, right?"

"Please," Georgia said.

Cate placed a white mug in front of her mom, then leaned back against the counter while she sipped her own drink. "What's new, Mother?"

"I hate when you call me that, Cate."

"Fine. What's up, Mom?"

"Well, since we're on the subject, I want to make sure that working is *really* your choice. Not your husband's."

Cate sighed. "You're still on that kick? After all these months? Yes, Mom, I choose to work. Joshua doesn't make me. I think I should earn my own way. And, I want to."

"Honestly, I don't know why either of you works, not when you have

26

that so-called inheritance."

"The money is real, Mom. It's sitting in our joint checking account, mocking me."

"Joint checking account?"

"Joshua gave us both access to the inheritance from his grandfather, but I know it's a test. He's trying to tempt me into spending *his* money so he has yet another reason to be mad at me."

"He's a peach," Georgia said between sips.

"Besides, it's not like it's enough to live on. Twenty-five thousand dollars? Please. And, Joshua would never give up being a cop. It gives him too much power."

"Honey, on a busy day, he may administer a Breathalyzer test or two. He's not saving the world, and he's sure as shit not protecting Perry's Creek. You just said it yourself: There's a killer on the loose."

Cate bit her lower lip. Her conversation with Matt from the night before came sprinting back to mind. "No matter what, he's never going to give up the badge."

"Is he still adamant about having a baby?"

Cate nodded. Her mother knew that was a sore subject with her, so why did she always insist on bringing it up? Of course Joshua still wanted to have a baby. Well, a baby boy, as if Cate had some control over the sex of the child.

"Does that mean you're actively trying?" Georgia asked.

"You mean," Cate corrected, "am I sleeping with my husband on a regular basis? I'm avoiding it as much as I can."

"Not even a year in, and you hate having sex with your husband already." Georgia raised her coffee mug and took a long gulp. "It usually takes a little longer than that."

"What can I say?" Cate shrugged. "He's not the man I thought he was."

"Most of them aren't. I thought I taught you that."

Cate pushed her half-empty mug away. She was shaking. The last thing she needed was more caffeine. "He's not going to change, Mom. I *know* he's not going to change. And, I refuse to bring a baby into our dynamic."

She felt the weight of tears beginning to form at the corners of her eyes. Cate didn't want to cry—she'd done that enough over Joshua—but she was so damned exhausted.

"Oh, honey." Georgia reached over the counter for Cate's hands.

"I mean, can you imagine? Joshua and me having a baby?"

"No, I can't," Georgia answered. "Maybe…maybe what happened on your honeymoon was a good thing."

Cate immediately slid her hands back and crossed her arms over her chest. "My husband started beating me on our honeymoon. For no reason. As soon as I said, "I do," Joshua began treating me like his property. And, because of it, because of his temper and unexplained cruelty, I lost…"

"I know, Cate. You don't have to say it."

"No, I think I do, Mother. I think I do need to say it." Her voice became louder, thicker. Cate didn't recognize it. "My husband started beating me on our honeymoon, and because of it, I lost my baby. How the hell is that a good thing?"

"I didn't mean it like that, Catie. What happened that night bothers me too, still. But, you said so yourself—"

"I'm sorry," Cate interrupted. "I'm just frustrated." She let her arms fall to her sides. Too embarrassed to look at anyone, especially her mother, she stared at the tile-covered floor. "I just don't know how I got here. How did I get to this suffocating place in my life?"

"Leave him."

Cate shook her head. "It's not that easy."

"It is, Cate. Don't make the same mistakes I made."

"I honestly don't have a choice in the matter. He won't let me leave."

"What does that mean?"

"He's a cop. I'm stuck. He may not have a lot of power, but he has enough. You don't know what Joshua can do, Mom. If I run, he'll find me. He won't divorce me and chance tarnishing his reputation or the memory of his parents. Don't you remember? He comes from a good, traditional Christian upbringing."

"Right." Georgia nodded. "Divorce may be frowned upon, but, by all means, raise a hand to your wife and no one will bat an eye."

"He married me so quickly because he got me pregnant. And, now that we've taken that vow—"

"He's going to kill you, Cate. Maybe not today or tomorrow, but eventually…"

"I know." Cate stopped her mother. "I'm beginning to realize that more and more."

Georgia stood and placed her hands on her hips. "Then there's only one thing to do."

"What?" Cate frowned.

"Kill him first."

"You're not serious?"

"Why wouldn't I be serious, Cate? Your husband is going to kill you one day, probably soon, and he'll make certain to get away with it. Do you want that to happen? Do you want to die?"

The room started to spin and Cate's vision became blurry. "No! How can you even say that? But, I can't kill my husband."

"Why not?"

"Because I'm not a murderer, Mother!"

"Yes, you are, Cate," Georgia said calmly. "You've killed before, and you can do it again. If you want to survive, you'll have to."

5

Truth be told, he was a drunk. It was that simple.

But, he wasn't just any old drunk; he was a great drunk. Over the years of choking down beer, rum, vodka, and his absolute favorite—whiskey—he'd learned to hide his addiction quite well. And, he was proud of that feat.

So, maybe, he contemplated, *"great" wasn't the best word to use*. No, Beau Reynolds wasn't a great drunk; he was a secret drunk. And, he worked overtime to make sure his little issue stayed that way.

Among the other issues in his life.

Of course, now that he no longer carried a badge, keeping his drinking problem under wraps wasn't as big of a necessity as it once was.

Still, Beau had a reputation to protect, and the last thing he wanted was to be caught in an act that would tarnish his image or take away from all of the good he'd done for the City of San Diego throughout his career.

He'd made an important decision a long time ago, a decision that was still in effect today: Beau only drank when he was home and alone. It was the only way to cover up his weakness.

Gone were the days of falling down drunk and chipping teeth, getting punched in the face by the wrong guy, and then later having to come up with a believable excuse as to why he had a black eye.

Hell, since he'd decided to make his drinking habits a party for one, he'd not only saved money and avoided embarrassing encounters, but Beau also managed to prove he didn't need anyone else around to have a good time. He was a loner, and it was by being alone that he'd managed to fuck up his life thoroughly.

Beau let his bare feet glide across the rough carpet of the seedy motel room. He knew better than to let flesh directly touch the dirty brown flooring, but at the moment, he was too drunk to care what was living in the shag fabric.

He made his way to the tall dresser where the half-empty bottle of amber liquor waited for him. *Just one more drink*, the glass container seemed to suggest. *Another big swig can finish me off.*

Beau staggered slightly as he reached for the whiskey. The paper cup in his left hand felt damp like it could fall apart at any given moment, but he didn't care. After all, the alcohol wouldn't be stationary for long. It was a quick trip from bottle to cup to lips.

The motion was fast and practiced, and Beau came alive after the hefty shot. Deciding not to waste any more time pouring, he let the paper cup fall to the floor, gripped the uncapped bottle, and walked backward until he fell on the bed.

He'd stayed in worse places, that was for sure, places that made the Dumpster in back alleys feel like five-star hotels. In his industry, it wasn't as if anyone willingly sprang for a room with the works. In fact, when he'd worked cases that required overnight travel, a room with a so-so warm bed and semi-clean shitter was considered accommodating.

The shitter in this room wasn't too bad, but the bed—could use some improvement. The ex-detective had never been a fan of lumpy mattresses, or, for that matter, white sheets. Seriously, did white sheets ever come clean?

Still, Beau knew he didn't have much of a choice. Perry's Creek offered only one option to visitors: Scott's Inn. And, that was exactly how he'd managed to find himself up a creek and without a paddle.

He had shelter—better shelter than he'd ever had growing up. Case closed.

Beau took another gulp from the whiskey bottle and then set it down by the plastic lamp on the nightstand. He picked up the manila folder that had the word "Confidential" stenciled across the cover.

It was time to get to work.

With his tie dangling loosely from around his neck and his dress shirt un-tucked and rolled up at the sleeves, Beau leaned back against the headboard and opened the file. He had two murders to solve.

The first victim, Stephanie Karr, had been strangled about two weeks ago on Friday, June 3. If the killer had left any sort of evidence behind, the person and responding deputy who had found the body wrecked it.

Karr had been discovered by her neighbor lady. No sign of forced entry, and the body had been on the living room floor. It appeared the killer had

'TIL DEATH

entered the home, crept up behind Karr, and squeezed the life out of her. Not hard to do to a twenty-five-year-old woman who stood five-foot-two and weighed less than one hundred pounds.

Time of death had been estimated between the hours of midnight and 2:00 a.m., leaving local authorities to believe Karr hadn't been able to sleep, and, therefore, had ventured downstairs to watch a little late-night TV, which had still been blaring the next morning, ultimately alerting the nosy neighbor lady.

The blonde-haired, blue-eyed Caucasian cashier hadn't had a boyfriend, girlfriend, or any known enemies, according to her parents and closest friends. It was more of a wrong time, wrong place, situation. Except the place had been the victim's own apartment.

Had Karr been mixed up with something unknowingly? Had she been watched, targeted? Had she been chosen at random?

Beau made a mental note. These questions topped his list.

He shuffled through the handful of photos that accompanied the file. Determining the motive behind Karr's murder was proving to be difficult.

Karr's clothing had been intact, her sleepwear of a pink tank top and matching shorts untouched. It was obvious the victim hadn't been raped or touched inappropriately. Just murdered.

The bruising around Karr's dainty neck had been thick: an angry shade of dark purple. However, there hadn't been any prints left on the body. The killer had been smart and put on gloves before completing the act of strangulation.

Though Beau had not personally seen inside the girl's home, according to the pictures he was still studying, Karr hadn't been known for being overly tidy.

What appeared to be a mixture of clean and dirty laundry littered the hallway, food-stained dishes were left out on the wooden countertop, and dust had settled across all the surfaces of the living room. Piles of mail and notices, including an unpaid speeding ticket, rested upon the dining room table.

Karr's lack of neatness made it hard to decide if the Perry's Creek Police Department was dealing with a robbery-turned-homicide or something else. Most likely something else, considering cash had been found in the victim's purse. Not to mention that other valuables had been left throughout the home.

However, something *had* been missing from the crime scene: Karr's left

32

earring.

An inexpensive piece of junk jewelry, Beau assumed the small pair of round, opal earrings could be purchased at any discount chain department store. Therefore, money hadn't been the purpose of the theft. The killer had taken a souvenir. But, why?

Beau made another mental note.

It could be argued that Karr had lost or misplaced one of her earrings, resulting in her only having one at the time of her death, but then victim two was found less than a week ago, on Monday, June 13, evoking the words that no one, specifically Mayor Jackson and Sheriff Sutton, wanted to hear: serial killer.

Sure, the killer would have to knock off a few more victims before the title could be rightfully earned, but Beau truly believed that was the game Perry's Creek killer was getting ready to play. And, Shelly Marthers helped prove it.

Like Karr, Marthers had been small—short and skinny—blonde, blue-eyed, and strangled to death. Her neck had also been bruised, but no prints were found on the body.

Again, there was no sign of forced entry into the home, leading Beau to believe that most of the town was either incompetent, living in a fantasy world, or both. Therefore, they didn't feel the need to lock any of their doors.

Beau knew otherwise. There was no such thing as a "safe" neighborhood.

Unlike the first victim, Marthers was found in bed, and it was likely she was awoken by her killer. Again, the time of death had been estimated between the hours of midnight and 2:00 a.m. Again, the girl's left earring—a small diamond stud, this time—had been taken.

Beau didn't believe in coincidences. The strangler was taking trophies. So, when they found the perpetrator, the victims' jewelry would be enough evidence to prove guilt.

But, first, of course, they had to *find* said perpetrator.

According to various notes and statements, the victims hadn't been friends. Sure, they'd most likely known each other, as did most people in Perry's Creek. They'd gone to high school together, but Karr had graduated a year ahead of Marthers. The two hadn't belonged to any of the same clubs or played any of the same sports.

Victim two, a nurse, had also lived alone, but in a different apartment complex. According to pictures, she'd been so organized that an obsessive-compulsive disorder was questioned.

Simply put, Karr and Marthers didn't seem to have too much in common, except for the fact that both victims had been blonde, blue-eyed, and shared the same body type. There was *that*, of course.

The killer had a type. Finally, something the Perry's Creek Police Department could work with.

Beau placed the reports, photographs, and other documents back in the folder, closed it, and tossed it onto the floor. He'd had enough shop for one night.

He bridged his hands together, placed them at the back of his neck, and stretched his legs across the queen-sized bed. One of the bonuses of being single his whole life, Beau had grown accustomed to sleeping the way he wanted to.

He contemplated turning on the sizeable flat-screen TV—the only amenity the room had to offer—but that would have required him to get up and walk back to the dresser to fetch the remote. Hell, Beau didn't even possess enough energy to roll over and finish off...

A noise! There was some sort of shuffling.

Someone was outside his motel room!

Beau was on his feet as if caffeine had suddenly replaced all of the alcohol in his body. Beau was together, alert, and ready to face the unknown.

He lunged for the leather suitcase he'd discarded earlier on the small chair by the dresser. He rifled through layers of socks and underwear before closing in on something cold and solid: his Glock.

Beau raised the registered piece. Yet another bad habit he'd never been able to break—the safety on his weapon was already off. He started for the entrance of the room.

He didn't bother messing around with the thick red curtain that blocked the front window. Beau wasn't interested in a sneak attack. Balls to the wall, he was going for broke.

In one swift movement, he released the chain and deadbolt and flung open the door. He looked into the black night and pointed his gun.

Shannon stared back at him.

"What the hell, Beau?" The sheriff, unarmed, raised his hands. "Have you been drinking? It's just me."

"Shannon?" Beau lowered his gun. "What are you doing here? It's past ten."

"I know, I know." The sheriff nodded. "I wasn't sure if you were up, so I stood outside and thought about—"

"You could have called or sent a text message."

"Right," the other man said breathlessly.

"Well, at least come in." Beau opened the door wider. "Tell me what's going on."

Shannon didn't move a muscle. Eyes wide, he didn't even blink. "We've got a problem," he said in one quick exhale. "She knows."

6

Someone was in her house! She just knew it!

Georgia stood in the kitchen with her back pressed firmly against the stainless-steel refrigerator. She had a decision to make, and not much time to make it: fish around in her purse for her cell phone or dart out the back door.

She glanced over the granite countertop where her bag lay open. Could she find her phone, dial 9-1-1, and then hide? Or was she better off taking her chances out in the dark all alone?

The day's previous events flashed in front of her mind's eye. How had she gotten here?

Spending quality time with Cate had been a disappointing bust. It wasn't as if Georgia hadn't noted all of the girl's hard work. Of course she was proud of her daughter. Lately, though, Georgia felt like she and Cate were slipping apart, losing a chunk of that close bond the two of them had always shared.

Did having a career in this day and age mean having to forfeit relationships? Change who you were, your lifestyle? Did it mean no longer having adequate time to spend with your own mother? Georgia refused to believe it. Still, Cate had been insistent on going to the coffee house and working her shift, resulting in Georgia spending the entire day alone.

Georgia had begun her adventure with a manicure and pedicure. She'd chosen an appropriate light pink hue for summer, naturally.

For about a year now, Perfection Nails had proven itself a relaxing and pampering atmosphere, and today was no different. There was just something so calming—or was it empowering?—about having another person massage your feet and decorate your nails. Georgia reveled in the opportunity.

Next, she'd gone to lunch. Again, by herself. Her late husband had rarely allowed her to eat out at restaurants, so Georgia tried to indulge in the act as much as her fixed income would allow. After all, lavish meals weren't quite the necessity that beauty maintenance and personal upkeep were to her.

Then again, Perry's Creek wasn't exactly known for gourmet meals or a wide variety of menus.

Georgia had gone to a popular eatery in the middle of town, a place that served breakfast twenty-four-seven, didn't have tablecloths, and offered a view of the small courthouse. At least the establishment had its liquor license. Georgia treated herself to a glass of pinot with her Greek salad.

She'd left her car in the parking lot in favor of walking to the locally owned shops across the street. Not that she was overly excited about handmade jewelry produced from various beads and fishing wire, or clothing that was either overpriced or lacked any sort of appeal for women over forty who weren't into lace or fringe. Typical boutiques. Georgia often wondered how they managed to stay out of the red.

Nonetheless, she liked supporting her own, especially when her own meant avoiding a thirty-minute drive to the nearest mall. Though she'd wandered through the line of brick stores optimistically, having purchased a belt and a few cute trinkets in the past, she'd ultimately gone back to her car empty-handed.

A late afternoon movie followed at the town's cinema that usually received films a month after their initial release, and then she'd gone to the store to grab a few items for dinner.

Georgia had just placed her plate and bowl in the dishwasher when she heard the footsteps.

"Dammit!" She'd crossed to the fridge and tried to peer down the dark hallway that led to the entrance of her house.

What was her next move?

It was obvious she was home. The overhead light in the kitchen was shining, and she was almost positive she'd left the television on in the front living room. If the intruder's agenda was robbery, he'd been gutsy enough to choose a home that wasn't empty.

Unless he also wasn't afraid to commit murder.

Georgia's heart started pounding. For a second, she thought it was going to burst right out of her chest. Cate had just mentioned the killer in Perry's Creek. Two women had recently been strangled.

Is that what this was about? Nothing to do with robbery at all. Was Georgia next on the murderer's list?

She took another quick peek at her purse but forced herself to come to terms with reality. There was no way the cops could get to her in time. At best, she lived fifteen minutes from the police department. She didn't know for certain but guessed it only took seconds to squeeze the life out of someone.

She had a new decision to make: run or stay. If she ran, where would she go? And if she stayed, did she hide? Or try and fight?

Another ear-splitting noise. This time, it was a *creaking* sound. Georgia placed it at the center of the house, the stairs. He was less than one hundred feet away from her—but was he going up or coming down?

Georgia eased away from the appliance she'd backed herself against. She prayed silently that the hardwood floor underneath her bare feet wouldn't alert the intruder of her whereabouts. She was going to make a run for it. Georgia knew that was her best bet for survival.

She peered down the dark hallway again. The dim light from the stairs created a large shadow against the far wall. Whoever was in her house wasn't moving. They were stationary. Perhaps contemplating their next move?

Georgia pivoted, reached for her purse on the counter, threw the strap over her arm, and darted for the back door. She twisted the deadbolt, turned the round knob, and that's when it happened: the quick, heavy thuds.

The intruder was running down the stairs!

Georgia swung open the door. The late-night, summer air hit her in the face. It was cool, and her entire body shivered.

Georgia heard the intruder hit the first-floor landing. He was moving. But, not toward her. His echoing steps were easy to place. He was moving to the front of the house.

Georgia froze. Was he leaving?

The footsteps thudded down the short hallway. The front door burst open and then slammed shut. An immediate stillness filled the house.

Georgia was afraid to breathe. Her jaw hung open loosely. Still standing in the doorway, she again found herself plagued with not knowing what to do.

Seconds ticked by, causing the hair on Georgia's bare arms to stand tall. The slow ticking sound from the oval clock above the sink had her wanting to scream in agony. Was this what torture felt like? Goosebumps covered every inch of her, and sweat formed at the small of her back.

And then Georgia had a thought: *What if he was coming around to this side of the house? What if the intruder was headed for the backdoor?*

She didn't waste another moment. Georgia stepped back into the kitchen and shut and locked the door. She pushed away the checkered curtain and looked out the small glass window beside the door, but she couldn't see anything. Just darkness.

Georgia felt trapped. Her bag became heavy suddenly as if it had been filled with a large number of bricks. She let it fall to the floor before cupping her face in the palms of her hands. She ran her fingers through her thick hair. She was stalling, but for what? Until she was attacked?

Finally, she'd had enough. Georgia turned around and started for the front of the house. She'd deadbolt the door, and then she'd call the police. Problem solved.

Georgia tiptoed down the hallway, holding onto the gray wall for support. The door directly in front of her was closed, and the stairs to her left were empty. She considered...wait! She stopped. The stairs weren't empty.

Something lay on the carpet of the bottom step, a sheet of white notebook paper. It had been ripped in half. Words were printed across the page, but Georgia couldn't quite make all of them out.

She bent down to grab the sheet, feeling the roughness of the tear. She brought the paper closer to her face. Eyes wide, she read the statement.

A gasp escaped her quivering lips, and her left hand automatically shot up to cover her mouth. She dropped the sheet and it slowly glided to the floor.

Georgia could no longer read the threat, but the black ink was stained into her mind:

I know what you did! I'm going to make you pay!

"Why is my bacon cold?"

Cate didn't answer her husband—at least, not right away. She was too busy staring into her coffee mug, contemplating what her mother said to her yesterday.

You've killed before and you can do it again. The words still pierced Cate's mind as if they were part of a bad pop song some cruel radio host had set on repeat. She couldn't quite shake them.

"Cate? Are you listening to me, Cate?"

That night was stuck in her memory; she'd never be able to forget it. Cate had come to terms with the fact a long time ago. Like an unfortunate birthmark that couldn't be removed, that ill-fated event would always be a part of her. In a way, it now defined her. But, that didn't mean it was necessary to talk about it.

When Cate and her mother left Arizona a year ago, they'd agreed to leave the past in the past and never talk about that night again. Perry's Creek was supposed to be a new start, a new life. The last thing they needed was that life plagued by prior ghosts.

So, why had her mother broken their code of silence?

After all, that night *had* been an accident. It wasn't as if Cate could or would commit murder again.

"Ignoring me, Catie? I asked you a question."

"Ah!" Cate screamed. "You're hurting me, Joshua!"

"Not the best way to start your morning, Catie."

Joshua had managed to sneak up behind her. He had gripped a fist full of her hair, and every time he said her name, he gave it a tight pull.

Fearful she might slip off the barstool, Cate reached out and grabbed the counter for support.

"Please, Joshua," she begged. "Let go."

"First, answer my question," he ordered.

Cate's neck jerked back stiffly and her head started pounding. "Please…"

"Answer my question."

"I-I-I don't know what you asked."

"So," Joshua taunted in a low voice, "you weren't listening to me. You *were* ignoring me."

"No, Joshua, I wasn't—"

"No?" He gave her hair another tug. "And now you're arguing with me."

"I'm sorry," Cate whispered. "I didn't mean to—"

"Why do you constantly insist on making me mad, Cate? Do you like it when I get mad? Do you like it when I have to punish you?"

"No." Her voice rose. "Of course not."

"Then why do you keep doing it?"

"I'm not trying to make you mad, Joshua."

He let go of her hair. Before she had time to breathe a sigh of relief, Joshua's right hand flew up and the back struck her cheek swiftly.

Cate fell to the floor. The strike to her face stung, and she touched the raw skin immediately, praying a bruise or welt wouldn't form. She had to be at work soon, and Jerry would *definitely* notice a mark.

"Get up!" Joshua demanded.

Cate found her footing and stood slowly. Tears burned at the corners of her eyes and begged for release. She ignored them. Cate refused to give Joshua the satisfaction of showing him the smack had hurt.

Truth be told, the blow had hurt—a lot—but Cate had been expecting it. Over the course of their short marriage, Joshua had become transparent. Already tightly wound, he was getting worse. Cate wasn't sure why, exactly, but she had her suspicions.

"You made me do that to you, Cate."

She didn't respond. Cate stood tall, shoulders back, completely motionless. She stared into her husband's dark, rage-filled eyes. She breathed in his nauseating musk scent. There was something unnatural about him, inhuman. Joshua didn't just have a hunger to be in control; it was much more than that. It was something deeper. He enjoyed hurting her. He seemed to get off on creating pain.

"Are you okay, Cate?"

41

"I'm fine." She knew she'd chosen the wrong tone immediately. She couldn't help but assume he was going to hit her again.

And, he did.

The back of his hand connected with her face once more, the same soft spot as before. However, this time, Cate didn't go down. She'd been ready for the blow. She reached out for the barstool, gripped it, and managed to hold herself up.

"Good reflexes," Joshua stated. "It looks like someone is catching on. Now, if you could only learn to control that mouth."

Cate pushed her hair out of her face. Joshua's fingernail had caught her cheek and ripped the flesh. She felt a small trickle of blood as it slowly began coursing down toward her chin. The sensation was almost ticklish.

"I'm sorry, Joshua." She swiped at the blood. Cate was relieved to discover she wouldn't need a bandage. It was more of a scratch than a cut, and Cate knew the blemish would be easy to conceal.

Torn between wanting to be brave and stand up to her attacker, but also needing to protect herself from being Joshua's personal punching bag, Cate reached for her coffee mug and sidestepped her husband. She started for the kitchen.

Distance—no matter how much—was definitely a tool of survival. If Joshua wasn't within arm's length of her, he couldn't lash out and hit her sporadically.

"I should have been listening to you." She poured the rest of what was sure to be ice-cold coffee into the sink. "Again, I'm sorry."

Survival Tip Number Two: Always admit you're wrong and then apologize. Then, when you're done doing that, apologize again. Survival Tip Number Three.

"It's a learning process, Catie." Joshua crossed his arms. "Apparently, a slow process, but you do learn something new every single day."

It used to be difficult to look at him after he beat her, especially when he was in uniform. As her husband, he was supposed to protect her and keep her safe, but as a cop, it was his profession. However, in the short ten months they'd been married, Cate had gotten pretty damned good at swallowing the irony of the situation. As if she really had a choice.

"I want some more coffee."

"Coming right up." Cate didn't miss a beat. She grabbed Joshua's mug from the counter, turned, and took a few steps to the other side of the kitchen where the pot was stationed.

She'd been smart to brew another pot after frying the bacon and scrambling the eggs. Joshua liked to take a thermos to work with him. Again, Cate had had to learn that the hard way. Now, there was enough coffee for him to have another mug or two at home, as well as plenty to get him to the police department.

Mug full and warm to the touch, Cate placed it in front of him. He'd resumed his seat at the counter, but not before pushing his plate of bacon to the side. Cate reached for it and then went to the sink.

"Are you throwing that out?"

Cate stopped. She stared down at the bacon as if the meat might contain the answer that Joshua wanted to hear. Most likely a trick question. Cate quickly contemplated how to respond to it.

Her heart began fluttering. The wrong answer could send Joshua into a fit of rage, but silence...silence could...

He cleared his throat. She almost dropped the glass plate.

"I-I-I thought you were done," she whispered. "Y-y-you pushed the plate—"

"You're damn right I did," he interrupted. "I'm not going to eat cold food."

"I'm sorry," she repeated. Cate tried to survive; she *wanted* to survive. The tips had to work.

"I don't like it when you're wasteful, Cate. Remember?"

"I'll do better next time, Joshua. I promise."

"I hope so. I really do."

Cate let the conversation die with his warning. She opened the lower cabinet, tossed the handful of bacon pieces into the white garbage can, and then placed the plate in the sink. She'd wash the dishes after Joshua left for work, which she hoped would be any minute.

"You'll be home tonight when I get home, right?"

"Yes," she said. "I'm only working till four."

"Good." Joshua stood. To her surprise, he gulped down what remained in his mug even though the coffee had to still be hot. He then turned to the kitchen. He was coming for her. "I hope you're planning something good for dinner."

Backed against the kitchen sink, he had her cornered. She'd just broken the first—and maybe the most important—survival tip.

"Yes." With her palms pressed against the smooth countertop that lined the lightly damp sink, she braced herself for the unknown.

43

He nodded his approval. He was getting closer. His dark, crisp uniform was just inches away from colliding with her. Her mind screamed.

What was Joshua going to do now?

"I was actually thinking about inviting Matt and Kathy over to join us tonight."

He smirked. Some girls would have found the gesture sexy, but Cate knew what was lurking behind it: pure evil.

Still holding the coffee mug, he raised his hand. Cate held her breath. This time, she flinched. He was coming right toward her, the mug nearing her face. She couldn't fight fear, not anymore. Cate bit her lower lip, immediately tasting the metallic thickness of her own blood.

Seriously, her insides begged, *what was her husband planning on doing?*

Cate didn't have time to move. An image filled her mind: the mug smashing into her face, tiny glass shards cutting into her skin before she collapsed to the cool, tiled floor while Joshua stood over her, laughing.

The thought never became a reality. Instead, Joshua lifted the mug over her shoulder and placed it in the sink. He took a step back and then crossed his arms.

"Are you all right, Cate? You suddenly look a little pale."

"I'm fine," she lied. Cate exhaled, finally, ran her shaking fingers through her hair, and then steadied them together in front of her stomach. "I was just thinking about dinner and what I should—"

"We're not having Matt and Kathy over tonight."

"Why not?" As if it had had its own agenda, the question flew out of Cate's mouth. She couldn't have stopped it.

Now, the damage was done.

Joshua took a step forward. His hands lowered to his sides, but just as fast, his right hand came up again. His fingers grazed her chin gently before taking a stronger grip, guiding her face closer to him.

"Because I want to spend the night with you," Joshua whispered. "Just you. I think we could use some alone time." Then he bent down and his lips stopped in front of hers.

Cate knew what was coming next. Sometimes, she dreaded it more than the abuse. Joshua kissed her. His thin tongue pushed into her mouth and began poking around aimlessly. The gesture felt like an invasion, but she remained still. Cate let Joshua finish.

Moments later, he pulled back. The schoolboy grin he sported across his face showed he was proud of the sloppy kiss.

Cate choked back a cough and forced a smile. She played along.

"I want a baby, Cate. Are you going to give me a baby?"

She didn't know what to say but felt her eyebrows shoot up instantly. Some things were harder to fake than others.

Joshua looked down at his watch. "Damn!"

Had she gotten lucky? Was she actually going to get to avoid the question? Cate tried not to get her hopes up.

"I have to go," he said. "The sheriff's butt buddy will be all over my ass if I'm late." He bent down again and gave her another peck on the lips. "Don't worry about my coffee for the road. I'll be fine."

"Oh." Cate blinked. "Okay."

"One other thing. Make sure you put some concealer over that cut on your cheek. You don't want people to start talking." Then Joshua turned, rounded the kitchen, and headed for the front door.

When he was out of view, finally, Cate shook her head. There went her husband, one of Perry Creek's finest, dressed in dark blue, his weapon loaded, ready to save the day.

* * *

She was ten minutes late. How was that for being professional? Just yesterday, Cate chastised one of her employees for showing up late to his shift. Now, here she was, the boss, doing the exact same thing.

Cate believed that you led by example. What kind of example was she setting in being late?

She rolled back her shoulders and shook away the question. Not today. She'd had more than her share of heavy blows this morning. She was done. This internal battle would have to be resumed another day.

"Good morning, Cate."

"Hi, Jerry. Sorry, I know I'm—"

"Don't worry about it," he said. "The place didn't burn down and everything is fine. Besides, you're here now."

She enjoyed working at Filled to the Brim. Sure, Jerry was probably one of the easiest bosses to work for, but, beyond that, the coffee shop gave Cate a purpose. It gave her a home, a safe place where she felt respected and needed.

Built within walking distance of the local high school, the Brim—for short—was a popular hangout from fall to spring after 3:00 p.m., when all the classes had ended. Summertime, though, offered some gradually busy moments, too.

Now was not one of those moments, which resulted in Cate feeling a little less guilty for being late to work.

She dodged the small, empty table for two in the back, rounded the wooden counter, and reached for one of the green aprons hanging loosely on the back wall. She placed the garment over her white T-shirt and blue jeans, pushed her blonde hair back into a messy ponytail, and then took a look around the shop to see what needed to be done.

According to building codes and regulations, the Brim's maximum capacity was forty-eight, though Cate was pretty sure she'd seen as many as seventy people in the shop at once. This morning, however, there were five.

Jerry and his late wife had bought the coffee shop a little over a year ago, opting to leave it pretty much the same as it had always been. That was one thing about Perry's Creek—change was rarely considered a good thing.

The original black-and-white checkered floor now had bright yellow, green, and blue rugs spread out sparingly on top of it, creating a pop of color. That had been Sarah's idea, no doubt.

The glass doors to the entrance advertised the shop's logo: a giant, overflowing mug of coffee with thick waves of steam surrounding it. Upon walking into the Brim, guests had the choice of sitting on a ripped leather sofa, overstuffed chair, or at one of the handfuls of mismatched tables and stools scattered throughout.

Across from the ordering counter on the right, a dozen or so randomly collected paperbacks sat on a small shelf that had most likely been purchased at a garage sale and then painted to give it a whole other look. Framed photographs of different famous destinations decorated the off-white walls. The subtle lighting mixed with the even softer background music helped to establish a place where all types and ages felt welcomed.

But, the smell was still the Brim's biggest incentive. It was even better than the assortment of homemade cookies and cupcakes a local older woman made and stocked the shop with. At least, Cate thought so.

She stood behind the counter and let the rich hazelnut scent fill her body. The heavy aroma almost felt like a drug: addictive, mouthwatering, mood-altering. Even though Cate knew all too well that there were worse things in life to be addicted to, she still tried to limit her caffeine intake while at work. She had a business to help run and a husband who didn't like it when she came home at night bursting with energy.

46

From her position, she could see the entire layout of the Brim. It looked as if more sugar packets needed to be added to...wait!

Cate's attention shifted suddenly. The man beside the bookshelf, standing in front of the milk station and adding cream to his to-go cup...who was he?

"Cate?"

She ignored Jerry and kept staring at the man. He looked so familiar, just like...no! It couldn't be him, could it? There was no way!

Cate felt lightheaded. The thick coffee smell was no longer appealing but close to making her sick. Dark spots rotated tediously around her line of vision, and she thought she was going to lose it completely and pass out. Those dark green eyes couldn't be a mistake.

"Cate? Are you all right, Cate?"

She turned to Jerry. Mouth painfully dry, she asked in a breathy voice, "Who is that?"

"Who's who?"

"Over there, at the milk station." Cate spun back around and raised a finger to point, but the man was gone. "Dammit! He was just there."

"What's wrong, Cate? You look like you've seen a ghost."

Jerry had no idea how right on the money he was. "How busy has the shop been this morning? All regulars? Anyone you've never seen here before?"

"I don't know." Jerry shook his head. "I wasn't paying too much attention. I guess there have been a few new customers today. Why? What's this about, Cate?"

She swallowed the lump that had formed in her throat and then shrugged. *Is this what going crazy feels like?* There was no possible way that could have been *him.*

"Cate?"

"Nothing." Her voice was sharper than she'd intended. "It's nothing. I just...too much coffee this morning." She faked a smile.

Jerry frowned. Thin lines formed on his small face, and he looked to be in his late thirties. "Well, switch to decaf." Then he offered his very own genuine smile.

Cate stared at him. It was no mystery to anyone who frequented the Brim routinely that he had a small crush on her. Intelligent and kind, with a full head of dark hair, and a body that seemed to be in pretty decent shape, Cate found him attractive, too. Close to being ten years older than she, Cate knew her mother would have approved of her being with a more mature man.

However, Jerry's fascination with her was tricky. Cate was married, so there was that obstacle. Still, even if a relationship with her boss had been an option, Cate was stuck trying to decide if Jerry's draw to her was authentic or if the man was simply lonely and missing his wife.

"What happened to your cheek?"

Before she could come up with a quick excuse, he was touching her. His hand seemed to be both soft and strong at the same time as he traced the scratch across her face.

"I…must have done that in my sleep. I woke up this morning and had the scratch." Ten months of being abused, and she still hadn't gotten good at lying.

It was clear from Jerry's inhalation that he didn't believe her. Then again, who would believe such a lame excuse? Cate knew one of two things was going to have to happen: She was either going to have to become a better storyteller, or she was going to have to learn some new makeup tricks.

He didn't question her. Jerry dropped his hand. "I'm going to get some more sugar packets from the back." He left her standing behind the counter all alone.

Cate took the moment of solitude to compose herself. She reminded herself that she was at work. Nothing good ever happened by mixing business with personal baggage. Being professional was key and an absolute must if she was going to keep her less-than-perfect marriage under wraps.

"Cate! I'm so glad you're here!"

Cate looked up at the entrance of the shop. Her mother was storming toward her. The woman's eyes were red and looked a little puffy. Had she been crying?

"We need to talk, Cate."

Cate wanted to scream. She knew the release wouldn't make the day any worse. *Just how many things could go wrong in one morning?*

"Now isn't a good time, Mom," she said through gritted teeth. Cate picked up a cloth rag Jerry had left on the counter. Maybe if she made herself look busy, then…

"I tried calling you last night, but your phone was off," Georgia continued. "And then, this morning—"

"I was running late this morning," Cate interrupted. "I didn't have time to chitchat. Whatever this is, I'm sure it can wait."

"Someone knows, Cate."

"Knows what? What are you talking about?"

Georgia unzipped the middle compartment of her bag and dug through it.

Cate felt her back muscles tighten immediately. Her frustration was growing, coming dangerously close to reaching a boiling point.

"Here." Finally, her mother produced a half sheet of paper and handed it to her. "Someone knows."

Cate took the sheet and read it aloud. "Oh, my God!" Cate dropped the sheet. Instinctively, her hand flew up to cover her still-open mouth.

Georgia nodded. "I don't know who left the note for me, or why, but—"

"I do," Cate whispered.

"What?"

"I know who wrote that threat." Her mind traveled back to just minutes before. Her ghost. Now she knew for sure that it had been *him*.

Except he wasn't a ghost at all. The man was very much alive, and he was in Perry's Creek.

8

Her door was unlocked. *Interesting*, he thought.

Sure, it was the middle of the day, and Perry's Creek was about as dangerous as a child's playground, but Collins still had trouble believing that people didn't lock their doors. Especially when the house was empty. It was the modern age. Wasn't that just asking for trouble?

"I have to be at the bar in an hour," the bartender said. "I'm working both the afternoon and evening shifts tonight."

"Fine." He honestly didn't give a shit where she had to go. He hadn't asked for her itinerary, and there was no way in hell he was planning on spending an hour with her, anyway.

"I could tell you liked me," she said through a lipstick-stained smile. She stepped into the apartment. "And, I knew you'd be back."

"Right." He told the girl what she wanted to hear as he followed her through the doorway and into what appeared to be a living room.

Collins *had* gone back to Tammi's Pub the previous day to see her, but he'd had an agenda. First, he'd learned her name: Tara Burns. Secondly, and more importantly, he'd gotten her phone number.

He'd called her this morning and mentioned in a roundabout way that he wanted to see her. Collins was careful not to invite her to breakfast, as this in no way, shape, or form was about dating. The last thing he wanted to do was buy her a meal. She'd suggested a walk at one of the Creek's hiking trails a few miles outside town. Collins agreed, and, after stopping to indulge in a morning cup of joe, met up with her. They'd been on the trail for maybe ten minutes before Tara turned to him, kissed him with an awkwardly open mouth, and invited him back to her place.

Jackpot!

Collins had never been one to enjoy outdoor activities. Still, it wasn't as if he could have asked her back to his motel room. That was *his* personal space.

So, he'd made an effort to play the game, and, lucky for him, he hadn't had to play that long.

"Do you want something to drink? I have—"

"I want you." Collins grabbed Tara's arm and pulled her close. Up against his hard chest, she felt small, even frail. He liked that. There was no confusion as to who was in control.

Her berry blend body scent was the same as the first time he'd met her, but, today, and for some reason, he found it less arousing. Even the fact that she was wearing a tiny pair of pink shorts and a white, virtually see-through T-shirt, didn't seem powerful enough to turn him on.

Something was wrong. Did his mind need to be altered with booze or marijuana to find the backwoods, tattoo-ridden whore doable?

Definitely not. Throughout his life, he'd gone home with less attractive women than the bartender he was with now. After all, he was a man with needs, and he'd discovered early on that if he closed his eyes, a female's touch was a female's touch. Imagination was a very powerful tool.

No, his issues went deeper than appearances, and he was almost positive where they originated from: his revenge plan. Recent events were weighing on his mind heavily, leaving him—and other parts of him—paralyzed.

"Is everything okay?" Tara pulled back and looked down.

"Fine," he lied. Apparently, he hadn't given her enough credit. Maybe this bartender did have a clue. Then again, it wasn't that hard to know if a man was into you or not.

"Do you want to go into the bedroom?" She reached for his hands as if *that* gesture was really going to make him want to jump her bones.

Collins shook his head. "On second thought, water would be good."

"You got it." She walked less than ten paces and then turned the corner.

One of the advantages of living in an apartment the size of a toddler's shoebox: nothing was ever out of reach. Collins knew the fact to be true from experience.

He decided to try and make himself feel a little more comfortable. Collins lowered himself to the pleather couch and took in his surroundings. He always found it so fascinating to discover how other people chose to live.

Tara was in her mid-twenties, and her apartment more than reflected that. Her furniture was cheap and disposable. Her TV was too small for the room and had most likely been purchased from a store offering a Black Friday sale. Half-melted, dollar-store candles littered every flat surface he could see, including one directly under her low-hanging curtains.

Okay, he considered, *maybe she wasn't all that bright.*

The carpet was brown, cheesy celebrity magazines filled one side of the coffee table, and a black laptop computer was plugged into the socket against the far wall. Not exactly his idea of "living the dream." Then again, Tara's situation was much better than his at the moment.

"I made an executive decision: beer instead of water." Tara stepped into view. She was holding a glass bottle. Except for what appeared to be ridiculously cheap earrings, she was completely naked. "I thought we should speed things up a bit."

Collins accepted the opened beer and then almost dropped it immediately as she jumped into his lap and straddled him. Her bare, pasty skin looked even whiter against his all-black clothing.

She pressed herself harder against him as she moved in for a kiss, but he avoided it. Instead, he turned his head and took a swig of his beer. Ice-cold, but it didn't even seem to hit the spot. He just wasn't feeling it. None of it.

"You know, if we're going to do this, then we need to get started. I only have an hour until—"

"You have to be at work," Collins finished for her. "I know." He took another gulp of the beer because, well, it was there. If only that rule could be applied to another issue he was being plagued with currently.

"Well, that," Tara began, "but also, Jed will be home soon."

"Who's Jed?"

"My boyfriend."

"Boyfriend?" Collins repeated. "You never told me you had a boyfriend."

"You never asked. Besides, it's fine. It's not like we're married or anything. He's most likely out there fucking random people, too."

Collins set the bottle down on the cluttered table to his right, and then, both hands completely free, gripped her hips and pulled her up and off himself. As if he needed another reason not to sleep with her, the bartender's naked flesh felt scaly to the touch.

"What in the hell are you doing?"

"This was a bad idea." Collins stood and started for the door.

"What?" She pushed her blonde hair from her eyes. "All of a sudden, you have a conscious?"

"I don't care how many people you screw in this shithole town," he called over his shoulder. "I would've been more than happy to have been another notch in your *barely* held together belt. But, I'm not messing around with another guy's girl. And, definitely not in his own home."

"Please," she said through a thick laugh. "You couldn't even get it up! What kind of a man are you?"

"I'm leaving, Tara."

"Fuck you!"

"Not today." Collins opened the door and stepped out of the apartment. He half expected her to follow him and was relieved when he took five steps away from the apartment and she never emerged.

Collins was a lot of things. More recently, drug dealer and felon topped the list. However, he wasn't the type of scumbag to knowingly sleep with another guy's broad. Call it ironic that he actually had standards, but he did.

Not to mention, he had enough crazy staining his life. The last thing he needed was to add to the drama, and the more he thought about it, the more he believed that Tara was a bitch who was certainly full of drama. She was a big red rash that even the best of creams wouldn't be able to make go away.

"Hey, pal. Watch where you're going."

"Sorry," Collins mumbled. He'd been so lost in thought that he hadn't even realized someone else had been walking up the stone pathway and almost bumped right into him.

Collins nonchalantly took in the other guy's appearance: tall, wide frame, and light brown hair an inch or two away from entering mullet territory. He probably had a mouth full of chewing tobacco.

"Only in East-fucking-County," Collins spat under his breath.

For some reason, Collins couldn't help but stay focused on the man as he walked by and started for apartment Number Five, the same one he had just exited.

The man stopped, opened the door, and then turned and made direct eye contact with Collins. He knew.

Collins didn't waste a second. He rounded the corner of the stucco building and picked up his pace as he headed for his Honda. There was no way in hell he was going to give the redneck version of G.I. Joe a chance at a confrontation. Especially not over someone as unimportant as Tara.

He pulled out of the complex's parking lot. Collins knew he only had himself to blame for dodging a bullet—or, more appropriately, an ironclad fist. He'd come to Perry's Creek for a very specific reason—for revenge, not to get his dick played with. Mistakes like that could blow his cover. He didn't have the time or resources to be driving off course.

He'd screwed up once already, and, though he wasn't entirely sure he'd been made, he had learned a lesson: be more careful. There was no such thing as being *too* cautious. Not when he was a known and convicted criminal.

Collins turned left onto Lincoln Street and headed toward Scott's Inn. He felt like he needed a shower, maybe even a nap. He had lots to do, but he knew damn well he wasn't going to be able to accomplish jack shit if he wasn't one hundred percent rested.

Suddenly, an impulse buzzed in his head. He paused at the stop sign and considered the thought.

He had a good friend who would be more than willing to lend a helping hand. Truth be told, Richie would be chomping at the bit to get caught up in some action. Especially if that action ended in a big payday.

Collins shifted the car into park and killed the engine. He tossed around the notion of bringing in a partner for another minute and then squashed it.

When you added teammates to your roster, you opened the door for unwanted and unnecessary trouble. Though Richie could definitely be of some assistance, he could also be a huge liability.

Then, of course, there was the payment factor. No one, Richie included, worked for free. Collins wasn't fond of even entertaining the idea of sharing his money. It was his hard work, patience, and skills that had gotten him here. Why in hell should someone else reap the rewards?

It's settled. Until he was backed into a tight corner and faced with no other option but to bring in a partner, he'd continue to fly solo. Richie would be his ace in the hole. Everyone needed one, just in case.

Collins opened the driver's side door and stepped out of the car. He ignored the empty, forty-ounce beer can that followed him and rolled down the blacktopped lot.

He stretched and reached high toward the dull, blue sky before running his hands through his thin hair. He needed a shower—a cold one—and a nap. Hell, maybe he'd even have a little lunch.

Then it would be time to focus. It would be time to get back to work and take the next step in executing his revenge plan successfully.

And, that step was paying *her* another visit.

9

"**A**re you having an affair with Cate?"

"Excuse me?" Matt wasn't sure he'd heard her correctly. There was no possible way she'd just asked him that.

"Are you having an affair with Cate?" she repeated the question, only slower this time.

"You can't be serious, Kathy."

"Why wouldn't I be, Matt? Late-night phone calls. Not to mention, you're always working her into the conversation. I have a right to know if something is going on between you two."

"That's ridiculous." Matt balled his hands into tight fists. "She's married."

"Yes." Kathy nodded. "She's married to your best friend and partner. And, *you* have a girlfriend. But, you still didn't answer my question."

A stillness fell over the table. Had he known Kathy was going to come at him with guns a-blazing, he wouldn't have bothered inviting her to lunch. Live and learn.

Matt looked into Kathy's light, accusing eyes. "I'm not sleeping with Cate."

"Don't lie to my face!"

And, just like that, the uncomfortable silence was back.

Matt leaned back into the red vinyl booth, pinched the bridge of his nose, and then stared down at the checkered tablecloth. What did she want from him?

Was he attracted to Cate? Yes. Did he enjoy talking to her and being around her? Yes. But, would he ever make a move on her? Probably not.

Matt sighed, and then to avoid further eye contact with Kathy, took a look around the restaurant. He'd been looking forward to pizza all morning, but now his appetite had completely evaporated. His father—married *and* divorced four times now—told him repeatedly that women could often have that effect on a man.

The place was busy, but it usually was around noon, especially in the summertime. The pizza wasn't only good and made quickly, but it was also cheap. A deadly combination that would make any carb-free advocate cave.

Add in a couple of pinball machines, big-screen TVs, and an old jukebox in the corner that only played the classics, and you had your very own slice of Italy right there in Perry's Creek, California.

Or, maybe the design was more caveman-focused. Either way, there was a make-your-own salad bar, plenty of entertainment for the kids, and ice-cold beer on tap for the dads and single twenty-somethings who refused to grow up. A family-oriented environment mixed with a dash of appeal for those who had either been rebuffed by marriage completely or hadn't yet conformed, plus enough cool air to cut sharply through the thick June smog that had recently grown to be suffocating. It all ensured that Crusts wasn't just another regular "pizza joint," but a town landmark.

Except Matt couldn't enjoy any of it. The woman he'd asked to lunch, the woman he'd been seeing for about a month now, was pissed at him. Thanks to the buckets of free advice his father had handed out happily over the years regarding the subject of women, Matt knew if he wanted to enjoy a meal any time soon, he'd better start apologizing. Even though he was almost one hundred percent sure he'd done nothing wrong.

This had nothing to do with growing up and taking responsibility and *everything* to do with being in a relationship.

Jesus H. Christ.

"If I gave you the impression that I'm into Cate or any other girl, I'm sorry. I didn't mean to hurt your feelings, Kathy."

She didn't respond right away. Instead, she remained quiet. Matt watched as Kathy turned her attention away from him and began focusing on the toddler playing with his doughy breadsticks at the next table.

Matt liked Kathy. How much did he like her, exactly? Well, he wasn't quite sure yet, but he was enjoying her company more and more.

Kathy was very pretty, but her beauty was rather subtle. The entire month Matt had known her, she'd kept her hair and makeup the same. Her dark hair was styled into a stiff bob, and her makeup was always minimal and natural-looking. An avid runner, Kathy was thin. She also never seemed to eat too much, so that obviously contributed to her shape, and she was always conscious of her nails. They were trimmed consistently and painted basic tones that didn't draw a lot of attention.

A paralegal who commuted to San Diego three days a week for part-time work, Kathy was the same age as he and had moved to Perry's Creek recently to "get away from the city."

She certainly had a professional manner to her, most of the time opting to wear conservative clothing that revealed little to no skin, like the pair of khaki slacks she wore even now in the raging heat. Hell, her jewelry was simple and classic, too: small gold wristwatch and matching, chandelier-style earrings.

Kathy wasn't like most girls her age. Matt was drawn to her mature quality. He wasn't sure where their relationship was going, or how far he wanted it to go. Matt just liked her. It was that simple.

"You didn't hurt my feelings," Kathy said. "But, I needed some reassurance. Cate seems to have some sort of hold over you—"

"Fine. You want to know the truth?" Matt interrupted. He never gave her a chance to answer. "O.J. is beating Cate. And, for some reason, she's decided to confide in me."

Kathy's eyebrows shot up. "Is that true?"

"That my best friend and partner is beating his wife?" Matt shrugged. "I don't know. I've never *seen* him do it, but Cate has shown me bruises and claims they're from him."

"Well, have you confronted O.J.? Asked him point-blank if he is or has ever hit his wife?"

"You're joking, right?" Matt shook his head. "Look at the position I'm in. How can I possibly ask him that?"

Kathy slowly folded her hands on the table. "You said Cate is your friend. If that's true—"

"It is true. But, O.J. is my friend, too. My oldest friend. He's like my brother."

"Do you believe Cate?"

"I don't know." He purposely enunciated each word. "I have a hard time believing Cate would lie about something like that. What could be her motive? But, on the other hand, it's also hard to swallow the idea that O.J. is some kind of monster who enjoys beating his wife."

"Well, has she told anyone else? Filed a complaint? Actually reported the—?"

"That would only make matters worse."

"Right," she agreed. "You guys tend to protect your own."

Matt frowned at her. "That's not fair, Kathy."

"You're right," she sighed. "I'm sorry. But, coming from a legal background, if there isn't documentation of the abuse, then…"

"I know, I know." Matt hated to admit it, but Kathy was right. He didn't agree with it—at all—but that was how the legal system worked.

As a paralegal, she'd been offering her point of view on the matter, which only highlighted Matt's reasons for avoiding getting romantically involved with women in her profession. Honestly, he didn't even care to have friends who worked in the legal field. As a cop—but, more so, as a human being—he rarely saw things in straight black and white.

"In the meantime," Kathy continued, "you're stuck in the middle, playing both sides. And, O.J. is none the wiser."

Because he didn't know how to respond, Matt just nodded. He wasn't even going to consider telling her the rest, that Cate thought O.J. could be responsible for the recent murders of two women.

"Why do you think Cate came to you?" Kathy pressed on. "She knows your relationship with O.J. She's well aware of how close you two are and the bond you guys share. Didn't she stop to think this would make things awkward for you? Don't you think she's a tad selfish for doing this to you?"

"No, I don't," Matt argued. He crossed his arms. "I think she's scared. I think she feels all alone. I don't think Cate really knew what to do, so she came to me to—"

"Help her," Kathy finished for him. "She came to you to help her, Matt. So, help her. She's your friend, and she's in need. Do something about it."

He released a built-up breath. "It's not that simple."

"It is that simple," Kathy countered. "You and Cate are making the situation entirely more difficult than what it needs to be. Help your friend. Or, at least, help her to help herself."

"What does that mean?"

"It means that Cate is a big girl, and Cate needs to defend herself. Instead of running around town, whispering all of her problems to you, she needs to confront them head-on."

"Not everyone is that strong, Kathy."

"Maybe not," she agreed. "But, it's not fair that you keep sticking up for her. You're *my* boyfriend. Remember?"

"I am your boyfriend, Kathy. This isn't a contest. It's not about who I help more. You know if you needed me, I'd be there."

"Do I?"

"You should. Let's be honest: This has nothing to do with Cate. This is all about you. You're insecure—"

"Don't you dare say that word to me, Matt." Her right hand flew up. "Don't make me sound crazy like I'm creating all of this in my head. You know—"

"Are you two ready to order?"

Matt looked up at the teenage waiter. Until now, he'd forgotten they were in a restaurant with witnesses, causing a scene.

Relationships, his father had warned, weren't for everyone.

"Can we have a few more minutes?" Kathy asked.

"Of course," the boy answered and walked away quickly. He looked relieved to leave.

Because Matt didn't know quite what to say, he apologized...again. "I'm sorry, Kathy."

"I love you," she said.

Matt thought he was going to fall out of the booth. That hadn't been the response he'd been expecting. "What did you say?"

"I love you," she said again. "I know it's early, Matt. I know we've only been seeing each other for a month, but it's true. I love you."

"I-I-I don't know what—"

"You don't have to say anything," she finished for him. Kathy reached for her leather purse on the floor and stood up. "Call me when you're ready to talk about this." She gave him a soft kiss on the cheek and then walked to the glass exit and left the restaurant.

Matt sat in silence. He didn't know what to say. A hefty, blanketing smell of grease floated from the back kitchen and hovered over his table, but his appetite was still nonexistent.

The last thing he wanted to do was hurt Kathy—she didn't deserve that—and though he would have liked to have appeased her and repeated the sentiment, he couldn't. Matt didn't love her, not yet. He wasn't sure if he ever would.

And now, more than ever, he was starting to understand why.

10

"**A**re you saying you lied yesterday? You lied to me? To my team? Is that what you're telling me, Beau?"

"Don't be ridiculous, Shannon. I didn't lie to anyone."

"Then explain it to me again," the sheriff ordered, "because I'm confused."

Beau released a thick, built-up breath and then flopped down into the soft chair in front of Shannon's desk. "Fine." He nodded.

Truth be told, it was more than a little odd that he and Shannon had not only become such great friends but also remained so close throughout the years. Beau had accepted that oddness but still wasn't sure he understood it.

Shannon Sutton was kind of a strange man. First, there was the simple fact that his parents had burdened him with a girl's name. Cruel joke? Or had the pair known such a great and powerful person named Shannon that they'd just had to name their kid after him?

Beau had always wondered but had never found out. He assumed his friend had never solved the great mystery, either. The sheriff's parents had both been killed in a single-car crash when he'd been twelve.

"Are you going to start talking any time today, Beau?"

"Right. Sorry." Beau crossed one leg over the other and leaned back in his chair. "I don't know who the killer is. Not yet."

"So you've mentioned." The sheriff nodded.

"That doesn't mean I can't solve this case with the two victims we have now. I still believe what I said yesterday: We should be able to find the killer with what he's left us. I just need more time."

"How much more time?" Shannon glided his hands into a steeple and placed them on the flat surface of his metal desk. "I just got off the phone with Mayor Jackson. He's not happy."

"Of course not," Beau agreed. "There's some psycho in town who's offing young blonde women. But, solving murder investigations can take time. Especially when you've got limited resources."

"Unfortunately, Mayor Jackson doesn't understand that."

"He wouldn't," Beau said. "So, we go back to what I said before: We work with what the killer has left us."

"Which isn't a damn thing!" Shannon roared. "He didn't even leave behind a thumbprint. He strangles his victims and then takes one of their earrings. What the hell? Seriously, what does that even mean? How can that information help us find the killer?"

"I don't know yet," Beau admitted. "But, it's something to go on. Believe it or not, it *does* mean something."

"Yeah, it means we're dealing with some fruitcake who probably likes dressing up in women's clothing."

Beau didn't respond. He made awkward eye contact with his friend, frowned, and then looked away.

The sheriff's office didn't in fact reflect Shannon's tastes, which led Beau to believe one thing: The man hadn't decorated the space. His wife had.

A handful of plaques and awards—all in matching silver frames—hung on one wall. A detailed painting of what Beau assumed was Perry's Creek back in the day had been placed behind Shannon's desk. A large black printer sat in the corner of the room, and a maroon rug with fringes covered most of the hardwood flooring.

Beau sat in the only chair the office had to offer besides the sheriff's leather one. The only piece of furniture that seemed to be new in the room was the desk, which was completely bare except for a wide day planner.

Clutter-free, Beau thought. That detail was definitely Shannon's doing, as was the stench of stale coffee.

The sheriff cleared his throat, breaking the silence. "I'm sorry, Beau. I shouldn't have said…"

Beau shrugged. "You don't have to apologize. I agree. The earring bit is different. But, if we figure out why the killer is taking the jewelry as a trophy, then we might be able to identify him."

"Or her," Shannon suggested.

"What?"

"Well, the killer could easily be female, right?"

61

Beau bit his lower lip. "I never really considered that idea."

Shannon smiled. "When it comes to crime, anything is possible. You taught me that."

Beau looked at the sheriff and returned his friend's gesture. "Most serial killers are white males, typically. However, anything *is* possible."

"Wait." Shannon sat up in his chair. "You think we're dealing with a potential serial killer?"

"In a word," Beau said, "yes."

"Fuck!"

"Come on, Shannon. You've seen the case files. The killer has a type— attractive blonde women—and a pattern. What did you think we were dealing with?"

"Honestly, I don't know," the sheriff admitted. He shook his head slowly. "I mean, maybe it was wishful thinking, but I was hoping for robberies turned homicides. Maybe even domestic violence situations that ended…"

Beau couldn't help it; he started laughing. The low-pitch, dry chuckle immediately silenced the sheriff. After a few moments, Beau managed to compose himself. He straightened his striped tie and then folded his hands in his lap. "I'm sorry, Shannon. I didn't mean to—"

"Laugh in my face?"

Beau tilted his head to the left. Surely, his friend hadn't been serious. "Now is not the time to be naive, Shannon. I realize Perry's Creek isn't exactly—"

"I've never worked a murder case before, Beau," the sheriff confessed. "Not like this one."

Shannon's tone had been soft. Beau knew his friend was feeling vulnerable. He felt weighed down with guilt for laughing at him.

"That doesn't matter, Shannon. You're smart, and you're a good cop. And, like I said yesterday, a lack of experience might work to our advantage in this case."

"How's that?"

"Because you've never really worked a homicide before, you've got nothing to compare this one to, no preconceived notions. I know that may not make a whole lot of sense now, but I truly believe that you and your team putting fresh eyes on this will aid the case, not hinder it."

Shannon shrugged. "I'd never thought of it that way. Maybe."

"That's not all," Beau said. "There's more."

"Which is?"

"Perry's Creek is a very small town. That works in our favor. You or someone from the department most likely knows the killer."

"You think so?"

"Yes," Beau verified. "Now, have you noticed any strange behavior or incidents since the first murder took place?"

"You mean besides the murder itself? No."

"No other reports of crime? No bizarre outsiders or visitors to have come to Perry's Creek? No one new in town?"

"Well." Shannon smirked. "Just one name comes to mind."

"Okay. Who?"

"You."

Beau rolled his eyes. "Okay. Well, would you like me to leave, then?"

"Certainly not," Shannon said. His smirk was gone. "I'm glad you're here. And, I know I've said it a few dozen times already, but I'd like to say it again: Thank you for coming."

Beau waved away the compliment. "You don't have to thank me, Shannon. At least, not until I catch the killer."

"You have no idea how much you're helping me. You're really saving my ass with the mayor. And, the fact that you're here of your own free will, well—"

"Are you kidding?" Beau interrupted. "I love this kind of stuff. I *live* for it. Besides, you'd have done the same thing for me."

The silence was back, invading the already too-stiff atmosphere, creating even more tension between the two men.

Shannon turned his head, no doubt to avoid eye contact, but Beau didn't follow suit. Instead, he took a moment to study his friend's face.

Deep lines cut across the sheriff's face, mostly around his eyes and in the middle of his forehead. Shannon was tired, Beau knew, probably even verging on exhausted. Still, Beau also knew that that exhaustion had nothing to do with the current case. It was no secret that Shannon had been exhausted for quite some time now.

This time, Beau was the first to speak up. "Should we talk about last night?"

Shannon's attention remained on the small window, gazing out at God knew what. "Yes," he said. "We probably should." He turned his head and looked at Beau. "But, not now, and definitely not here."

"Then when?" Beau stood up. He began pacing the office nervously.

"And, where? Should I come by your house tonight? Maybe around dinnertime? I'm sure Diane would love that."

"Stop it, Beau," the sheriff ordered. "Just knock it off!"

Beau sighed. "What happened back then…"

"Is in the past," Shannon finished. "It happened a long time ago."

Beau shook his head. He took a step toward the sheriff's desk and then gripped the edge of it. "You know that's not true," he whispered. "We need to talk about this. I *want* to talk about this." He opened his hands—palms up—and rested them on the smooth surface in front of Shannon. "Please."

There was a quick knock at the door, and then it flew open. "Sheriff Sutton?"

Shannon pushed his chair back from his desk and fumbled to stand up straight. He cleared his throat and said, "What is it, Deputy Benson?"

"Sheriff," the deputy stated, "we have a situation."

"Another murder?" Beau turned to the young cop, his hands now placed firmly in the pockets of his gray dress pants.

"Oh, no." Benson shook his head. "Mayor Jackson is here."

"Dammit," the sheriff muttered. "I just got off the phone with him. Why in the hell is he here?"

"Sir?"

"Right," Shannon answered. "Offer him something to drink and tell him I'll be there in a minute."

The deputy left the office and shut the door.

"I can't deal with this right now, Beau. I have a murder investigation to run. Can we please focus on *that* for the time being?"

Beau nodded. "It's why I'm here. I gave you my word that I'd help you and your team solve this case." He paused before adding, "But, there was one condition."

"I know, I know." Shannon raised his hand. "I'll follow through with my part of the deal. But, first, let's catch this monster."

11

Cate reached for her wine glass, brought it up to her thirsty lips, and took a long gulp. She knew better than to drink too quickly. It was smarter to preserve the merlot, make it last. But, she enjoyed the smoky flavor too much to just sip it.

"That's all you've had to drink today, right? Just the one glass?"

"Yes, Joshua," she answered.

"Good."

Even before he'd made the fact known that he wanted to have a baby, he'd been mindful of her drinking. Not that she had a problem with alcohol—by any standards—but he didn't approve of her consuming something that could alter her behavior. Or, so he'd said on many, many occasions.

Cate knew it was just another control tactic. In some way, Joshua always had to be telling her what to do...or say...or wear. She could only imagine how much worse things would get if she were to become pregnant.

Cate refused to let that happen.

"How was your day?" She traded her wine glass for a fork. "Anything exciting happen? Any big news on the case?" Cate couldn't win. Making small talk with her husband was just as painful as the bitter silence.

"The day was fine," he said between mouthfuls of pasta. "Uneventful, really. I think Matt wrote a parking ticket. That's about as exciting as things got."

"Hmm." She bit into her salad. The lettuce was nice and crisp, even a little refreshing, but it definitely could have used some more Italian dressing. She used her fork to roam around in the bowl for a cherry tomato. "And, the new guy, the sheriff's friend, how are things with him? Any better?"

"Nope." Joshua went for his beer bottle. "He's still a prick. We had another briefing this afternoon. The guy doesn't know his ass from a hole in the ground. For the life of me, I can't figure out why Sheriff Sutton brought him on board."

Cate shrugged. "Maybe he just needs time to get his bearings. Once he's adjusted—"

"Why are you sticking up for a man you don't even know?"

"I'm not." Cate immediately bit her tongue. The action stung. "I mean…" She searched for the right words, anything that would make Joshua believe she hadn't been arguing with him. "I-I-I didn't mean to stick up for him. I'm sorry."

Joshua sighed and then shook his head. "It's okay, Cate. I'm kind of getting used to it." He took another drink of his beer.

No longer interested in her salad, Cate set her fork down on the table. Somehow, her plan to shift the direction of Joshua's temper away from her had blown up in her face. She'd tried so hard to ensure it didn't happen, but she'd failed.

Knowing how much Joshua couldn't stand that ex-detective in town, she'd purposely dragged him into the conversation, hoping all of her husband's negative energy would center around him instead of its usual destination: her. Now, it was time for another tactic.

"How's the pasta?" she tried. "I know the sauce is your—"

"It's good," he said.

At least she'd given it a shot. She went back to digging around in her salad.

Cate didn't like mushrooms. Joshua refused to eat the fettuccine dish without them, and until Cate could learn to eat the meal the way it had been intended, the way he'd grown up eating it, he'd told her she'd just have to go without. So, every time she made the meal—his absolute favorite—she did. Cate got a salad for dinner while her husband enjoyed the pasta and sauce with extra mushrooms.

Cate didn't usually mind it, especially tonight. After the brutal start to her morning, the blast from the past at the coffee shop, and then learning about the threat her mother had received, food was the last thing Cate was concerned about. She didn't even have an appetite, though another glass of wine would have definitely filled a craving.

She'd attempted to cancel dinner, but Joshua hadn't approved. He couldn't have cared less that her mother had had an emergency and needed her. He'd explained to her that, above all else, she was a wife, and, as a wife—*his* wife—she was to make him dinner, clean up after the meal, and then join him in bed.

Cate was all too familiar with the motive behind Joshua's last order: a baby.

She silently prayed the Ambien kicked in, and fast. She wasn't in the right headspace for Joshua's advances, and certainly not now.

Normally, she had no problem bluffing her affection for him, moaning and imitating bliss every time his rough, calloused hands caressed her bare skin. Cate was so good sometimes that she could even trick Joshua into making him believe she was actually enjoying his misguided thrusts and sweaty body writhing around on top of her. She would pant and smile as if he was seriously giving her pleasure.

Sex with Joshua always left Cate feeling violated, but she endured it, because, really, what was her other option?

Tonight, though, she didn't have the energy to fake anything. Least of all that she liked or was even remotely into making love to her husband.

I know what you did! I'm going to make you pay!

Like a bad storm warning, the words flashed in front of Cate's eyes. Whoever said, *You can't escape your past,* well, they'd been one hundred percent right. She knew that from experience. Cate and her mother *had* tried to outrun their past in Arizona, but it had finally caught up with them.

"I'd like another beer," Joshua said.

"Sure." Cate stood from the dining room table, grabbed his empty bottle, and then started for the kitchen. She considered questioning his daily alcohol intake, but then quickly shook the idea away. After all, Cate liked her face exactly where it was, and she didn't want to chance it being pounded by Joshua's fist as if it were a piece of tough meat he was trying to tenderize.

Her focus went back to the threat her mother had received the other night. The more Cate contemplated it, the more she realized that anyone could have typed it up, printed it out, and delivered it. Sure, the culprit behind the act could have been her original assumption, but how likely was that?

Not too likely. She opened the refrigerator door. The guy she'd suspected…well, notes weren't really his style. Or, they hadn't been. He'd always been a more direct type of person, wanting immediate reactions and

67

results. None of this "more to come" implication crap.

Then again, a lot of time had passed since Cate last saw him. He could have changed. People, she knew, did, change.

"Here you go." She returned to the table, placed the cold bottle in front of Joshua, and then resumed her seat. People did change, but seldom for the better.

Maybe that was someone else at the Brim this morning. After all, she'd been late, flustered, and had just gotten into a fight with her husband where she'd been verbally and physically abused. It only made sense that Cate's mind had been elsewhere and her imagination was playing a cruel joke on her.

It had to have been someone else at the Brim this morning.

Almost immediately, her breathing became shallow and her vision blurry. Cate knew she was just telling herself what she wanted to hear. She *wanted* it to have been someone else.

"You seem to be somewhere else tonight. What are you thinking about?"

She shrugged and took a moment to choose her lie wisely. "Nothing, really. Just work stuff."

"It's not too stressful over there for you, is it?" he asked. "Jerry's not giving you too much to do?"

"No," Cate answered, "of course not. We've just been adding some new features to the shop—"

"I don't want you working there if you're going to be stressed out all day long and then come home completely exhausted."

"You don't have to worry, Joshua," she said. "I'm not overstressed; I'm fine. I wouldn't say I'm exhausted. I mean, I'm tired, yes, but—"

"Your main focus should be getting pregnant, Cate. I want that to be your top priority. Understand?" He raised his beer bottle to his mouth.

"I do, Joshua."

"If that means you need to quit that little coffee shop job that's meant for teenagers, so be it. And, if Jerry gets mad, fuck him. You've lost one baby. I don't want that to happen again."

Cate stared at him. Eyes wide, she willed herself not to cry. Not now. She'd come too far, been too strong to give in and show weakness. She refused to let him win.

Still, he'd brought up her unborn baby, and now Cate felt herself breaking apart piece by piece, slowly shattering from the inside out. Starting with her heart.

Joshua never mentioned their honeymoon or what had happened on it, and for good reason. Cate had trouble swallowing the sour moment even now. Why? What was her husband trying to accomplish?

"If you're going to properly take care of our baby, then you're going to have to start taking care of yourself first. Understand?" He took the last bite of his pasta and then pushed the plate away, signaling that the conversation was over.

However, for Cate, it was far from over. In fact, it was just getting started.

"No, I don't understand, Joshua." She forced her voice to be steady. "Does that mean that once I'm pregnant, you're going to stop beating me?"

"Cate," he warned.

"Please, enlighten me," she continued. "I think I have a right to know. When I get pregnant again, are you actually going to give this baby a chance to live? Or are you going to keep on—?"

Joshua's plate connected with the floor, shattering. The sound made her stop. Cate's mouth hung open mid-sentence as Joshua planted his hands on the edge of the table and pushed himself back. His chair flipped over in the process, creating a *banging* sound. He was behind her instantly. He leaned over her and screamed into her ear.

"Why must you always disrespect me, Cate? And, in my own home?" He grabbed a handful of her hair and pulled her out of her seat. "Do you like making me mad? Do you want me to hurt you?"

She knew talking would only make the situation worse. Cate bit her lower lip and forced herself to remain quiet. Normally, that wasn't a problem. Cate knew all too well what Joshua was capable of doing—what he *would* do when he got upset—but the baby, *her* baby…he'd accused her of being responsible for its…Cate couldn't bear to finish the thought.

She'd seen red, and, as a result, she'd let her emotions get the best of her. Cate knew better than to speak out against her husband, but he'd crossed a line, and she'd reached her breaking point.

"You will learn to respect me, Cate. I'll make sure of it!" He pushed her into the broken shards of glass that littered the floor.

"Please! No!" Cate used her hands to try and stop the fall. She hit the floor and a thin shaving of glass immediately sliced into her left palm.

"Don't cry, Cate," he ordered. "Tears will only make it worse."

She didn't look up at Joshua; she couldn't. Instead, she stared down at the mess on the floor: the broken glass, the pasta sauce, and, now, smears of her own blood.

This mess was her life.

"Why can't you just keep your mouth shut, Catie?" He crouched down beside her. "Why can't you just shut the fuck up?" Joshua's coarse hand was at the base of her neck suddenly. He pushed her face down toward the floor. "Is it really that important for you to get the last word?"

"I'm sorry, Joshua," she mumbled. Cate closed her eyes. She felt herself getting dangerously close to the sharp pieces of the broken plate. The ripe, earthy stench of the mushroom sauce filled her nostrils. Cate began to gag.

"You should be sorry, Catie." Her nose was just inches from the floor, but he held her in place, gripping her neck even tighter. "I don't deserve to be treated this way. Not by you, not by anyone."

"I-I-I know," she managed. Tears started to stream down her cheeks, and her nose was running. "It's my fault, Joshua. It's all my fault. I should have kept quiet. I should have just—"

"You're damn right you should have! Do you know how lucky you are? Do you know how many blonde-haired, blue-eyed bitches I could get to replace you?"

"I'm sorry," she repeated. "I'm so sorry." Her neck felt tightly pinched like he could snap it at any second. Another control measure, Cate knew. Joshua was *physically* proving that he had complete control over her life.

"I believe you, Catie," he whispered. He finally let go of her neck and stood up. "I know you're sorry. I just wish you'd quit putting yourself through this torture. It's really not necessary."

She gulped for air. In and out, in and out. She turned her face away from the smell of their dinner. Cate looked down at her hand to assess the severity of her injury. It was nothing she couldn't handle—at least she wouldn't need stitches. It was only a minor cut…this time. Cate didn't even see any glass sticking out of the wound. She'd gotten off easy.

She used the back of her right hand to wipe away her tears, and then, still on the floor, she grabbed her napkin from the table and went to work on her nose.

Joshua stood with his back to her. Feet planted shoulder-wide, his hands on his hips, he appeared to gaze at the blank wall.

The Ambien had to take effect soon. It was her only hope. Cate needed rest, and after tonight, there was no way she could force herself to be intimate with her husband. She'd have to refuse, and then Cate could only imagine the repercussions that would follow.

"All right." Joshua turned around and clasped his hands together. His dark eyes locked on hers, and even though she desperately wanted to look away, she couldn't. The sides of his head glistened. He'd started sweating.

Perhaps tonight's abuse had taken it out of him.

"All right," he said again. "Clean up this mess, get yourself together, and then meet me in the bedroom. I'll be waiting for you, so hurry."

Cate didn't have time to agree or disagree. Joshua turned and was already heading for the stairs.

After a few moments of holding onto the table for support, she managed to drag herself to her feet. She looked back down at the floor. She'd have to clean quickly. Joshua hated it when she made him wait.

'Til death do us part, she thought as she started for the kitchen closet where she kept the broom and dustpan. Joshua seemed to be reminding her of the vow constantly. He'd made it quite clear—more than once—that death was the only factor that could separate them.

Her mother's advice from the other day rushed into her head. The words were so clear, almost as if they'd once again been spoken to her.

There was only one way out of her marriage. If Cate wanted to survive, she knew what she was going to have to do.

12

Her life sucked. That much was obvious.

She'd had dreams and goals and hopes to one day get out of Perry's Creek, like every other unlucky bastard who'd had the misfortune of growing up here. No one *chose* to live in this godforsaken place, and if they said otherwise, they were either lying or needed their head examined.

But, like so many before her—and after her—she'd gotten stuck in the sharp metal teeth of the bear trap that was this damned town. Now, as a result, she only had two things to show for herself: a tattoo that was fading and the lone skill of fetching cold beer for crusty men.

Her parents would have been so proud.

So, life wasn't some Julia Roberts rom-com. Big deal. So, she hadn't gotten the man, the house, the kids, or a career to brag about at her upcoming high school reunion. She'd learned a long time ago to make do. Besides, she was doing pretty well for herself.

Okay, maybe "well" was a strong word, but Tara Burns was young. She still had plenty of time to figure it all out—to conquer the world *and* learn how to cook.

Her aching body craved a shower, and a hot meal didn't sound too bad, either. Yet, the first thing Tara did after she entered her apartment was fall down onto her pleather couch and prop her tired feet up on the coffee table. She needed a moment to relax, and she felt she'd earned it.

Tammi's Pub had drawn quite a crowd for a Tuesday. Then again, it'd been a hot afternoon, and even those with a basic GED education knew that the best medicine for sticky air and sweat-soaked skin was a frozen mason jar full of whichever tap brew happened to be the special.

Most of her regulars had stopped by, some to get in a couple of games of pool, more often to complain about the heat. All in all, she'd spent most of her shift running around, busting her cute little ass, but at least now she had a pocket stuffed with cash to show for her efforts. Tara considered that a win.

One man hadn't bothered to show his face, though. As Tara crossed her arms and released a built-up breath, she realized she wasn't sure how she felt about that now.

It was a pride thing, she figured as she closed her eyes and leaned back on the not-so-soft couch. Collins had turned her down, and Tara wasn't used to something like that happening. Honestly, she didn't much care for it.

Sure, the sexless afternoon had ended up being a good thing since Jed had gotten a bug up his ass and decided to come home early. But, still. She'd never been hit over the head with rejection so blatantly before, and she was going to make damn well sure it never happened again.

Since working at the Pub, Tara had grown accustomed to having her pick of the men in Perry's Creek who came into the bar regularly. And, while none of the balding, out-of-shape, no-manners-to-be-found guys resembled Prince Charming, she'd still had a lot of fun over the years—fun that was always on her terms.

When she'd seen Collins the other day, Tara had wanted him instantly. She found him to be sexy in a don't-fuck-with-me-because-I'm-a-very-bad-boy sort of way. Sitting at the bar and ordering beer, he'd looked like a felon, but Tara hadn't cared. That minor detail had only added to the attraction. She'd planned on getting him, and she almost had.

Until he'd turned her down.

Collins, she thought now, *what a bullshit name.* Hell, she didn't even know if it was his first or last and probably never would. He hadn't had the balls to come into the pub tonight, which led Tara to believe that he most likely wouldn't be back. A newbie to the Creek, she figured he'd seen enough, and like others before him, was on his way to his next stop. Still, he could have at least dropped by and apologized for not passing through *her* before leaving.

Tara yawned, stood, and headed for the kitchen. Deep down, she knew worrying about Collins wasn't only a waste of time but also just plain stupid. She had more important things to focus on, like her boyfriend and paying next month's rent. Plus, deciding if she wanted to end her night with a beer or a glass of wine.

Tara opened the refrigerator door, glad she was no longer hungry. She was able to make a few basic meals but highly doubted there was much she could do with expired cottage cheese and pepperoni slices. She frowned at the last two beer bottles and then shut the fridge door. Wine sounded better and would hopefully help her relax.

Yet, when she turned around and faced the small shelf above the stove, she noticed quickly that something was missing. There was no wine.

"Dammit!" Tara muttered.

Jed, she knew. He was the guilty party. He was always finishing off her supermarket selections, never once having the common courtesy to replace them.

Well, fuck him. She went back to the refrigerator and grabbed a beer. Maybe she'd show him and just smoke the rest of his stash. Of course, to do that, she'd have to find out where he'd hidden it.

Seemed like a lot of extra work when she could just yell at him later. So, that's what she planned to do. Tara unscrewed the top of her beer bottle, threw it onto the ceramic countertop, where it landed in a pile of takeout napkins, and then resumed her spot on the couch.

Yes, she'd wait and attack Jed when he got home…whenever that was.

Oh, Jed, she thought as she closed her eyes once again. He was a lot of things, *definitely* a little stupid. Still, it wasn't like it took a college degree to determine what she'd been up to earlier. He'd passed Collins in the hallway and then walked into the apartment to find her hair down and ass out. He'd known but had kept quiet. Well, except for mumbling "whore" under his breath before slamming the door shut to the back bedroom.

Still, what could he have said without sounding like a complete hypocrite? Okay, so he'd never brought a woman back to their apartment. However, he'd come into the pub tonight—just like he did most nights— and made it as clear as glass that he had no respect for her, or, really, any woman.

In between buying shots and fruity drinks for three or four different girls who'd just barely turned twenty-one (she'd eagerly checked all of their IDs), Jed had taken turns groping each of them on the makeshift dance floor before choosing one and "teaching" her how to shoot a better pool game.

Then, to add insult to injury, the bastard hadn't even bothered to leave her a tip on his $88.00 tab. Thankfully, she'd had the good sense to charge him double on the shots. Then, still keeping with his popular nightly

74

routine, he'd picked one of the lucky skanks at random to go home with. A damn creature of habit, Tara assumed he was with her now and wouldn't be home until dawn. Typical.

Somewhere between hating Jed and wanting him dead, her beer had gone flat. Tara placed the half-empty bottle on the table and stood up. She began studying herself in the large rectangular mirror that hung over the couch. Even through the streaks that stained the glass, Tara saw herself, and, truth be told, she wasn't that impressed. This was the youngest she was ever going to be, so didn't that mean she should also look her hottest?

Tara didn't feel hot at the moment—just the opposite.

She wanted extensions desperately, now cursing her so-called friend and new beauty school enrollee for talking her into the less-than-flattering pixie cut. The short blonde 'do, combined with her non-existent hips and small boobs, created a look that wasn't all that feminine, or hot.

She'd started her fake tit fund when she'd been eighteen. Now, after saving money on and off for a handful of years, it looked as if she'd finally be able to afford a new set of jugs when she was in her fifties. And, by then, what would be the fucking point?

Tara was proud of her tattoo, though. She felt like it gave her much-needed character. Lightly tracing the tail of the purple lizard, she caught herself smiling. She'd chosen the reptile for a couple of different reasons, but mostly because it was her body and she could put whatever she wanted on it. She'd been drawn to the fact that lizards like herself were known for their skin. Tara had had to learn at a very young age that if she wanted to survive, she'd need to grow a thick skin.

She continued looking at herself. The task seemed to be getting easier.

Tara didn't wear much makeup, mainly because she was lazy and cheap, but also because she'd never really thought that she needed it. Sure, she didn't consider herself a beauty queen, not by a long shot, but she preferred the plain, natural look. It seemed to suit her. Plenty of guys seemed to think so, too. After all, her bedpost had pretty much been notched down to a toothpick.

Then again, if she went back and looked at the quality of her many manly companions, that was hardly a compliment. Most guys didn't care about hair, tattoos, or makeup. Ultimately, they were looking for a place to "put it," and they'd found that place with Tara.

Her jewelry was always minimal, too. She wore a ring she'd gotten on her sixteenth birthday—instead of a car—and a pair of gold hoop earrings she'd stolen at the mall last year. She wasn't a bling-bling sort of girl. One, she couldn't afford it, and, two, she found it unnecessary. Jewelry was for rich people who wanted to show off, and she didn't fit into either of those categories.

She rolled her eyes, shrugged, and then turned her back to the mirror. That was more than enough torture for one night.

Her mind quickly traveled back to her boyfriend—or, more appropriately, her roommate. She'd loved Jed once upon a time, or, at least, she'd thought she had. But, at some point in their relationship, they'd become roommates and had stopped caring about each other in *that* sort of way. Tara couldn't even remember the last time they'd gone on a date. Or had sex. But, such was life, she figured. Or such was her life.

And, it sucked.

She started down the short hallway. She wasn't going to get a hot meal, not tonight, but she still craved a shower and hoped it would hit the spot.

The bathroom was—so small it didn't even offer a tub, just a red-tiled shower. Though it was sometimes a pain to not have a choice, tonight she didn't care. Sitting, standing, Tara didn't give a rat's ass; she wanted to be clean. She wanted to scrub away the sweat and grime of the pub, and then, if she had even an ounce of luck in her, get a decent night's sleep.

Tara kicked off her leather boots and traded her dark skinny jeans and black tank top for a tiny cloth robe that barely reached her thighs. Pink was hardly her color, but it had been a gift—from Jed, no less—and, well, free was free.

Back in the hallway, she headed for the kitchen. With one lone beer remaining, Tara knew it would taste better under the thick spray of the showerhead. *Locking the apartment door probably wouldn't be a bad idea, either*, she thought.

That was a habit she needed to get into—especially now. Jed had a key, obviously, and if he was too drunk or stupid to remember where he kept it and ended up having to sleep in the back of his truck, then that was just the way the cookie crumbled. It would serve him right.

Tara reached the door but frowned in confusion. The deadbolt and locking chain were both already in place.

She spun around swiftly and leaned against the door, her back flat against it. Was she not alone in the apartment?

"Jed?" she called out. "Are you here, Jed?"

Nothing. No answer. Stillness.

76

Surely, he would have said something if he'd come home and saw she was still awake? *Then again, this is Jed.* If he had come home, he would have snuck in like the piece of shit he was and gone to the bedroom directly.

Still, how had she not seen or heard him? She'd only been in the bathroom for a few minutes. Had he really moved that quickly and quietly?

"Jed?" she tried again. Nothing.

The living room was how she'd left it, down to her beer bottle still staring at her from its place on the table.

Tara hit the switch to her left. The overhead light went out and she was surrounded by complete darkness. Jed was no doubt up to something, and she wasn't going to fall for it. Not this time.

"Fuck you," she muttered. She walked into the kitchen.

Tara found the room empty, but she knew she would. Jed hadn't stopped in the kitchen on his way to the bedroom, but, if he had, he at least had had enough consideration to not take the last beer. Quite the gentleman, that Jed.

Back in the hallway, beer in hand, that's when she heard what sounded like he was snoring already. Drunk and passed out, she figured. Tara shook her head. Perhaps she'd get lucky and he'd choke on his own vomit.

She sighed. No, she couldn't let that happen. She was a lot of things, but she wasn't a monster. Well, not *all* of the time.

However, as soon as she entered the bedroom, she noticed it was empty. Jed wasn't in bed. No one was.

"What the hell?" Tara set her beer bottle down on the oak dresser. Something wasn't right.

Had she imagined the noise? Had it just been her sleepy mind playing a trick on her?

Tara had to be sure she was truly alone. She set out to search the room.

Closet—*clear.*

Under the bed—*clear.*

Behind the door—*clear.*

She was starting to lose it. She needed sleep—and that second beer.

Tara tiptoed across the rough carpet, entered the bathroom, and then shut and locked the door. She placed the beer bottle on the edge of the sink and the glass made a *clinking* sound.

She looked in the mirror. "Get it together," she warned herself.

The dark circles under her blue eyes proved she was lacking in the sleep department. She would rest. First, though, she would shower.

She pivoted around. Tara pulled back the polka-dotted curtain in one swift motion.

She was no longer alone.

13

Matt couldn't lie: Waking up next to someone was pretty nice. He may not have known where his relationship with Kathy was going—or if it was going anywhere—but, for the moment, he was enjoying just being *with* someone. He liked having her as company. He also happened to like that his company was in bed and completely naked.

"I'm glad you called me last night." She rolled toward him. "It was nice that you invited me over, even if it was late."

He smiled and pulled her in close to his bare chest. "You know it often takes guys a while to come to their senses."

"You called me at 2:00 a.m., and I came running. What's that say about me?"

"Hmm," he stated, "that you like to cuddle?"

She propped herself up on her right elbow. "Oh, we did a lot more than cuddling. Don't tell me you've forgotten already?"

"I was hoping you could refresh my memory." He leaned down and placed his dry lips on hers.

Kathy drew back instantly. "I want to talk, Matt."

He sighed. Of course she wanted to talk. Matt wasn't surprised, and he honestly didn't blame her. They did have a lot to talk about, but he was still disappointed. No man wanted to begin his morning by taking part in a deep conversation. Where was the fun in that?

He hadn't meant to use Kathy; that had never been his intention. Still, Matt feared that that was exactly what he'd done, and he hated himself for it now.

He'd called her last night, genuinely missing her. Spending time with Kathy was always nice, but he was beginning to see that their time together meant more to her than it did to him.

Of course, he'd known that yesterday when she'd confessed her love for him and he hadn't returned the gesture. He'd hoped to explore her feelings further, but that hadn't exactly happened when she'd come over in the middle of the night.

Go figure. Now that she was ready to talk, that was the farthest thing from his mind...and other parts of him.

Maybe he was a typical man. Matt didn't want to be. A caring, respectable gentleman was what he'd always aimed for—at least, he'd thought so, until now. Until Kathy.

In reality, whether he meant to or not, he was hurting Kathy. He was going to keep on hurting her until he made a clean break. He was treating her like a rubber band, pulling her forward, then letting her snap back. Sooner or later, Kathy was going to snap, and he'd be one hundred percent responsible for it.

"We need to discuss what I said yesterday."

"Okay," he agreed.

"I mean, that's why you called, right? You're ready to talk about this? About us?"

Matt nodded. "Yes." He was ready to talk. He just wasn't sure how to say what was on his mind—not without crushing her completely. Kathy deserved the truth, but could she handle it?

"I guess I should start." She sat up taller. "What I said yesterday about loving you—I meant it. I love you, Matt. Now, I need to know if you think you could ever love me. It doesn't have to be today or tomorrow, but, eventually, do you see yourself loving me?"

He couldn't look at her. Maybe that made him a coward, but he couldn't stare into her doe-like eyes knowing they'd reveal all. Her voice had been so soft, so vulnerable. It was hard telling what her eyes would say, exactly, but he had a good idea. So, Matt looked away.

He stared down at the beige sheet that covered both of their bodies. It was hard to believe that just hours ago, that same sheet had been a tangled knot between them as they'd attacked one another hungrily, each of their mouths craving the other. Neither of them had been talking then. Matt wanted to go back to that time. The thick scent of sweat and sex still hung in the air, torturing him.

Yes, he desperately wanted to go back.

Why couldn't Kathy just want to have fun? Seriously, what was wrong with just having a bit of fun these days? Why did there have to be such a focus on the actual relationship part? And, the future. Why was that always such a big issue?

Dammit! Was it really *that* hard to live in the present? To live for the now?

Matt would have loved for things to be different. Having stronger feelings for Kathy would have made his life easier. Unfortunately, that just wasn't the case.

"You can be honest, Matt," she offered. "Don't be afraid you might hurt my feelings. Just tell me the truth. Let me know if I'm wasting my time."

He went back to focusing on everything in the room except for her. Matt didn't give her eye contact, but he could feel her dark pupils burning holes into him.

First, his gaze traveled to the white walls that needed painting, then the pile of files on the metal desk that begged to be organized. Finally, he stared up at the ceiling fan that was spinning in what seemed to be slow motion. He couldn't remember the last time he'd dusted…

"Are you listening to me, Matt?"

"Yes." He forced himself to look at her. "I was just thinking."

"Okay," she nodded. "Care to share?"

How could he tell her that he had feelings for Cate? She'd asked him yesterday point-blank, and he'd lied to her face. If he told her the truth now, well, it wasn't that hard to guess how she'd react.

Matt's attraction to Cate was new—well, semi-new. He placed its origin right around the time she'd started confiding in him about O.J. about her less-than-perfect marriage. Sure, he'd always been drawn to Cate and found her cute. Most men did. But, it hadn't been until she'd acted like she *needed* him that Matt began feeling differently about Cate, to see her in a whole new light.

Maybe that was his purpose in life, who he was: a protector. He was someone to defend those in need. He was, after all, a cop. Still, this was the first time he'd been connected to a woman who needed to be rescued, and it was driving him absolutely crazy.

Then, of course, there was the million-dollar question: If he really liked Cate, had feelings for her, and believed she was in danger by staying with O.J., then why wasn't he trying to save her?

Kathy released a heavy sigh, and her nostrils started to flare ever so slightly. He had to say something. Now!

"I like you, Kathy." Matt released her hand. "I like spending time with you and getting to know you, and it's always great having you here."

"But?" "There's no 'but,'" he countered. "Honestly, I'm having a lot of fun, and I'd like to keep having fun."

She let go of his hand. "That's great, Matt, but that doesn't answer my question."

No, it didn't. To properly answer her question, he'd have to tell her that he'd hoped by dating her, his feelings for Cate would go away, just evaporate of their own accord.

Well, so far, *that* hadn't happened. He couldn't trick his head—or heart—into replacing Kathy with Cate. Not yet, anyway, and he probably never would.

That was what he needed to tell Kathy. That's what she'd asked to hear. Yet, Matt couldn't make himself form the words and speak them aloud. Just bouncing them around in his mind, they seemed cruel and insensitive. Then again, the brutal truth usually was cruel and insensitive.

"I know I didn't answer your question," he said, "but I'm trying to."

"It's not that difficult, Matt." She crossed her arms over her sheet-covered chest. "In fact, the more you stall, the more I think—"

"Can't we just keep doing what we're doing?" he interrupted. "Let's continue to get to know one another and—"

"I already know you, Matt. Or, I know enough. I can see myself with you for a while, maybe even..." Kathy let her words trail off. "If you can't see yourself with me long-term, then there's no reason for me to stay. I'm just going to get my hopes up and my heart broken."

A sharp guilt erupted in Matt's stomach. He had a sickening feeling that the former had already taken place and that the latter was close behind.

"It's fine, really." Kathy shifted her body and pushed her legs to the side of the bed. "I don't blame you. This is my fault. I-I-I knew yesterday, *before* yesterday, even. It's Cate." She stood and started for the adjacent bathroom. "I knew better than to come here last night."

Cate. There was her name again. *Cate.*

Cate was O.J.'s wife. O.J. was his best friend, his partner...his brother, or the closest thing he'd ever had to one. They weren't bound by blood, technically, but they might as well have been.

He and Cate were never going to be able to be together. It was as simple as that. Not if he expected O.J. to be in his life. Besides, he didn't even know if Cate felt the same way about him. For all he knew, she thought of him as a friend, or a big brother, even. That's why she'd chosen to confide in him in the first place.

Matt needed to move on. He needed to find someone else—and there was no reason why that someone else shouldn't be Kathy.

"Wait." He looked over at her. Standing in the doorway of the bathroom, she'd already managed to put on her jeans and T-shirt and was now pushing her hair back into a ponytail. "Don't go," he ordered. "Please stay."

"I can't, Matt." She shrugged. "It's not fair."

"I want to make this work. I *do* like you, Kathy. And, I really would like to see where this is going."

She smiled and dropped her hands to her sides. "Yeah?" She took a small step toward the bed.

It was probably wrong, but Matt didn't know what else to do. His father had been right: Relationships weren't for everyone.

"Yes." He returned her smile. "Now, come back to bed."

Before she'd even hit the mattress, his cell phone rang. Matt knew from experience that phone calls before 8:00 a.m. never brought good news.

He turned to his nightstand, grabbed the phone, and looked down at the number. Matt immediately recognized it and his heart began pounding.

"This is Deputy Combs," he answered.

"It's Sheriff Sutton."

"Good morning, Sheriff."

"Not for somebody," the man said in a dry tone. "There's been another murder, Matt. Victim number three. It looks like Perry's Creek has its first official serial killer."

"Shit," Matt muttered.

"I've already contacted O.J. I need you two to work the crime scene. Now."

"Right." Matt stepped out of the bed. "What's the address? We'll see you there."

"No, you won't," the sheriff argued. "Beau and I are getting ready to question the killer down at the police department." He paused for a brief moment and then added, "We got him, Matt!"

"He wants ten thousand dollars."

"That's what the new note said?"

"Here." Georgia passed the sheet across the glass to Cate.

It was almost 8:00 in the morning, and she hadn't had one drop of caffeine. Cate knew it was going to be a long day.

She accepted the paper from her mother and gave it a quick look. Sure enough, whoever had left the first threat had dropped off a new one, and he or she was now demanding ten grand to keep quiet.

Cate had to deliver another blow to her mother.

"The man I suggested yesterday, well, I don't think he's responsible for the notes."

"What?" Georgia asked. "You were so sure of it. What changed?"

Cate shrugged. She sat at the table in her mother's kitchen, searching for the right words to explain her theory. She wasn't sure there were any—not that that would make her mom understand.

"If not him," Georgia said, "then who? Why would—?"

"I don't know, Mom, but can you please stop throwing so many questions at me?" Cate began massaging her temple slowly. The pressure in her head was heavy, and she didn't know if she wanted to cry or scream. Maybe both.

Cate hadn't been at her mother's for even ten minutes and she was regretting coming. Her mom had called her in a panic this morning. She'd found another message. This time, it had been taped to her refrigerator. Someone had been in her home again, only they'd been creeping around while Georgia had been sleeping.

Her mother had been spooked, to say the least, and, as soon as Joshua left after receiving an emergency phone call from the sheriff, Cate had come running. Now, she was reconsidering those actions. What could she offer her mother that would help the situation besides what now seemed to be doubt and confusion?

"I've been thinking about it," Cate spoke finally, "and it doesn't make sense that Collins would be in Perry's Creek."

"You're confusing me, Cate." Georgia balled her hands into fists. "Did you see Collins at the coffee shop yesterday or not?"

"I don't know," Cate admitted. "I don't think so. I mean, yes, at first I thought I'd seen him. You came in and told me about the threat. It all seemed to fit."

"Yes." Georgia nodded.

"But then, I got to thinking," Cate continued. "I'd been tired and upset yesterday. Not to mention, I'd only seen the side of the man's face. I think I might have jumped to a conclusion too soon."

Georgia sighed. "I can't believe this is happening."

Cate stared across the table, taking in her mother's appearance. The woman looked exhausted. She'd aged in the past forty-eight hours. The dark circles under her eyes and the extra lines around her mouth more than proved that.

"Yesterday, after you suggested Collins left the note, it was as if I could suddenly see the threat. I don't need to tell you why it seemed so obvious that he was at the center of all of this."

In an attempt to avoid eye contact, Cate turned away from her mother. Longing for a distraction, she let her gaze settle on the coffee pot by the stove in the corner of the kitchen. The brew seemed to be mocking her. The more she craved it, the slower it seemed to drip. When would the damn pot be filled already?

She and her mother had agreed to never talk about that night, but, yet again, Georgia was referring to it. The past was getting harder and harder to stay buried.

"I know it would be a living hell if Collins was to come back into our lives, but I can't figure out who else could have delivered the threats, or even why."

"Seriously?" Cate asked. "You've had to have pissed off tons of people in your life. I'm sure you've done something that warrants revenge."

"Yeah, well, only one murder comes to mind."

"Is that necessary, Mom?" Cate couldn't hold back anymore. Her head no longer felt heavy; it was throbbing angrily. She knew she was about to lose it, but staying quiet was no longer an option. "We said we'd never talk about that night again. So, please, *stop* talking about it!"

As soon as she'd heard her own bitter tone, Cate felt guilty. She crouched lower in the cloth chair as if she could become invisible. She hadn't meant to yell at her mother. The words had just flown out, dripping with fury and frustration, and now she wished she could disappear because disrespecting her mother was never a wise thing to do.

However, Georgia didn't respond. She remained silent. The only sound she made was with her right hand when she drummed her fingers softly on the glass in front of her.

The tapping noise was making Cate go crazy. It was even worse than the awkward stillness. Still, Cate remained button-lipped, and she was going to stay that way. Cate knew that she'd sooner pull her hair out than criticize her mother again.

Finally, to avoid the unsettling moment altogether, Cate stood. She walked to the coffee pot and busied herself with pouring a mug of joe. Just for a second, she inhaled the dark roast scent, reveling in the richness of it. She allowed it to take her to someplace else, someplace other than her mother's kitchen where she was getting the third degree.

"Fine," she said, her back still to her mother. "When's the last time you saw Collins? Or even heard from him?"

"It's been a while," Georgia sighed. Her tapping stopped. "Honestly, it's probably been a couple of years since I've seen or heard from him. The last I knew, Collins was still on heroin, dating that frigid bitch, Hannah Harper."

"I remember."

"Maybe you're right," Georgia said. "If Collins is still an addict, then he's probably not even in the right mindset to be in Perry's Creek, delivering threatening notes."

"Collins would have taken a more direct approach." Cate turned around to face her mom. "Don't you think? He would have confronted you—or even me—head-on. And, it would have been years ago. That is, if he *truly* knows what we did."

Georgia nodded. "You're right, Cate. When you put it like that, you're absolutely right."

Even though the dust had settled and all seemed to be right again, that rusty can of worms had still been pried open. Cate couldn't control herself and asked, "Do you ever feel guilty, Mom, about what we did?"

Georgia didn't blink. "Not once," she said in an even tone. "I haven't lost one night's sleepover that bastard. I hope you haven't, either. He got what he deserved."

Perhaps, Cate thought. There'd been so much violence and pain throughout her entire life. Still, did two wrongs truly make a right?

Cate shook her head. She couldn't go down that path. She refused to. If Cate unraveled just one tiny thread, then the whole rug covering the rough, uneven floorboards of her life would come undone. That couldn't happen. Cate wouldn't *let* it happen.

"We need to think about who else could have left the notes and why." Cate decided to move on as she rejoined her mom at the table. "If we find the motive behind the threats, we find the culprit."

"Okay," Georgia said. "I'll do some thinking, try and come up with a list of possible suspects."

"That will be helpful." Cate set her mug down on the table. "Can I get you some?"

"No." Georgia shook her head. "My nerves are already buzzing. Caffeine won't help. I made the coffee for you."

"Thank you."

"So." Georgia folded her hands on her silk-robe-covered lap. "How're things with Joshua? Any baby news?"

"I don't want to talk about him." Cate made sure her voice was as soft as possible. "Not right now. One crisis at a time."

"Fair enough."

Before another uncomfortable moment of silence could creep in and fester, Cate asked, "What if you just ignored the threats? Threw them in the garbage and forgot about them?"

"Easier said than done," Georgia argued. "Someone has been in my house—twice. What if this person decides to turn violent? It might be best to just give him what he wants and get it over with."

"Well, do you have an extra ten thousand dollars lying around?"

"No, not exactly," she admitted. "But, I do have an idea. You're just not going to like it."

* * *

It was on days like today that she was grateful to have a job. Between her growing issues with Joshua, and now the mysterious drama with her mother, Cate knew the worst thing she could do was sit at home all alone and reflect on things. Just the thought of it made her shiver. Work was certainly a less grueling option. Being at the Brim even made her smile.

From behind the counter, Cate stared out into the shop. Some people in Perry's Creek seemed to be having a good morning. The handful of customers who sat sipping lattes or nibbling on chocolate cupcakes either didn't have a care in the world or were masters at hiding it. Happiness—maybe it wasn't completely lost.

The sun was already starting to creep in through the large glass windows in the front and blast heat into the shop. It was going to be another beautiful summer day. Living on the outskirts of San Diego definitely had its perks, and though Cate couldn't quite recall the last time she'd been to the beach to breathe in the crisp, salty air that hovered over the ocean water, it was still nice to know that the option was always there.

"Think it's going to be a busy day?"

Cate turned to Jerry and smiled. "Here's hoping. I suspect most people already know that mornings are much better with a big cup of coffee."

"Definitely." Jerry nodded. "When you have a second, Cate, I'd really like to talk to you about something."

"Sure. Is it about the new system? Because—"

"No," Jerry interrupted. "It's not work-related."

"Oh, okay." She felt her stomach drop. What kind of news was Jerry going to deliver? Whatever it was, she knew it wasn't going to be good. Otherwise, he would have spat it out already.

"I don't really want to talk here, though. The back?"

"We have customers, Jerry."

"They'll be fine, and we'll be able to hear if anyone comes into the shop," he said. "This won't take long."

Cate frowned. *Was this necessary?* Yet she ultimately gave in and followed him to the back of the shop.

Jerry stood in place, his hands shoved deep in his pockets and his back pressed flat against one of the metal storage cabinets. Dressed in jeans and a short-sleeved, collared shirt—his usual work attire—Jerry seemed to be concerned about something. His light eyes were wide but still offered a certain softness. His bottom lip was pointed downward, almost as if he was battling with himself to get the words out and say whatever it was he had to say.

"What's going on, Jerry? Is everything okay?" Cate took a defensive stance. She crossed her arms over her apron-covered chest.

"I don't know, Cate," he answered. "Is it?"

She felt her eyes narrow in confusion. "What are you talking about?"

"I'm worried about you, Cate."

She uncrossed her arms and placed her hands on her hips. "Worried about me? Why?"

"Come on, Cate," he sighed. "You can talk to me, confide in me."

"I don't know what you're talking about, Jerry, but I'd really like to get back to work."

He took a step forward. "I'm not trying to scare you or make you feel uncomfortable," he offered, his tone smooth. "But, I'm not stupid, Cate, or blind, for that matter. I've seen—"

"Please, Jerry," Cate begged. She didn't want to go to *that* place, not today, and certainly not with him. "I don't think…"

"I just want you to know that I'm here for you." He took another step toward her. His hands were now out in front of him almost as if he was going to grab her.

"I appreciate that, Jerry. Thank you. Now…"

"If you ever want to talk, or if you ever need anything—*anything* at all—let me know."

"T-t-thank you," she repeated. Cate tried to angle her body away from him, but she couldn't. There was no place for her to go. He was just feet away from her. Jerry had her trapped.

"I know I may not look it, Cate, but I'm a very capable man. I can help make sure that you're being treated right. After all, you deserve the best." He reached out and grabbed her right hand.

"This isn't appropriate, Jerry." She wanted to be nice and professional, but he was making her feel uncomfortable.

Suddenly, her skin felt itchy. She wanted to scratch, but she couldn't. Somehow, he had her frozen, immobile. Jerry was pulling her in closer and closer. His rising chest was touching her, and his breath—she could feel his hot, sour breath on her face. Was he going to—?

The bell from the front of the shop chimed. They had a new customer.

"I'll handle that." Jerry stepped back. "Take a moment and think about what I said."

As soon as he was gone, Cate exhaled. Until then, she hadn't even realized she'd been holding her breath.

"Dammit," she whispered. As if she didn't already have enough on her overfilled plate, now this.

It was bad that Jerry, her boss, had just made a pass at her, but he also knew that she was being abused, that Joshua was beating her. Would he tell someone? Would he take matters into his own hands?

How was Jerry going to react next? More importantly, what was Joshua going to do once he found out that people in town were starting to notice his work?

Cate knew the answer already, and it chilled her to the bone.

Beau shook his head. "I'm telling you: *He's* not the killer."

"What do you mean? He was found standing over the victim."

"He found the victim, yes. But, he didn't kill her."

"Come on, Beau," Shannon pleaded. "This has to be our guy. It makes perfect sense. It's so easy."

"It's *too* easy. We still need to question him, but I'm warning you, don't get your hopes up."

Beau hated to be the bearer of bad news, but his friend needed to know the truth. Sure, Shannon and Mayor Jackson wanted this case to be solved already, wrapped up nice and tight with a little red bow on top, but Beau refused to let someone innocent take the fall for three murders just so an arrest could be made. He didn't work like that.

Besides, if the real killer wasn't put behind bars, then what was the point?

"Okay." Shannon dropped into the chair behind his desk. "At least tell me this: Why are you so sure he's not the killer? We haven't even talked to him yet."

"I already told you." Beau took the seat opposite the sheriff. "It's too easy. The guy strangles two women, leaving nothing behind, not even a thumbprint. Then, he murders a third girl and is dumb enough to be found standing over the body? No. That doesn't add up. We're looking for someone a lot smarter than Jed Turner."

"But—"

"And, you're overlooking the fact that we can't even connect him to the first two victims. He has no motive for doing this."

"Yet," Shannon corrected. "We can't connect him to the other women.

Yet. But, we will." He reached for the coffee mug in the center of his desk but didn't bring it up to his lips. The sheriff just gripped the dark handle. "Look, maybe Jed wanted his girlfriend dead all along. Maybe that was his plan. So, he murders the first two women to create a serial killer, and then murders his girlfriend to make it look like she was just part of—"

"You've got to be kidding me!" Beau exploded. "Are you even listening to yourself, Shannon?"

"What?" The sheriff's tone became thicker, more defensive. "It's possible. It's happened before."

"Yeah," Beau mocked, "in Lifetime movies. Besides, I highly doubt this Turner guy is clever enough to come up with such an intricate plan."

Shannon sighed. "Well, *I* need to come up with something. So far, I've been pretty lucky. The community hasn't really responded to the murders. Only the mayor is acting irrationally. Thankfully, the newspaper doesn't know all of the details about the crimes yet and hasn't blown the story out of proportion completely. With a third victim and the mention of a serial killer…it's hard to predict how people will react. But, it won't be pretty, Beau. In fact, it's probably going to be downright ugly."

"I understand." Beau leaned forward in his chair. "I get that the mayor is hounding you to make an arrest before this case explodes. I used to do this for a living, remember? But, think of the false hope you'll create if you arrest the wrong man. And then, all of the repercussions. It'll only make things that much worse."

"Fuck!" The sheriff threw his arms into the air. "What about the earrings?" He sat up straighter in his chair. "I've got Abbott and Combs over there now. They're looking for the missing earrings. They could find…"

Beau shook his head again.

"Okay, so what now, then?" Shannon asked. "You seem to know it all. What do we do now? Just send the guy on his way? Thank him for his time and let him walk right out of here?"

Beau let the dig slide. He knew his friend was feeling the pressure. Still, Shannon was going to have to get it together, and quickly. After all, Beau was still doing the man a favor, and Beau was good at his job. Wasn't that a good thing?

"Of course we're still going to question him," Beau answered. "We'll make him think he's a suspect, see what he knows. He might be able to tell us something."

"Unless he can tell us who the fucking killer is, it will be a waste of time."

"What's wrong with you?" Beaus asked finally. He rose to his feet. "It's like you're afraid to do some actual police work."

"Excuse me?"

"Since I've been here, you've had this attitude, this expectation. You want the case to be solved right now, but you don't want to do any work to solve it. The killer isn't going to just stop strangling women one day, or get bored and miraculously turn himself in. That's not how this works."

"Thank you, Beau," the sheriff snapped, "but I know how this works."

Beau shrugged. "You could have fooled me. I'm not sure if it's from being married to Diane for so many years or it's because you're running a town like Perry's Creek, but you've gotten soft."

"Go to hell, Beau!" Shannon stood. "You know, you're in my office. You could have some damn respect."

Beau pivoted around, turning his back on the sheriff. He didn't say anything. Instead, he raked his hands through his hair before bridging them together and placing them at the back of his taut neck.

He needed a drink. Maybe two.

Had it been a mistake to come here? Beau had had some reservations when Shannon first asked him to come to Perry's Creek, and for good reason, but he'd shaken every last doubt away. He'd wanted to see his friend, and he'd wanted to help. Now, though, Beau couldn't help but feel as if he'd made a big mistake.

Unfortunately, Beau needed to come to terms with the fact that sometimes it didn't matter how hard you fought. You could claw, bite, kick—hell, even pray—the past could never be changed.

Maybe that was for the best. What had happened was done and over with, and there was no going back now. No amount of childish insults or ridicule would make the situation any better.

It was time to move on. It was way *past* time to move on.

"I'm sorry," Beau whispered. "I shouldn't have said that about Diane. It was out of line."

Shannon sighed. "I'm sorry, too."

Beau felt his head drop in confusion. He turned around, finally. "What? Why are you sorry? You didn't—"

"I asked you to come here," Shannon said. "I asked for your help, and now that I'm getting it, I'm arguing with you. I'm fighting you, and I don't know why."

"Because you want this all to be over," Beau provided. "The sooner you arrest someone, the sooner—"

"But, like you said, it won't do me or the Creek any good to arrest the wrong guy."

Beau wasn't sure what to say, so he just shrugged.

"And, maybe it was a little selfish of me to ask you to come here," Shannon continued. "I know it hasn't been easy, and I haven't really been—"

"You don't have to go there." Beau raised his right hand. "It's fine." He wasn't sure he was ready for *that* uncomfortable conversation, not when he was supposed to be preparing mentally for an interrogation.

Some things needed to be said. That was the main reason Beau had agreed to come to Perry's Creek in the first place. Still, there was a time and place for everything, and, right now, Beau's main concern was catching a killer.

Not to mention, Beau was terrified of what Shannon was going to say. His insides were doing summersaults already, and an awful, nails-down-a-chalkboard-like sound was screeching in and out of his head.

That's a whole other type of conversation to prepare for mentally, he thought.

"We can talk later," Beau said. "But, for now, let's go see what that piece of shit has to share with us."

* * *

The air in the small room was thick and stuffy as if it hadn't been used in a few months. Then again, Beau assumed that not many interrogations took place at the Perry's Creek Police Department. The notion explained the stack of water-stained boxes in the corner. This space wasn't used as a place to question suspects but as a storage facility.

The interrogation/storage room didn't offer a window, just a small round table with a few mismatched chairs positioned around it, which Beau guessed had been brought in this morning by Deputy Benson or some other low-on-the-totem-pole employee.

He tugged at his tie to loosen the knot. Beau felt better almost instantly. Without a doubt, three was a crowd, Beau decided, as he stepped in behind the sheriff. He took inventory of Jed Turner immediately.

Turner looked completely miserable as he tapped his large booted foot against the brown linoleum floor. His nose was wrinkled. It was impossible to ignore the musty, mildew stench, but at least someone had fetched him a small paper cup of water. Jed Turner wasn't going to die of thirst. Although he most likely wasn't a murderer or the one *they* were searching for, he looked the part with his sleeveless flannel shirt and bad haircut.

"Hi, Jed," Shannon started. "We appreciate—"

"Is this going to take long? I've got stuff to do today."

"We just want to ask you a few questions." Shannon pulled out one of the small chairs and took a seat. "Of course, the more you cooperate, the faster all of this will go. Understand?"

"Yes." Jed rolled his eyes. "I'm not an idiot. What do you want to know?"

"First, what can you tell us about Tara?"

"Well, I didn't kill her, which I'm guessing is what you really want to know."

"Do you have any proof of that?" Beau spoke up finally. He'd purposely let the sheriff lead the interrogation, but he was getting annoyed, and fast. Turner had that typical "badass" attitude, and Beau was more than ready to tackle it straight on.

What was the deal with these defensive scumbags? He'd seen it a million times. Turner was being questioned about a murder. Was it actually that hard to be polite and helpful? Wouldn't someone with even half a brain want to assist the police?

"I was at Tammi's Pub for most of the night," Jed answered. "And then, I went home with some girl. I don't remember her name."

"Did you get her phone number?" Beau still hadn't joined Shannon and Jed at the table but remained at the closed door with his back pressed against it. He could already feel sweat starting to form.

"What do you think?" Jed pointed his chin toward Beau.

Beau crossed his arms. "I think it's interesting that you have a girlfriend, a live-in girlfriend, no less, but went home with someone else. What's that all about, Jed?"

"None of your fucking business."

"Well, we're making it our fucking business," Shannon spoke up. "So, how about you drop the attitude and help us? Otherwise, you're going down for—"

"Are you serious?" Jed yelled. "I had no reason to kill Tara."

"Really?" Beau leaned forward. "Let's see." He rubbed the edge of his chin. "Tara finds out you slept with another woman. You come home, get into an argument, and then strangle her. Seems pretty cut and dried to me."

"That's bullshit, man." Jed shook his head. "Whoever strangled Tara strangled those other two girls, and I didn't do that. None of it."

"What makes you think that whoever killed Tara killed the others?" Beau asked. "Strangulation is a pretty common method of murder." Not to mention, the bit about the victims' earrings being taken hadn't been released to the public. A tactic used to help flush out the real killer, nobody knew about the stolen jewelry being a trophy except for the Perry's Creek Police Department. Well, and the murderer, of course.

Therefore, Beau couldn't help but feel that Turner's connect-the-dots conclusion was quite presumptuous, and, as far as the man knew, completely inaccurate.

"You mean there's more than one person strangling women in Perry's Creek? Okay," Jed mocked.

Beau took a step forward. "Listen, you dumb—"

"You don't seem too upset about your girlfriend's death," the sheriff interrupted. "Why is that?"

Jed shrugged. "We weren't dating. We lived together, sure, but Tara and I did our own things. We had a sort of mutual understanding."

"Are you even the tiniest bit upset that your 'roommate with benefits' was murdered?" Shannon asked.

Jed shrugged again. "Look." He folded his hands on the table. "Tara didn't deserve to be strangled, but am I sad? Will I lose any sleep over the fact that she's dead? I'll need to find a new roommate. But, honestly, Tara was only good at two things: giving head and collecting parking tickets. That's it."

Interesting, Beau thought, *and extremely grotesque.*

"Like I already told you," Jed began again, "I didn't kill Tara. I came home this morning and found her body in the bathroom, but that's it...."

Beau ran his shaking hands through his hair. It was definitely time for some booze.

Just as suspected, Turner was a dead end, a complete waste of time. He was a pig, but he wasn't a killer, and, as it'd turned out, he couldn't even offer up a sliver of help. That was the way too many interrogations seemed to go, Beau knew. So, now what were they going to do with him?

"Is there anything you can tell us?" Shannon's voice was too soft; it was almost on the verge of pleading as if he were begging for assistance from the man. "Anything at all that might be able to help us?"

"Well," Jed said through a toothy smile, "I may know who killed Tara."

"What?" Beau's eyebrows shot up with interest.

"Tara had someone at the apartment yesterday afternoon. I'm guessing they were sleeping together," he explained. "He probably had something to do with her murder. And, before you ask, no, I don't know his name or phone number."

Beau rolled his eyes, and his shoulders slumped. Were they ever going to catch a break?

"But," Jed went on, "I think I do know how to help you find him."

"**I**t was Joshua! I'm telling you! He strangled that bartender. He murdered the other two women, too. It makes sense."

"Why?" Matt asked. "How? Where's the proof?"

Cate took a deep breath and then exhaled slowly. She reached for a wine glass that wasn't there. *Habit*, she thought.

Cate had had a large glass of merlot with dinner, which Joshua had questioned. In fear that he'd measured the bottle and knew how much was left, she'd stopped herself from having more now. Still, that didn't mean she didn't want more. Cate's craving for more wine was strong, almost unbearable.

"Cate?" Matt asked. "You still there?"

"Yes." She gripped her cell phone tighter. "Joshua and I got into a fight last night. I took an Ambien and passed out. He could have snuck out of the house and killed that girl."

"Again, Cate, why?"

"I don't know," she admitted. "Well…" She bit her lower lip. "…I've been considering it, and I may have come up with something, but you might think it's crazy or a bit of a stretch."

"Tell me."

"Okay." She rolled back her tense shoulders. "Like me, all of the victims have had blonde hair and blue eyes. What if Joshua is strangling them in some weird, symbolic way of strangling me?"

"Cate…"

"Just let me finish." She had the guts to share her theory, finally, and she didn't want to stop now. "He hates me, right? But, is he going to kill me and get away with it? So, to fulfill his therapeutic needs, he kills women

98

that *look* like me. What if it's like he's killing me without *really* killing me?"

Matt was silent on the other end of the line, most likely pinching the bridge of his nose and shaking his head. Yet, seconds later, he said, "Unfortunately, you can't solve a murder investigation with 'what if.' You need facts, Cate. You need evidence. There's no evidence that points to O.J."

Ultimately, Matt was right. Cate had to come to terms with that. No evidence pointed to Joshua being the killer, just her feelings and beliefs, and Cate was well aware of the situation: She was biased. She *wanted* Joshua to be guilty.

"I'm still trying to come up with a way to confront O.J.," Matt said. "I want to talk to him. I want to help. I'm just not sure how to go about it. You know it's difficult," he admitted. "I'm kind of in an awkward place."

"I know," Cate said. "And, I'm sorry I confided in you and dragged you into my mess. It wasn't fair."

"Why did you?" Matt asked. "I mean, I'm not upset you told me. You had to tell someone. But, why did you choose me?"

Cate shrugged. "Well, it's not like I have a girlfriend to talk to or even a close friend. I've told my mother, obviously, but…"

"I get it," Matt said.

"There was another reason," Cate added slowly. She wasn't sure how to say this next part exactly but knew she now had no choice but to finish what she'd started.

"What was it?" Matt prompted.

"I figured you might be the only one who could help me." As she had expected, Matt became completely silent. Cate knew he hadn't hung up; she could still hear his deep breathing, but he said nothing.

She sat on the barstool in front of the counter and took a glance around the dark, empty kitchen. The only light came from the microwave flashing the time in a green glow. Cate realized she was starting to develop a pattern: Cook dinner for Joshua, clean up after Joshua, wait for Joshua to pass out, then sneak downstairs and call Matt. This was the second time this week she'd reached out to him, and while Cate knew the act wasn't right, she also seemed to have no control over it.

Her mind went back to wine. Just a sip would help to relax her, but Cate knew that she couldn't chance it. The risk just wasn't worth it. After all, she and Joshua had had a nice dinner, as nice as a dinner could be when you were sitting across from a man who enjoyed beating you, a man who was known to turn on a dime and snap without warning.

Cate had chosen to make a pot roast, and even in the suffocating heat, the dinner had still tasted good and had been a hit with Joshua. He'd talked throughout the entire meal, sharing details about his day, including the new murder, and Cate's mind had instantly begun to spin.

Surprisingly, Joshua had even stuck around and chatted, watching as she cleared the table and loaded the dishwasher. He'd been in an oddly good mood—for him—and hadn't raised his voice at her once the whole evening.

The unnatural behavior put Cate on edge, and because it happened so infrequently, she still hadn't gotten used to the times when Joshua acted that way. He wanted something or was planning something. Either way, Cate had been relieved when he'd announced an hour later that he was going out for a run. She knew what this meant: He'd be gone for forty minutes, come home, take a quick shower, and then go to bed, leaving her alone for the rest of the night. Well, until he woke up, crept down the stairs, and ordered her to join him in the bedroom.

The thick, beefy scent from dinner still hung strongly in the air, but Cate welcomed it. The smell reminded her of home—the good times, anyway. The times when her mother would make a big meal and they would all sit around the table, eating, smiling, and enjoying small talk, *pretending* to be a family.

The good ol' days, she thought, *before the bad took over and left its mark.*

Suddenly, Cate was plagued with a burning question: Should she inform Matt about the threatening blackmail notes her mother had received? She'd already made the decision not to tell Joshua. How could he possibly help? He'd most likely only get angry and then find a way to blame her for the entire mess.

Matt, on the other hand…could he offer assistance somehow?

She shook the idea away as quickly as it popped into her head. First off, Matt had done absolutely nothing to solve her other problem, so why would this new issue have a different result?

Secondly, sharing the threats with Matt could lead to her having no choice but to open the sealed file on her past, and she wasn't prepared to do that. Cate *wouldn't* share that secret; it would cost her too much.

Some things were just better left unsaid. Besides, Georgia had a plan for dealing with the demand from the second note. While Cate knew it would never work—not in a million years—at least it was a plan to work with. At the moment, it was their only option.

"You have no idea how bad I want to help you, Cate," he whispered. "Seriously."

She almost dropped her phone. Cate had been so lost in the darkness of her own mind that she'd forgotten Matt was on the other end of the line.

"I'm sure," Cate said flatly. She wanted to believe Matt, but he was making it too difficult.

Yes, he was Joshua's friend and partner. Yes, she'd put him in a difficult position. Yes, it made her a little bit selfish. Still, he was supposed to be her friend, too, and she needed help.

"Really," Matt continued. "I'm going to help you. I'll find a way. But, I have to be honest: I don't think O.J. killed that bartender or the other two women. Sheriff Sutton got a really good lead today."

"Joshua didn't mention that part tonight," she said. "What happened? What's the lead?"

"The bartender had a boyfriend," Matt explained. "Yesterday, the boyfriend saw some guy leaving her apartment. The sheriff thinks it could be the killer. And, that ex-detective, the sheriff's friend, thinks that that could be how the killer becomes familiar with his victims: He befriends or seduces them before going back to strangle them. He earns their trust."

"Interesting," Cate offered. "Who is the guy? Do you know him?"

"The boyfriend didn't recognize him. He thinks he might be new in town."

"Then how are you going to catch him?" she asked in confusion.

"The boyfriend is going to help," Matt answered. "He's guessing the guy will pay another visit to Tammi's Pub where the last victim worked."

"Doesn't that seem a little unlikely? I mean, if he killed this girl, would he go to the place where she worked?"

"I don't know," Matt said, and his voice sounded as if it was edged with razor blades. "The guy slipped up. He was seen outside of the victim's apartment before the murder, so maybe he'll make another mistake. Right now, it's the only thing we have to go on."

Cate didn't respond, mainly because she wasn't sure what to say. Matt was acting aggravated with the case. Or with her. Or both. Either way, she realized now that it was a mistake to have called him.

"Are you still there?"

"I'm still here," she sighed. Cate held the phone to her ear with her right shoulder and used her free hands to gently rub her bare arms. She knew she should have put a light sweater on over her T-shirt.

"I didn't mean to sound so heated," Matt said. "It's been a long day and I'm tired."

"I understand," Cate mumbled.

It had been a long day for her, too: the conversation with her mother, Jerry's advances, and then the discussion about the new murder over dinner. *When did life get easier?* Did it get easier? Or did you just grow more accustomed to all of the shit and learn how to swallow it down without a chaser?

"What do you think would happen if you threatened O.J.?"

"Excuse me?" Cate was positive she hadn't heard him correctly.

"What if you told O.J. that you were going to the police? Or that you were going to tell someone about the abuse?" Matt suggested. "What do you think would happen? What do you think he would do?"

Cate had to cough back a laugh. "You're joking, right? You know Joshua better than anyone—probably even better than me. What do you honestly think he'd do…?"

"I know he's got a temper, and sometimes a bad attitude, but…"

"If I told Joshua that the next time he hit me, he'd probably smile," Cate said. "Then, he'd most likely hit me harder than he's ever hit me before."

"You really—?"

"Why do you think I haven't gone to the police already?" Cate felt herself stand up. No longer cold, her body was now on fire. Matt had struck a nerve. "Joshua *is* the police. And, even if someone down at the department did believe me, you think that would stop Joshua? He'd come up with some sort of plan to make me look crazy. He doesn't lose, Matt. Ever."

"I understand," he said slowly. "But, his abuse isn't on record, so if you ever—"

"What? If I ever want to press charges? Get a restraining order? Get real, Matt!"

Cate started pacing. Her feet sank into the soft carpet as she crossed the length of her home—kitchen to dining room to living room—before pivoting around and repeating the course. It didn't matter that the entire house was dark. She knew the route well and had walked it many times in the late evening.

"I'm sorry, Cate. I didn't mean—"

"Maybe that's why I told you about Joshua," she said. "Maybe I thought you'd be able to talk to him, get him to stop beating me. But, we'll never know. You're too loyal to your abusive friend and partner."

"That's not fair, Cate!" Matt fired back. "You said it yourself. Involving me wasn't—"

"It's late," Cate said. "I should let you go. Give Kathy my best." She ended the call. "Dammit!" She tossed her cell onto the dining room table. "Dammit!"

Her last comment had been unnecessary, a low blow. Bringing Kathy into the conversation had been childish. Why had she done it?

Cate was well aware of the answer, and it terrified her. Mainly because it was ridiculous, but also because there was nothing she could do about it.

She and Matt were never going to be together. He would never be her man. End of story.

In all honesty, that was probably the last thing she needed, anyway. It was time to stop thinking about a man and hope that one might be able to save her.

Matt was a good guy, but he was Joshua's friend and always would be. That was never going to change. When it came to picking a side, Matt had already chosen his, and it wasn't hers. Cate had to move on.

If her mother had taught her anything, it was how to survive. Or, more importantly, how to survive without a man. That's what Cate was going to do. She was going to survive, and she had a plan that would help her do just that.

chapter 17

"**A**re you beating Cate?"

He stopped dead in his tracks. "You want to ask me that again?"

Matt shrugged. He did his best to avoid eye contact with O.J. He hadn't meant for the question to come out like that—so blatant and dripping with blame—but it had. Matt had been wrestling with the notion all morning, and ever since his conversation with Cate last night, he'd decided he was going to confront O.J. Now that he had, Matt wished he'd chosen a different tactic to address the issue.

"I have a hard time believing you'd ask me something like that," O.J. said. "You better explain yourself, Matt. Quickly."

Dammit! He was already off to a bad start.

"Matt?"

"Right." Matt nodded. "I guess that came out wrong. I didn't mean—"

"To accuse me of abusing my wife?" O.J. finished for him. "Why would you ask me something like that? Have you been talking to Cate? Did she give you the impression—?"

"No," Matt lied, "of course not. Cate hasn't said anything to me."

"Okay, then why did you ask me that?" O.J. frowned.

Matt pinched the bridge of his nose. He searched for something—anything—that would come off as even the slightest true. "I was at the Brim the other day and saw Cate. She was acting strange, even quiet. She had a small bruise and—"

"And you just assumed that I had hit her?"

"No," Matt argued. "It's not like that."

"Actually, it's *exactly* like that," O.J. argued.

Matt wasn't sure how to respond. The two of them stood in the police department's parking lot, facing each other. Embarrassed, and maybe a little worried, Matt stared down at the asphalt but could still feel O.J.'s gaze burning a hole into his own flesh. His best friend and partner wasn't going to back down. Typical O.J.

"Maybe it's best if we changed the subject," Matt suggested.

"Good idea." O.J. picked up his pace once again.

Matt followed suit. He knew he most likely hadn't helped Cate but made her life a lot worse. He'd have to do some major damage control. But, how?

The two headed toward the black and white police cruiser in complete silence. It wasn't even noon and the sun was already proving to be difficult, shining down angrily and burning the ground beneath their boots. When was the summer heat going to take a vacation?

Matt opened the passenger side door. "For what it's worth, I'm sorry. I didn't mean to…it was wrong for me to jump to conclusions. I hope we can move on and forget that I said anything."

O.J. positioned himself in the driver's seat. "Look, Cate and I have had our problems, that's no secret. We got married too quickly, but as you know, we really didn't have much of a choice."

Matt nodded.

"And then, she lost the baby on our honeymoon. Now, we're trying to have another baby, but it hasn't been easy. In fact, it's been rough, but I'm not going to run away from my problems. And, I'm certainly not going to try and beat them away."

"Right." Matt reached for the seat belt. "Again, I shouldn't have said—"

"I think Cate might be hurting herself."

"What?" The pitch of Matt's voice rose, and he felt his forehead wrinkle. "Cate wouldn't hurt herself." He stopped and took a quick second to compose himself. Matt heard his own defensive tone. He needed to dial it back and watch himself. The thin ice he was skating on could easily break at any given moment.

"You think you know Cate," O.J. explained, "but you don't. Not the way I do."

"Why would Cate hurt herself? I don't understand."

"I think she's stressed." O.J. placed the key in the ignition and started the car. "I think she blames herself for losing the baby, and for not being able to get pregnant again. Cate hasn't said too much to me about it, but that would explain the bruise you described."

"Yeah, sure," Matt said slowly. He sounded as neutral as possible. "I suppose that makes sense."

"Of course it does." O.J. shifted the car into drive and pulled out of the parking lot. "Come to think of it, I'm glad you said something. You've made me realize I need to talk to Cate. She's my wife, and I can't have her upset. Or worse, strutting around town like some damaged piece of fruit, making people think I beat her," he added with a chuckle.

Matt tried to swallow the lump that had formed in his throat, but he couldn't. It was too big. To keep his hands steady, he folded them tightly in his lap.

The heat in the small, enclosed space was worse than it had been outside the car. Though a strong blast of cool air poured in through the open vents, it still wasn't enough to offer any sort of relief. Matt could feel the slick sweat forming at the base of his neck.

Someone was lying to him—Cate or O.J.—and was playing him for a fool, a pawn in this wicked and twisted game, but which one of them was it? And, why?

To protect himself fully, Matt knew he wasn't going to be able to trust either of them. One of them had an agenda, and he needed to find out who.

"You okay?" O.J. asked. "You're pretty quiet."

"Yeah, I'm fine." Matt looked down. "I was just thinking—"

"How long have we known each other, Matt? We grew up together. We're practically brothers. I'm a lot of things, but do you think I'm capable of hurting my wife? Why would I ever want to hurt Cate? I love her."

That was rich, Matt thought. Just a couple of days ago, O.J. had warned him about the pitfalls of getting married. Yet, now, he seemed to be all for the act, declaring his love for his wife. Something didn't add up, but, then again, when it came to manipulation tactics, O.J. had always been a master.

Because he knew he needed to speak up, Matt said quickly, "No, I-I-I wasn't thinking about that. Actually, I was thinking about the suspect. Shouldn't we wait to hear from the sheriff before we go checking out the pub?"

"Definitely not." O.J. stomped on the gas. The car sped forward. "If we wait any longer, this guy could be gone by the time we get there. And then, we've lost him again."

"I know," Matt agreed, "but you heard Sutton this morning. If any news came in regarding the case, specifically about this unidentified suspect, he wanted to be notified immediately."

"And, we tried calling him," O.J. said, "several times. But, he didn't answer his phone. He and his *friend* went out for an early lunch, and now they're both MIA."

Matt shrugged. "Yeah, I guess that's true."

"Believe me, Matt, if we just sit on this tip, Sutton will have both of our heads. Besides, Benson is still trying to get in touch with the sheriff. And as soon as he does, he'll let Sutton know what's going down at the Pub."

Matt hated to admit it, but O.J. was right. The clock was ticking. They had no way of knowing how long their guy was going to be at Tammi's Pub. In all honesty, he could already be gone, but Matt highly doubted it.

He'd been the one to field the call when it came in some ten minutes ago. The latest victim's boyfriend—Jed Turner—tried to get a hold of the sheriff, but to no avail. So, instead, he'd dialed the Perry's Creek Police Department, hoping to find someone there who'd be excited about his big news: The man he'd seen leaving Tara's apartment the afternoon before her murder, the *only* suspect in the strangulation case, was sitting at the bar at the pub, having lunch and drinking a beer.

Matt warned Jed not to go near the suspect, who could very well be armed and dangerous. Although the boyfriend had given his word, Matt knew his word most likely didn't mean shit. Especially if the suspect tried to leave. Matt assumed Jed wouldn't allow *that* to happen.

It was hard telling what they'd find at the pub, or what condition anyone would be in, and they were still at least five minutes out.

"We got lucky." O.J. turned the corner and the wheels came off the ground slightly. "We didn't have to drag the rookie along with us."

Deputy Benson, Matt thought. O.J. had ordered him to stay put until his one and only task was complete: find the sheriff and inform him of what was happening.

Sure, Benson was wet behind the ears and needed someone to show him the ropes, but he also happened to be a pain in the ass that insisted on doing everything by the book, and because they had no idea what they were walking into at Tammi's Pub, the last thing Matt and O.J. needed was to be responsible for babysitting some kid who insisted on coloring inside the lines. Not today.

"I agree," Matt said finally. "He'll get his turn, but right now is certainly not the time."

"So," O.J. said, "what's your take on the situation? Is this guy *the* guy? Are we going to catch a killer?"

"I don't know." Matt's mind turned immediately to Cate. He thought about all of the times she'd accused O.J. of being the killer. "The sheriff seems to think so, but I also know he's desperate to make an arrest. What are your thoughts?"

"Seems a little easy to me." O.J. shrugged. "But, I guess we'll find out soon enough."

They sped past a line of telephone poles, made a sharp left turn, and then came to a sudden stop in the pub's almost full parking lot. Lunch hour. Matt hadn't considered that fact. The place would be packed inside.

O.J. killed the engine. As if on cue, someone came running up to the passenger side of the car. He was tall, big, and looked as if he was holding a cell phone. The device looked small in his hairy hand.

Matt opened the door. "Jed?" He stepped up to the man.

"It's about time," the man answered. "Good thing there wasn't a murder in progress. You two would have another body on your hands."

Matt let the insult go. He didn't have time to get involved in any sort of pissing contest. "Is he still here?" As he got closer to Jed, the stale stench of booze became stronger.

"Sitting at the bar," Jed replied. "He's had a few drinks."

He's not the only one, Matt thought. *A witness who was under the influence—that would look great in court.*

"What can you tell us about him?" O.J. came around the front of the car. "Can you describe him? Tell us what he's wearing?"

"I can do better than that." Jed hit a button on his phone. "I can show you. I was able to snap a few pictures of Collins without him noticing. Ain't technology fantastic?"

"Collins?" Matt frowned. "Is that his name?"

Jed shrugged. "I guess so. That's what I heard the bartender call him, anyway."

"Show us the pictures," O.J. demanded.

"We never discussed this, but do I get some sort of reward for helping you guys out?"

"Yes, of course." O.J. crossed his arms. "If this Collins guy proves to be the killer, the reward is that we won't arrest *you* for murdering your girlfriend."

"That's fucking bullshit," Jed yelled. He took a step back. "I told the sheriff already that I had an alibi."

"Yeah," Matt nodded, "but your alibi isn't all that reliable. So, shut your mouth, show us the damn pictures, and let us do our job." Then there were times when you had no choice but to prove you could, in fact, piss the farthest.

Matt and O.J. huddled over the silver phone in Jed's open palm. The man they were staring at—Collins, apparently—wore a black T-shirt, matching pants, and boots. It was difficult to determine his height as he was sitting on a barstool, his legs crossed at the ankle. If the pictures were accurate, then he most likely wasn't concealing a weapon.

His eyes. Matt couldn't help but notice his dark green eyes. *They* were definitely concealing some sort of secret.

"Good work, Jed," O.J. offered. "Now, you wait here. You'll need to make an official statement, and we'll need copies of those photos."

"I'd prefer to go back inside." Jed shoved his phone into the front pocket of his jeans. "It's hot as hell out here, and I'd like another beer."

"Just wait here," O.J. repeated. "We'll be back soon enough."

"How do you want to play this?" Matt followed O.J. up the gravel path toward the pub's entrance.

"Quick and easy." O.J. reached the double glass doors of the brick building. "He's going to see us coming. Hopefully, he cooperates. But, no matter what happens, I've got your back, partner." He turned around, grasped Matt's shoulder, and gave it a tight squeeze.

Matt nodded. "Let's do this." He took a deep breath.

With O.J. in the lead, they shuffled into the pub. Matt's eyes bounced around the room, registering several different things at once: scattered baskets of greasy food on top of a handful of tables; two men in stained and faded mechanic's jumpsuits playing a game of pool in the corner; a young bartender whose wide eyes and creased forehead proved that she was most likely new and overwhelmed; and a man who'd recently been identified as Collins darting toward the back kitchen.

They'd been spotted, all right. Now, they had a runner.

ollins hit the metal exit door, shoved the heavy barrier open, and bounded into the alley. His breathing was already turning into shallow gasps and wheezes. He wasn't going to make it.

"Stop! Police!"

Did anyone actually obey that ridiculous command? Collins wasn't about to. He didn't even bother to look over his shoulder to see which deputy had yelled at him. Collins just kept running. He had no idea where he was going and only had one goal in mind: to put as much distance between himself and the two men in blue as he possibly could.

With a belly full of draft beer and onion rings, the mission wasn't going to be easy to accomplish, but he wasn't about to give up. He didn't know what the police wanted, and he wasn't sticking around to find out.

He made a quick left. He found himself on another street, and the back end of a half a dozen brick and stucco buildings faced him.

"Fuck!" Collins screamed. His side was burning, and sharp pains were shooting up and down both of his legs. He was too out of shape for any sort of extracurricular activity that involved outrunning the police. He was going to have to hide. But, where?

"Stop, Collins! We just want to talk to you!"

Shit! They knew his name. How in the hell did they know his name? That was definitely going to screw up his plans.

"Just shoot the motherfucker, Matt! That'll make him stop!"

This was serious: life or death. If he didn't get away now, he was done. He was all too familiar with how these pursuits ended. Not to mention, he was unarmed. He wouldn't even be able to put up a decent fight.

Collins went back to his original idea: he had to hide. Now, he just had to find a place.

He considered trying one of the doors on either side of him—he had a lot to choose from—but where did they lead? Would he just be trapping himself? Making it easier for the police to catch him? What if there were people inside those buildings? Collins knew that crowds would only create a much worse situation.

No, it made more sense to stay away from enclosed spaces. He wasn't about to make anyone's job easier—and he wasn't going back to prison. That wasn't an option.

Collins knew what he needed to get out of this mess: his car. Not that he was gunning for some big freeway chase with helicopters and roadblocks and an appearance on the evening news, but if he could just circle back to the pub's parking lot and get to his vehicle, then he could drive to his motel room and lie low for a while.

So, how in hell was he going to do that?

He took another fast turn. A new stretch of road greeted him. More buildings, more doors, and, up ahead…was that a clearing? A way out of this rat-like maze he'd found himself in?

He staggered but pushed forward. The two men were out of sight for now, but he still wasn't sure he was going to make it. His entire body was on fire, and it begged him for a break. Sweat dripped down from his thin hair and landed in his eyes. It stung. If only he could…

Over there! Twenty feet ahead, there was a large green Dumpster. Collins saw an opportunity and sprinted toward it. He didn't give the hiding place another thought. With every ounce of energy he had left in him, he lifted the top. He tried not to inhale the rotten stench of spoiled food and what had to be dirty diapers and dove in.

He covered his mouth with both hands to silence his heavy breathing and managed to ignore the files buzzing around him greedily as if he were fresh meat. Annoying little insects with wings? He could handle that. No problem. But, two men with guns, handcuffs, and the power to lock him up and throw away the key? Not so much.

Now, Collins was going to find out exactly who he was dealing with and just how smart the men of the Perry's Creek Police Department truly were.

"I don't see him," one of the deputies called out in a deep voice. "Where the fuck did he go?"

"He could have gone anywhere," the other deputy answered. "In one of those buildings or up ahead through that opening and over to the next street."

"Fuck!" the deputy with the deep voice said again.

"He couldn't have gotten far. We need to split up and keep looking." This one spoke softer, and his voice was a little steadier. He sounded positive, maybe even hopeful as if they might actually catch the "bad guy."

Well, not if Collins could help it.

"We'll find him! You keep going forward. Check the next street over. And, ask around. Maybe someone saw him."

"What about you? What are you going to do?"

"I'm going into some of these buildings, have a look around. He's here somewhere, O.J. We'll find him."

After that, except for the buzzing of the flies, Collins heard nothing. The alley had grown silent once again. The two deputies had each gone their separate ways, hoping to accomplish the same objective, leaving him with a brief opportunity to tackle his.

Collins would get to his car. He would make it safely back to his motel room, and then he would regroup and re-evaluate the situation. He'd come to Perry's Creek with a purpose, and no one was going to stop him from fulfilling that purpose. He was too determined. He would get what he wanted. He would make the guilty parties pay.

But, first things first. He had to get out of this damned Dumpster. He didn't waste time trying to be sneaky. Now, it was all about being quick. He thrust both of his arms upward, connected with the top of the Dumpster, and pushed. The warmth and brightness of the sun hit him almost immediately, and the fresh air...he'd never been so happy to inhale such a pure scent in his entire life. Collins didn't realize how much he took it for granted—and he'd spent time in prison.

Within seconds, Collins was out of the Dumpster. He wiped at various smudges and streaks that stained his bare arms. A long shower would help, he knew, but it would have to wait. One crisis at a time.

He retraced his steps back toward the pub. Collins even picked up the pace. He'd tasted freedom and wasn't about to give it up. Not again.

He was getting closer. He hadn't strayed that far from Tammi's to begin with, and he guessed that if he stopped looking back to see if he was being followed, he could reach his car within seconds.

So, he kept moving. He even managed to keep his balance as he dug down into his front pocket and grasped the lone key.

Most of the parking lot had cleared out. His Honda was still there, along with a black and white cruiser stationed in a front spot, but the car was empty. The two deputies were still out looking for him, and they either hadn't bothered to call for backup, or it hadn't arrived yet. It didn't matter, and Collins didn't actually care. Luck was on his side, finally. He was going to get out of this mess unscathed.

He slowed down to take a much-needed breath.

"Hey, Collins!"

"Fuck!" he screamed.

He'd been cocky and had let his guard down too soon. As a result, he'd broken one of his cardinal rules: Don't assume you're out of the woods until you *actually* are. Even then, always be mindful of your surroundings.

He took a quick look around to see who had called his name. Was it the police again? Had they managed to circle back around to the pub to surprise him with a sneak attack?

No. Standing by the entrance to the pub was the big guy from Tara's apartment, the guy Collins had assumed was her boyfriend. He'd picked a hell of a time for revenge. And, how had the hick figured out his name? Collins had done a bang-up job of keeping a low profile.

"The police are looking for you. Did you kill Tara, you son of a bitch?"

Collins stopped. He stared at the man. He hadn't expected him to say that, and now he couldn't move. It was as if his legs had turned to stone. He was locked in place, watching the stranger move closer to him.

"How'd you manage to get out here?" His hands were balled into fists. He was now just an arm's length away. "It doesn't matter. You won't get away from me."

Collins found his footing. He took a step back. "What are you talking about? I didn't kill anybody."

"You're a fucking liar! And, you're going down!"

Collins took another step back. So that's why the Perry's Creek Police Department was after him: Everyone thought he'd killed Tara. He was a fucking murder suspect!

Wait! That meant Tara was dead. He'd expected to see her at the pub. It was the main reason he'd gone back in. Well, boredom *and* an attempt at another round with the skank.

Collins had thought it was odd that she hadn't been behind the bar but then figured she'd had the day off or called in sick. Frankly, he hadn't given it much thought.

He'd gone in to see her, and when she hadn't been there, he'd still ordered a beer and some lunch, and then blocked out his surroundings to better enjoy his afternoon. A skill he'd perfected in prison, he wished now that he'd been paying more attention to the bar scene. While he'd noticed Tara wasn't at Tammi's, he'd never once thought that it was because she was dead. Someone in the pub had to have been talking about it, and he should have been more mindful of what was going on around him. Doing so really could have saved him some time and hassle.

Too little, too late—and now he had another cage to escape from.

"I didn't kill Tara," he tried again.

"Keep telling yourself that!" The man's arm came up. He directed his thick fist right at Collins' nose.

Collins stepped out of the way and ducked down, then pivoted around. He faced his car and made a mad dash for it. His key was out and ready. He'd done it again. He'd escaped. Now if he could just get behind the wheel and onto the road, he'd be home free!

"Get back here, asshole!"

He jumped into the driver's seat. Doors locked and key in the ignition, Collins started the engine. He put the car in drive and stepped on the gas.

Bang!

The stranger was on the hood. Collins wasn't sure if he'd hit the man or if he'd jumped on the car willingly, but he was certainly an unwanted passenger.

Collins swerved left. The man flew off the Honda and landed in a ball on the gravel path. He didn't move.

Collins didn't bother waiting around for another obstacle to appear in his way. He peeled out of the parking lot. He didn't look back.

Collins didn't take a deep breath until he was sitting on the stiff comforter that covered the queen-sized bed in his motel room. He would have liked another beer to help calm his nerves, but there was no way in hell he was going to take any more risks today. He still had a difficult time believing he wasn't behind bars, and he wasn't about to risk his freedom by stopping at some gas station or grocery store for booze.

He'd find a way to take the edge off later. Right now, he had a phone call to make.

The man answered after the second ring. "Hello?"

"Richie, it's Collins."

"Well, holy shit!" Surprise filled the man's voice. "You're alive!"

"Yes." Collins nodded. "Look, I know it's been a while—"

"You're telling me," Richie agreed. "A long while. I heard you got out. What's been going on? How you been?"

"I need your help." Collins skipped right to the point. He'd never been a fan of small talk. There was simply no point to it. Dancing around an issue was a colossal waste of time, and Collins had never in his life liked to dance.

"Wow." Disappointment replaced the surprise in Richie's voice. "I see some things haven't changed."

"Look, Richie, I didn't mean—"

"By the way, I'm doing great. Thanks for asking." Richie exhaled on the other end. "Yeah, got a girl and a job. Life is good."

"I'm glad, Richie." Collins was only half listening. He hadn't called for the man's updated biography. He was in trouble and needed assistance. "Can you help me or not?"

"I don't know." Richie waited a beat, and then, "I don't think so, Collins. I'm trying to stay clean."

"You don't even know what I need help with yet," Collins argued. "It's not like last time. It's different."

"It's never different with you, Collins. Whatever it is, I'm sure it's illegal. And, like I said, I got a girl now. I'm trying to do right—"

"There's money," Collins interrupted. "Not a lot to begin with, but this project has the potential to be huge. We're talking big and consistent payoffs."

Richie laughed. "Project? Payoffs? What are you getting involved in? Some sort of extortion deal?"

"Everyone's got to eat," Collins said. "So, what do you think?"

He stood from the bed and started walking the length of the small room. The journey was quick—three big steps and he'd reached the door. He pulled the curtain a few inches away from the window to his left and peeked outside. The parking lot was the same as it had been ten minutes ago: free of Perry Creek's finest. They hadn't found him...yet.

"I'm still on the fence," Richie answered. "I don't think my girl would approve."

"Since when do you need a woman's approval?"

Richie laughed again, and the sound was like two cats clawing at each other. "I know, I know. But, I've changed, man. Macy has had quite an impact on me."

115

"Macy?" Collins asked.

"Yeah, Macy Caper," Richie confirmed. "That's my girl. I don't want to fuck things up with her," Richie went on. "We just began dating, so…"

"There's money," Collins repeated. When going for the closer, it was always important to rehash the best points of your case, which also happened to be Richie's weakness.

"How much?" Richie asked.

There it was, Collins thought. *Richie's weakness: greed.*

"I can give you two grand, but—"

"No way," Richie said flatly. "That's nothing."

"I told you there would be more money down the road. First, we have to create a foundation."

"Here's how it goes." Richie's voice was now stern. "If you want my help, it's going to cost you five grand."

"Five thousand dollars?" Collins exploded. "That's insane! I'm only making ten on the deal."

"Sounds fair to me," Richie argued. "Fifty-fifty. Besides, I didn't even ask what I'd have to do. I think you're getting off cheap."

Collins sat back down on the bed. He *hated* needing someone, but, right now, he needed Richie. The man had him by the balls, and he seemed only seconds away from giving them a tight squeeze. As a result, Collins knew what he was going to have to do: Share more of his money.

But, that was life. Collins couldn't be seen running around town, blackmailing people. Not now that he was wanted for murder. He wasn't sure how fast news could spread in this place, but he assumed his face—and name—would be everywhere soon. He'd made a mistake, and now that mistake was going to cost him more than he'd originally thought.

"Fine," Collins agreed, "five grand." He closed his eyes and fell backward. His big revenge plan was no longer tricky but now a pain in the ass. "Head to Perry's Creek and call me when you're close. And, Richie, bring beer."

19

"You don't think he's the killer, do you?"

Beau shrugged before looking over at the sheriff. "Do you want me to be honest?"

"Fuck," Shannon mumbled. He leaned back in his chair. "What's your issue with this Collins guy being guilty?"

Beau shrugged again. "It's just an instinct."

More often than not, that was what solved cases: instinct. Sure, evidence helped and looked great in court, but Beau knew that without a little instinct to initially go on, most cases didn't progress too quickly.

The sheriff shook his head, smiled, and then, "You're going to have to give me a little more than that, Beau."

Beau nodded and then returned Shannon's smile. "For me, it goes back to why I never thought Turner was the killer: brains."

"Brains?"

"Yes." Beau crossed one leg over the other. "Our killer is smart. He killed two women—three, counting Tara Burns—and left nothing behind. Would he be dumb enough to be seen outside a victim's apartment before strangling her?"

"Nobody's perfect," Shannon argued. "Maybe the killer made a mistake. Maybe Collins is the killer, and he didn't anticipate the boyfriend coming home so soon."

"That's a pretty big mistake."

"But, not uncommon, right?" the sheriff asked. "Aren't a lot of cases involving serial killers solved because the culprit turns out to *not* be perfect? They always slip up."

"I'd like to think that it's good old-fashioned police work that gets the job done," Beau admitted. "But, yes, both killers' slips and luck have been known to help solve cases from time to time."

"Real cases?" Shannon asked. "Or just cases in Lifetime movies?" He threw the dig from yesterday back at Beau and then added another smile.

Beau rolled his eyes. He knew if he smiled again, he wouldn't be able to wipe it away. He'd be stuck looking like a grinning fool. So, instead, he shifted his gaze down to the floor of the sheriff's office. There was nothing there to smile about.

Their lunch "meeting" had been good for Beau. Well, until they'd turned on their cell phones and realized a shitstorm had erupted. Until that moment, things had gone pretty well. Maybe even great. For the first time since being in Perry's Creek, Beau had been able to recognize his friend, and, though their conversation over a couple of iced teas and chicken breast salads hadn't been one hundred percent satisfying, it had certainly been a start.

"You know, sometimes I envy you, Beau," Shannon spoke up. "If I'd followed your lead and gotten out of law enforcement a while ago, well, then this Perry's Creek strangler would be someone else's problem."

"It's not like it was my choice to leave. I didn't want to retire, remember?" Beau said. "I was more or less forced out."

"Right." Shannon bit his lower lip. "Sorry."

Beau waved off the apology. He was over it, and there was absolutely nothing he could do about that now. Lord knew being angry hadn't helped the situation. Sad, bitter, and jealous hadn't offered much assistance, either. However, finding a bigger whiskey glass? That had offered the relief that Beau had been searching for.

"So, you think Collins is too stupid to be the killer?" Shannon brought the conversation back to point.

"I could be wrong," Beau offered. "Perhaps he did slip up. Like I said yesterday, it's possible he's sleeping with these women or befriending them before he strangles them. Hopefully, you'll have no trouble connecting him to the first two victims. He could have been seen with them, too."

"We'll see," Shannon said. "I've got Tweedledee and Tweedledum working on it now. I still can't believe they managed to let our only suspect slip away."

"How are you handling the search for Collins? What all are you doing?"

"His photo will be on the front page of the paper. Local news channels will make an announcement. There's radio, too. A social media campaign has already been started. You know, the works."

Beau nodded. "Well, if he's still in Perry's Creek, I'm sure you'll find him."

"You think he's gone already?" The sheriff frowned. "Not that I want a murderer in my town, but if he is guilty, I'd like to be the one to arrest him."

"This will be a true testament to how smart he is." Beau stood and paced the room. "If the cops were chasing after me, and I'd managed to get away, I wouldn't lift my foot off the gas pedal until I reached the border."

"Isn't that a sign of guilt right there? He ran."

"I don't know."

"Okay, maybe he is innocent," the sheriff sighed. "After all, why would he come to Perry's Creek to murder three strangers that, as far as we know, have nothing in common?"

"I don't know that either," Beau answered. "But, look at the bright side: Whether or not he's guilty of murder, you've got him for a hit and run."

The sheriff laughed, and when he did, the deep lines around his mouth expanded and became more prominent. He looked genuinely amused. "Attempted vehicular manslaughter," he corrected.

"How's Turner doing?" Beau asked.

"Just a broken leg. He'll be fine." Shannon answered. "He called a little while ago to say he'll be pressing charges."

"Someone will have to find Collins first."

"No kidding," Shannon agreed. "Is that his first name or last? We can't even do a background check on the guy. And, here I thought Jed had helped us. It's almost like he did the opposite and created more work for us."

"At least you have an update to give to the mayor."

"Silver lining. I'm heading over to his office soon. I imagine he won't take too kindly to the fact that we had Collins in our grasps and let him get away."

"No," Beau agreed. "Unfortunately, that doesn't look too good, but maybe you can spin it a different way. Tell Mayor Jackson that—"

"Beau, if Collins isn't the killer, then who is? Who's doing this? Why? And how in the hell are we going to find him?"

Shannon had turned completely serious. No more smiling, no more laughing. He was back to pure cop mode. His friend was angry, that much was obvious, but even more so, Beau realized for the first time that Shannon was worried. The small quaver in his voice had proved it.

Of course, he was worried, Beau thought.

It was Shannon's job to protect the residents of Perry's Creek, and he currently wasn't succeeding. The mayor was more than likely going to come down hard on him in their meeting later, but Beau knew from experience that that wasn't all that was weighing heavy on the sheriff.

Guilt. Shannon had to be feeling guilty. Three innocent women had lost their lives, and the responsible party was nowhere near being brought to justice, meaning someone else could die, and probably would.

Beau had been in those tight, uncomfortable shoes before. Add feeling like a total failure to the mix, and life was just an utter ball of joy.

"We'll find him," Beau answered finally. "It may take a little bit of extra work—and luck—but we'll catch him."

"We have to."

"I'll go over the files again, see what Tara Burns adds to the mix. I'll try to come up with a potential motive. *Why* these girls were killed, and what the killer wants."

"I appreciate that." The sheriff steadied his hands on the surface of his desk. "If I'm being honest, Beau, I hope you're wrong. I hope we locate him soon, and I hope he proves to be the killer."

"I hope I'm wrong, too." Beau returned to his chair and then folded his hands in his lap. He took a deep breath. "It really would make all of our lives easier if Collins was guilty."

"Nothing in life is ever easy," Shannon stated. "So, he's probably innocent."

"Time will tell." Beau leaned back.

"Am I a bad cop, Beau?"

"Excuse me?"

"You can be honest," Shannon said. "I *want* you to be honest. Am I a bad cop?"

"Come on, Shannon." Beau's voice deepened. He didn't like where this was going. "Be serious."

"I am serious. If I was better at my job, I would have made an arrest by now."

"Don't say that!" Beau stood from the chair again. "You're not being fair to yourself. No one has been able to solve this case. That doesn't make you a bad cop. It just means—"

"But, this is my town, my home," Shannon explained. "I'm supposed to protect Perry's Creek. And, what happens? The first sign of something bad, the first time I get to prove my worth, I fail."

"You haven't failed!"

"Look at your career, Beau. Look at all the cases you've solved, all the lives you've saved. And, in San Diego. I'm in some podunk town, yet I can't even—"

"Stop!" Beau slammed both of his fists down on the sheriff's desk. He'd had enough of this "woe is me" crap. Shannon had never been this weak in the past—or this insecure. So, why now? It was pointless and unattractive, and Beau was over it.

"Beau…"

"No, Shannon," Beau fired back. "Yes, we chose different paths, and we've had two different professional experiences because of it, but that doesn't make me a better cop than you. Do you honestly think I've never struggled with a case, had a difficult time making sense of the clues, or in determining how I could get a leg up on the investigation?"

"But—"

"But, nothing!" Beau pushed away from the desk. "Now isn't the time to give up. You're smart and capable. You have the opportunity to prove you deserve to be sheriff. Don't you dare let it go to waste."

Beau watched as the smile gradually crept across Shannon's face once more. Signs of doubt began fading away as the sheriff sat up taller in his char. It appeared as if he'd gotten the ego boost he needed.

That was what friends were for, Beau thought. While it hadn't necessarily been in character for Shannon to have a small meltdown, Beau knew that with age, it was sometimes difficult to hold onto certain qualities like self-confidence. Not to mention, when trying to solve a murder investigation, and coming up empty-handed repeatedly, it was easy to let doubt seep in and take over.

Beau had been there before, too. The same wave of uncertainty had found him a handful of times in the past. Yet, he never let it deter his overall agenda: closing his case. Sure, he might have taken a few extra swigs from the bottle during those particularly stressful moments, but he'd always managed to stay on track. That was just his nature. He was disciplined and strong-willed like that.

Still, Beau had to admit that since he was getting older and was no longer considered an "asset" in his professional field—or hell, even in his personal life—feeling valuable was getting harder, and yet more important to him by the day. Beau realized that, soon enough, he'd be faced with a *burning* question: Would Shannon truly be there for him in *his* time of need?

Beau didn't want to think about the answer. Not today. There were far too many other things going on. Besides, the two had had a good lunch and a decent conversation this afternoon. Beau was perfectly okay with leaving it at that…for now.

"What time are you meeting with the mayor?"

The sheriff looked down at his left wrist. "Damn," he sighed. "I guess I should get going. I'm really not looking forward to this."

"It will be fine." Beau tried to make his voice sound light and reassuring but felt he'd failed. "Don't tell him there's a chance that Collins isn't the killer. Remember, he still very well could be."

"Yeah, right." Shannon stood. "Since when have you ever been wrong about these sorts of things? All joking aside, Beau, you've got killer instinct."

Beau shrugged and then offered his friend a sideways smirk. "Just don't give away any information you don't have to. Don't lie to the mayor, but don't be forthcoming, either."

"Thanks for the advice, Beau." Shannon walked around the front of his desk. "And, thanks for the pep talk, too. You always seem to have the answer."

Beau wasn't sure what to say, exactly. He looked back down at the floor. He could feel Shannon getting closer to him. Would a hug be too much? Perhaps a handshake or pat on the back would be more appropriate. They'd been friends for what seemed like an eternity, so the fact that this awkward sensation had washed over Beau spoke volumes. He didn't understand it fully, and he certainly didn't care for it.

"What are you going to do?" Shannon edged past Beau and took a step toward the closed door. "You sticking around here?"

Awkward moment over, Beau thought.

"Yes," Beau mumbled. "For a while, anyway. I'm going to take that second pass at the files and see what I can come up with. Who knows? Maybe I'll find something that specifically points to Collins.

"Here's hoping." Shannon reached for the door handle and pulled the door open. "I'm sure this goes without saying, but if you get any new information on Collins' whereabouts—"

"You'll be the first person I call," Beau finished for the sheriff.

"Thank you."

"Real smooth, Beau," he taunted himself after Shannon had left.

Beau walked around the desk and took a seat in Shannon's still-warm chair. He leaned back and closed his eyes.

So, this is what it was like to be in power, to run a whole town. Sure, he'd run his fair share of operations. He'd been in charge of many cases and had teams of people reporting to him and following his orders. Still, this was different. Or, it *felt* different.

As he sat in the sheriff's chair behind the broad desk, Beau couldn't help but consider the idea of being a big fish in a small pond, versus the opposite—a small fish in a big pond. While Beau had never regretted his choice or the wonderful experiences he'd had as a part of it, he did imagine how his life might have turned out differently.

He never heard the visitor enter the room. It was the scent he picked up on first: jasmine. He wasn't sure how long he'd been sitting in Shannon's chair with his eyes closed, imagining all the other scenarios of his life, but when he opened them finally and looked up, he saw her. Her dark gaze and deep frown proved she wasn't happy to see him.

"Comfortable?" she asked.

"Hi, Diane."

Beau couldn't remember the last time he'd seen her, but he knew it was quite a while ago. She looked the same, though: same light-colored, chin-length hair; same dark, hard eyes; same small nose that seemed to be constantly crinkled; and the same pale lips that were always pursed together in disgust.

Today was no different.

"Are you enjoying playing make-believe behind my husband's desk?"

He figured that was an invitation to move, but Beau didn't budge. "You just missed Shannon," he informed her. "He's meeting with the mayor."

"Oh." Diane pulled on the leather strap of her purse. "That must be why he's not answering my calls. And, what about earlier today? Do you know why his cell phone was off?"

"He was with me," Beau admitted. He tried his best to bite back a smile but found the task rather difficult. When Diane's thick eyebrows shot up, he almost lost it completely. "We were having lunch and discussing the case. You know, the latest victim and suspect."

"Right." She bobbed her head slowly. "The case."

"Is there a problem, Diane?"

Diane clasped her hands together and placed them in front of her small stomach. "I'm not sure. I mean, if I'm thinking out loud, I do find it rather interesting that as soon as you arrived in Perry's Creek, women started turning up strangled to death."

"You're mistaken, Diane." Beau stood up. "I didn't get into town until *after* the second murder. Not to mention, Shannon asked me to come here. He wants my help."

"Yes, your help." She shook her head slightly. "You know, Beau, I'm not stupid."

"Okay," he said, confusion staining his voice. Beau crossed his arms.

"And, I know what's going on here."

"What's that supposed to mean?"

Diane placed her hands on her hips. "Shannon and I have been married for a long time, over thirty-five years. And, there are no secrets between us. We tell each other everything."

"That's so sweet," Beau mocked. He put the right palm of his hand to his heart. "I bet you're proud of that, too."

She ignored the dig. "I know what happened between you two in the past, and I know the real reason you came here. You came to Perry's Creek with an agenda. You're hoping to—"

"You need to relax, Diane. Shannon and I have been friends for a really long time, and we—"

"I've never liked you," she admitted. "I've never trusted you. I don't like the person Shannon becomes when he's around you. You're grotesque, Beau, and you make me sick."

"Well, since we're being honest, I've never liked you, either." Beau paused and made sure his voice was completely steady. He'd wanted to say this for a while, and he wasn't about to show weakness. Not in front of her. "I've always wondered what Shannon saw in you. You're cold and bitter, and nothing but a big bitch. Shannon can do better."

"Stay away from my husband!" she ordered. Her tone was sharp enough to shred the thick air around them.

"I'm not afraid of you, Diane."

"You should be," she warned. "Shannon may be the sheriff, but I'm the wife, and that trumps everything, even your little friendship."

"Go to hell!"

"I'm serious." She spun on her heel and started for the door. "Stay away from Shannon, Beau. If you don't, I'll kill you."

20

She tried to back away from him, but his grip around her neck was getting tighter. Cate couldn't breathe, which also meant she couldn't scream. Then again, no one would hear her even if she did cry out for help. No one was going to rescue her, she knew, and, this time, Joshua's dark eyes looked intent on killing.

"I didn't say anything to anyone," Cate choked out the lie. "I s-s-swear it!"

"I don't believe you, Catie."

That damn nickname again. It was one thing coming from her mother. Even though Cate didn't like it, she'd accepted it and had learned to live with it.

However, when Joshua used it, Cate swore her ears started bleeding almost immediately. There was just something about the way he said "Catie"—mostly the way he enunciated the "ie" sound. She knew he did it on purpose. He wanted her to feel like a frightened, helpless little girl.

And, he succeeded every single time.

"I think you're lying to me, Catie."

She tried to keep her focus on him: deep voice; strong, rough hands; and garlic-strained breath. When Cate looked up at Joshua from her spot in the corner, she didn't see her husband, but her stepfather. *He* was the one reprimanding her, and the vision from the past made her gut burst with pain. She thought she might get sick. Cate closed her eyes and let the darkness consume her.

Joshua had blindsided her tonight. He'd let her serve him dinner, and then they'd been sitting at the table, eating and sharing bits and pieces of their day, when he took the last sip of his beer, stood, grabbed a fistful of her hair, and then ripped her out of the chair.

"Ahhh!" she'd screamed. "What are you doing, Joshua? You're hurting me!"

"And, you hurt me, Catie," he'd said calmly. He'd pushed her to the hard floor and grabbed for her neck. "I think it's only fair that I get to hurt you back."

"W-w-what? I don't understand. H-h-how did—?"

"You opened your big, fat mouth, didn't you? Whatever happened to privacy? We're a married couple, Catie. What happens behind the closed doors of this house is *our* business. No one else's."

"I didn't say anything, Joshua." She'd tried to crawl away, then. Cate would have crawled anywhere, but there'd been no place for her to go. Cate had been trapped, just like she'd been trapped so many times in the past.

This time, though, it was Joshua who had her, and he didn't show any signs of letting go.

"You should know by now that you can't lie to me." He let go of her neck, finally.

He kept his balance in a tight squat formation and leaned back. "You haven't been a good girl, Catie." He tsked.

She rested the back of her head against the wall and started gasping for air. Cate stared up at the ceiling fan, the blinding light flooding her vision, but Cate didn't mind. It proved she was still alive.

A few moments passed. Cate caught her breath, and her mind began to race.

What was Joshua talking about? Had someone confronted him about the abuse? Had they told him they knew his favorite pastime was beating his wife for sport?

Cate didn't have to rack her brain for very long. Only one name came to mind: Jerry.

Their conversation from earlier flashed in front of her eyes: Jerry had all but come out and told her he knew she was being beaten by her husband and that he was more than willing to do something about it. Had he?

"Tell me, Cate," Joshua stated, "why don't you respect me? I'm your husband. You're supposed to love, honor, and obey me. Remember?"

She nodded slowly. Cate knew by now that talking would only make her situation that much worse. When or *if* Joshua wanted her to respond, she'd know it, and while Cate was all too familiar with this fact, she was also tired of it.

She swallowed the large lump that had formed in her throat. "I told you, Joshua. I didn't say anything to anyone."

Cate never saw the blow coming.

The back of his hand came up quickly. She didn't have time to try and dodge it. He struck the side of her face and created a stinging sensation almost instantly. Then the tears came. Cate couldn't hold them back. She wasn't sure if they were due to the shock of the hit or the pain of it, maybe both. Either way, she couldn't make herself stop crying.

"Crying won't help you, Catie." He stood up. "You know what will? Keeping our business private."

"Please," she sobbed. "I didn't tell him. I swear it!"

Joshua lifted his foot. He was going in for a kick. Cate mashed her eyes closed. She raised both of her small hands to try and protect herself. She knew the weak shield wouldn't block much, but she at least had to try.

But, his boot never connected with any part of her. Joshua didn't follow through with the kick. Instead, he said, "Here, let me help you up." He stretched out his right arm.

Was this some sort of trap? As soon as she gave him her hand, was he going to snap her arm like some meaningless twig? Did he want to help her up just so he could knock her back down again?

Cate knew better than to trust him. Her husband didn't like helping people. Especially his wife.

"Come on, Catie. Take my hand. You can trust me."

It was as if he'd read her mind. This was classic Joshua, the ultimate manipulator. He'd want her to trust him, to feel safe and secure. Then, as soon as her guard was down, he'd get her with some sort of surprise attack. That was his MO. He liked creating that kind of fear.

"Joshua…"

"Take my hand," he repeated. His tone was more severe this time. He wasn't asking. He was demanding.

Cate did as she was told. She took Joshua's steady hand and let him pull her up to her feet. Tears still rolled down her cheeks, and they burned the place where he'd smacked her. Her throat was stiff and ached from him choking her, but she was still breathing…for now.

"I think there's a lesson to be learned here." He kept a firm hold on her hand. "Maybe you didn't actually *say* anything, Catie, but your wounds did. They spoke volumes to Matt, which is just as bad as if the words had come from your lips."

"What?" She frowned. "Matt was—?"

"He noticed you had a mark the last time he was at the Brim," Joshua said. "That, mixed with your quiet behavior, made him suspect something was up. He even had the audacity to ask if I was hurting you. Can you believe it?"

No, she couldn't. Matt had confronted Joshua, finally, but what had he said? And, why hadn't Matt given her some sort of head's up? It seemed like he had spun the story a little bit, probably in an attempt to try and protect her. That had been very mindful of him, even though it had still resulted in her taking a bad beating.

"I warned you about covering up," Joshua continued. "I told you people in town were going to start talking, didn't I?"

"Yes," she whispered.

"And, you knew I didn't want that, right? I don't like other people knowing my business."

"I know, Joshua."

"Well, good," he said. "I'm glad you know that now and can recognize it."

She bit down on her lower lip. Joshua most likely wanted an apology. In his eyes, she'd done wrong. She'd been the one to screw up and wear her abuse publicly like it was some scarlet letter for all of Perry's Creek to see.

However, Cate couldn't do it. Not this time. She was the victim, not Joshua. Apologizing for something she didn't do would only give him more control, more power. At some point, enough had to be enough.

"Moving forward, what are we going to do to ensure this doesn't happen again?"

She shrugged. "This is just off the top of my head, but you could stop beating me."

Cate hadn't expected his reaction. He laughed. Joshua threw his head back and released a sound that caused the tiny hairs on the back of her neck to come to life. A cold chill overtook her entire body. While she couldn't predict his next move, she tried to prepare herself mentally for the absolute worst.

His grip tightened on her hand. He looked into her eyes. "Don't be silly, Catie."

"But—"

"Think of tonight as a little test. Let's see how well you cover up tomorrow."

Cate couldn't find her voice. She just nodded.

"And, if I were you, I'd try my very best. Understand?"

She looked down at the floor. "Yes, Joshua."

"I thought you would." He reached for her chin. "My good little girl." He gave her face a slight pinch and then released his hold on her. He turned around. "I'm going for a run. Make sure this place is cleaned up by the time I get back. And then, we're going to bed together. You still haven't given me a baby, Cate. That needs to change."

She didn't get the chance to argue or agree. He'd already started upstairs for the bedroom where he would exchange his police uniform for shorts and tennis shoes. Joshua had informed her of how the rest of the evening would go. That was that.

Cate looked down at the table and the dinner she hadn't been allowed to finish. She took a deep breath. She immediately recalled several other meals she hadn't finished due to some sort of fight or argument breaking out, and not just during her married life, but when she'd been younger, too.

Her mother had always prepared so much wonderful food in the evenings, almost as if each dinner was a celebration in some way. Or maybe a peace offering, now that Cate was contemplating it further. There'd always been salads and appetizers and tasty main courses, followed by elaborate desserts. Her mother had loved to cook and provide delicious meals for the family.

And, every single night, it would be a tossup as to whether or not the family would get to enjoy that meal. At least once, but mostly twice a week, her stepdad would come home in one of his "tornado moods." He'd attack everything and anything that got in his way. As a result, Cate would usually get sent to her bedroom, and all of the beautiful food her mother had spent hours working on would end up in the garbage.

She reached for the cold plate that still contained a piece of salmon and a spoonful of wild rice. Cate shook her head. She was so disappointed in herself, and when she caught a glimpse of her reflection in the glass table, she wanted to curl up in the fetal position under the covers and pretend life was going to change all of its own accord.

She'd told herself for years that history would not repeat itself, that she would not end up like her mother. Still, Cate knew that in a way, she was even worse off than her mom. She'd vowed to never be like the woman and had had plenty of opportunities to ensure their lives would never mirror each other.

Yet, here Cate was, married to Joshua. She'd chosen a man who was almost identical to her stepdad, right down to the use of her awful nickname.

Maybe this was her punishment for marrying a man after knowing him just a couple of months. Then again, she'd been in love...and pregnant. In all fairness, Joshua hadn't shown his true colors until after their "I dos" had been exchanged.

He was a stranger, a damn good actor who had created a persona and fairy tale she'd fallen for hook, line, and sinker—and now, well, she was sunk, all right.

It probably didn't much matter. Cate scraped the remaining bits from the plate into the garbage can. If Joshua hadn't come along, then someone else would have, and it was hard to predict what kind of guy that could have been. One perhaps even worse than Joshua, resulting in a whole different type of nightmare.

Besides, was it ever really possible to trust the person you laid down next to each night?

Table cleared and scrubbed down, dishes spinning in the dishwasher, Cate took a seat on one of the bar stools and rested her head on the countertop.

Oh, how she craved a break from her life. Was that even normal? Did other people want to be someone else or step into another life that was nothing like their own?

Not happy people.

She couldn't believe she'd tried sticking up for herself tonight, and how had Joshua reacted? He'd laughed in her face.

The reaction hadn't been that surprising. The surprising part was that he hadn't added a hit to accompany the laugh. If he'd been true to character, he'd have delivered another backhand to her face.

So, what did this mean? Was Joshua growing? Did even he think there was such a thing as being "too abusive?"

Cate knew better than to hold her breath. It had most likely been some new manipulation tactic to scare and confuse her further.

Maybe she'd been naive to think she could stop Joshua. Short of doing something drastic like going up the stairs, grabbing the spare gun from his nightstand dresser, and shooting him until he quit moving, Cate wasn't sure her husband could be stopped.

Yes, she had a plan, a way to hopefully take her life back, but she was becoming less and less sure that it was going to work, and if it didn't work, if it didn't end up all coming together, Cate knew she'd be worse off than she was now. Way worse.

Now, as if life hadn't hit her with enough punches, she had Matt and Jerry to consider.

Jerry, she knew, was a ticking time bomb. After the confrontation with him yesterday, Cate had to be ready for the explosion that could happen at any moment. While she didn't know what that entailed, exactly, if it had anything to do with talking to Joshua, well, the outcome wouldn't be pretty. Not for her, at least.

Then there was Matt. He'd come through, sort of. He'd at least tried to talk to Joshua...

She wanted to call him. Cate figured Joshua would be gone for another twenty-five minutes. She had time to make a quick call, to hear the full story of what had been discussed earlier today.

She found her phone at the bottom of her purse in the front living room. Within seconds, she'd entered Matt's number and put the cell up to her ear.

After four long rings, she heard his heavy voice mutter, "Hello?" on the other end.

"Matt, it's Cate." She knew that the last time they'd spoken, the conversation had ended awkwardly, but she hoped he was ready to move past that. After all, she had already.

"Oh, hey." His tone went up a notch. "Now isn't really a good time."

"Sorry." She frowned. "I don't mean to interrupt your night, but—"

"Yeah, sounds good," he cut her off. "We'll talk later. Bye." He hung up.

Cate dropped down onto the couch. She stared at her phone for a few moments and then tossed it back into her bag. She crossed her arms.

Kathy, Cate thought. Matt had to be with Kathy. It was the only thing that made sense. Still, wasn't Matt allowed to have friends? Was Kathy that type of person? So jealous and insecure that she had to keep him on a short leash?

Cate shrugged. Maybe there was no such thing as the "perfect relationship." Maybe every couple struggled in their own way. Though, some struggles were much worse than others, she knew.

She leaned back into the soft cushion of the couch. Cate took a deep breath and then exhaled slowly. At the moment, life seemed to be one big struggle.

She shifted her focus to the coffee table in front of her. Joshua must have brought home the evening paper. The big, bold headline didn't grab her attention so much as the large photo underneath it.

That really was Collins she'd seen at the Brim the other day. Now, he was wanted for questioning in the murder of a bartender from Tammi's Pub.

This proved it: he was out there somewhere in her town. Collins had to have been the one who left the threatening notes, too. *That* all made perfect sense now. What she'd been so afraid of seeing, and so quick to avoid, was officially staring her in the face.

But, murder? Why was Collins wanted for questioning in the Creek's latest murder? It didn't quite add up, and she didn't like it. Was he being tied to the other strangulations, too? If so, how?

She reached for her purse again. Cate had to get a hold of her mother. Georgia never bought the paper, so she probably hadn't seen the new development yet.

Cate's mind screamed as she turned the bag upside down and dumped it. Where in hell was her phone? She'd just had it.

This was bad.

Another one of life's cruel curveballs, she wondered how this one would work itself out, or if it even could. Cate highly doubted it.

Collins had followed her and her mom to Perry's Creek, which meant he *knew*. Cate could barely stomach the idea.

Her stepbrother was here, and he wanted revenge.

21

"That was Cate, wasn't it?"

He was completely serious about making it work with Kathy, so he didn't even consider lying as an option. "Yes," Matt answered.

"And, last night? When you snuck out of bed to take a phone call? Let me guess: Cate, too?" Kathy raised her eyebrows.

She'd heard him. Matt couldn't believe it. She'd been so still and quiet, her eyes closed and her breathing labored. He'd been positive that Kathy was fast asleep. Otherwise, he doubted he would have gotten up, thrown on some clothes, and crept out to his backyard to talk to Cate. Especially after the recent conversation he and Kathy had shared. They were giving this relationship a go.

Tonight, even if he'd been in the mood to talk to Cate—which he certainly hadn't been—there was no possible way he could have. Not only was Kathy awake, but Matt also happened to be at her house.

"You know, Matt," Kathy started, "I really don't want to be the bad guy, and I'm trying not to be, but you're making it pretty difficult."

"Cate did call me last night," he admitted. "But, she just wanted to talk about—"

"Her husband, right? Then why did she call you again tonight? Is this some sort of ritual? Do you two have to talk every single night?"

"No, of course not." Matt's voice became deeper. He knew on some level that Kathy was right. It probably wasn't fair for him to be talking so much to Cate, not if he was attempting to get serious with Kathy, but another part of him didn't enjoy the fact that he was a grown man being told what to do.

Was that how relationships worked? One person was the boss, and the other one was there to take orders? To obey?

Well, that wasn't Matt at all, and that was one thing that would never change.

"What did she want?" Kathy persisted.

"I don't know," Matt answered. "You heard me on the phone with her just now. I told her I couldn't talk. I mean, I practically hung up on her."

"Yes." Kathy nodded. "But, you didn't tell her why you couldn't talk. You didn't tell her you were with me, your girlfriend."

"Come on, Kathy. Please," Matt tried, "don't do this."

It had been an extremely long day.

First, the less than pleasant talk with O.J., followed by the pursuit of a suspect that hadn't ended successfully. Then, to put the big red cherry on top of the sundae, the tongue lashing from the sheriff.

A long, tiring day, indeed. Matt had been looking forward to his evening with Kathy, but, now, that was definitely shot to shit.

Matt reached for the green beer bottle. He didn't bother looking at her. He knew she'd be sporting a frown and her dark eyes would be full of disappointment. What did she want from him?

She was the one making this difficult. Did she have to be so uptight about things? He was having dinner with her. He'd told Cate he couldn't talk. He'd chosen Kathy. Wasn't that enough? Would anything he did ever be enough? Or was Kathy going to be jealous of Cate forever?

Matt glanced around Kathy's dining room. The surroundings didn't offer much insight into her character, but now he wondered if that was on purpose. Was Kathy trying to hide who she truly was? Or did she just lack personality?

The walls were all beige and didn't offer any sort of decoration—no paintings, family portraits, or even a mirror. The table was square, wooden, sat four, and had been placed on top of a rug that looked to be both prickly and expensive.

Then there was Kathy. She'd chosen wine over beer and had hardly touched her salad or lasagna. Was she just not hungry? Or was she too upset to eat? Matt was almost sure he knew the answer, and he didn't like it.

Kathy hadn't styled her hair but had just pushed it out of her face. She'd picked casual clothing for their dinner—jeans and a T-shirt—which matched Matt's outfit perfectly. Her makeup, as usual, was almost non-existent. Everything about Kathy tonight seemed relaxed and comfortable— except for her attitude. Her attitude was one hundred percent unattractive, and the pouty face she was making didn't help matters.

Matt had to say something. The silence was making him feel numb.

"I confronted O.J. today," he said finally.

The statement must have piqued her interest because she looked up at him. "And? Did he admit to beating his wife?"

"No." Matt shook his head. "He denied it, and now I think things might be weird between the two of us."

"Of course it's going to be weird." Kathy reached for her wine glass. "You accused your best friend of abusing his wife, of doing something that isn't true."

"Wait," Matt argued. "I didn't say it wasn't true. I just said he denied it. He could be lying."

"Do you think he's lying to you, Matt?"

Matt shrugged. "Honestly, I'm not sure."

"O.J. is your best friend. I would think you'd be able to tell when he's lying."

"Well, I can't," Matt admitted. "He said he's not hurting Cate, but something seemed off. His explanation for Cate's bruises—"

"Look, Matt." Kathy returned her glass to the table. "You did all you could do. You talked to O.J. You did the noble thing and tried to help Cate out, but your friend told you point-blank that he's not beating his wife, and you should respect him enough to believe him and now leave it alone."

"But, what if he's lying? Cate could be in trouble."

"What if Cate's the one lying? What if O.J. is telling the truth and Cate made the whole thing up?"

"I-I-I guess it's a possibility." He shrugged. "But, why would she do that? What's her motive behind it?"

"She gets you."

"Excuse me?"

"Think about it." Kathy pushed her plate away and folded her hands in its place. "That last few times we've been together, what's been our main topic of discussion? Cate. And, the last couple of times we've had an argument, who's been at the center of it? Cate. Don't you see it, Matt?"

"Not really. Why don't you just tell me what you want me to see, Kathy?"

She shook her head. "Cate wants you, Matt. It's pretty obvious to me. She's trying to get to you by getting your sympathy vote. And, quite frankly, I think she's succeeding."

"What are you talking about?" His voice became louder, and his head was starting to pound. Matt feared he was only seconds away from losing it.

"She's playing the victim. She wants you to feel sorry for her."

"I don't know if that's necessarily—"

"It is true." Kathy nodded. "And, it's working. You feel sorry for her."

"I don't," Matt protested, but even he didn't believe his words. It was a lie—and after he'd just told himself that he wasn't going to lie to her. He knew this wasn't going to end well. There was no possible way it could.

He began picking at the corner of the white label stretched across the glass of his beer bottle. A little at first, but once he got going, he couldn't stop. There was something oddly comforting about the act, but he finished when the sticky label was shredded.

"We shouldn't be arguing over Cate, Matt," Kathy said softly. "We shouldn't be talking about her at all. She's your friend, fine. But—"

"There's a little more to the story," Matt interrupted.

"Okay," Kathy sighed. "What is it?"

Matt took a deep breath. "Cate thinks O.J. strangled those three women. She has it in her head that he's the killer."

"Does she have any proof? Is there any evidence that O.J. is or could be involved with the murders?"

"No." Matt turned away. "Not exactly."

"But, you have a suspect for the murders, right? Or, at least a person of interest. Someone was seen outside of the last victim's apartment the day she was strangled."

"Yes," Matt answered.

Kathy shrugged. "You still can't see what she's doing? She's making her husband out to be some sort of monster—and for no reason. She doesn't even have any—"

"I didn't say I believed her about that," Matt said. "Honestly, no, I don't think O.J. strangled anybody. But, I do think he might be..."

"Beating her." Kathy nodded. "So you've said. Except you asked him, and he told you he wasn't. What more can you do?"

"I don't know yet, but I think I need to find out—"

"Find out which one of your friends is lying to you?"

"Please, Kathy."

"Why did she come to you, anyway?" Kathy rested her right hand on her chin. "Why not talk to a girlfriend or her family?"

"She doesn't have anyone else," Matt confessed. "Cate doesn't really have any girlfriends, and her mom can't do much for her."

"So you were her only option?"

"She thought I could help her because I'm O.J.'s friend."

"Right," Kathy agreed. "And, as O.J.'s friend, don't you find it strange you're talking to his wife behind his back?"

"It's not like that."

"It's exactly like that," Kathy pressed on. "You're sneaking around, having secret phone calls with your best friend and partner's wife. To make matters worse, you're accusing him of something he probably didn't even do."

"I don't think Cate is lying just to get me to feel sorry for her. I don't think she wants me. I think she's scared and alone and looking for help."

"I already told you how to help her." Kathy stood up.

"She's not going to file a complaint or get a restraining order," Matt said. "I asked her. She refused."

"Because she's lying about the abuse!" Kathy threw up her hands. "If she was really that scared or in any kind of danger, she'd get out of that house."

"You just don't understand." Matt stood, too.

"Something we can agree on, finally. You're right, Matt—I don't understand. I don't understand any of this. You're betraying your best friend, and you're choosing some other woman over your girlfriend."

"That's not true," Matt argued. "I'm not choosing any side."

"Well, you're going to have to."

"What?" Matt crossed his arms. "What are you talking about, Kathy?"

"Simply put, it's me or Cate."

"You can't be serious."

"Dead serious." She placed her hands on her hips. "I can't keep having this same fight with you. Cate asked for your help. Okay, fine. You talked to O.J., and he said there's no abuse going on. That should be the end of it."

"But—"

"But, instead, you're listening to some weak little girl who has no interest in helping herself. She's lying, Matt. She's trying to get to you, and you're letting her. And, worst of all, you're allowing her to come between not just one, but two of the closest people you have in your life."

Matt closed his eyes. His head was pounding full blast now. He wasn't too familiar with how relationships worked, but he didn't think new ones were supposed to go this way. Not in the beginning, at least. Didn't people usually wait a while before showing their true colors?

"I'm sorry, Matt." Kathy's voice was calmer. "I don't like being this person."

"Then stop being her."

Matt was all for giving this relationship a try, but not like this. He needed to get something more enjoyable out of it than a lasagna dinner. Not to mention, most of his days usually involved some sort of argument or hassle. He didn't want to come home to that life. He'd rather be alone.

"The only way I think I'll be able to stop is if you cut Cate out of your life." She waited a beat and then added, "For good."

"Kathy—"

"It may not seem fair to you," she went on, "but it's the only thing I can think of that may give us a chance. So, if you want to date me and give this relationship a shot, see if it's going anywhere, then you'll have to say goodbye to Cate."

Matt just stared at her. He didn't know what to say. He hated being told what to do, but he also knew that Kathy was ultimately right.

Matt had a decision to make. And, as tough as that decision was, he thought he knew how he was going to handle it.

22

"Thank you for coming on such short notice," he said. "I really appreciate it."

"Don't get too sentimental on me, Collins. Remember, you're paying me to be here."

How could he possibly forget? Richie seemed keen on reminding him every two minutes. Hell, Collins was sure Richie had added the twelve-pack of beer to his tab.

"You'll get paid just as soon as I do." Collins raised the can to his lips and took a long swig. It wasn't much of a surprise to learn his beer had grown warm.

The room didn't offer a refrigerator, and neither of them had volunteered to trek down to the first floor to get ice out of the machine. Still, Collins managed to overlook the temperature of the brew and took another swallow. After all, he'd consumed much worse things in his life.

"Tell me again why I'm here," Richie ordered in between burps. "You're wanted for murder, right? Did you strangle some girl, Collins?"

"No! Of course not!" Collins drained the last of the silver can and crumbled it. He'd forgotten what a big pain in the ass Richie could be. "I was in the girl's apartment, but when I left, she was very much alive."

"What were you doing there in the first place?"

"What do you think I was doing there?" Collins turned to his friend and frowned. "You got shit for brains all of a sudden? Maybe I called the wrong guy for help."

"I'm just trying to make sure I know what's going on, exactly. So you fucked her, but you didn't kill her."

"I didn't do either," Collins admitted. "It's a long story." He gave

Richie the Cliff's Notes version, and in a way that he hoped wouldn't evoke too many more questions. Collins was ready to move on, get serious, and get some work done.

"And, because you can't show your mug around here without getting picked up now that you've been branded the town strangler, I'm here to do your dirty work for you."

"Something like that." Collins nodded.

Richie reached for another beer. "But, if you didn't do it, why not turn yourself in? Clear your name and move on with whatever it is you came here to do?"

"It's not that simple. I didn't kill anybody, but I can't prove that. Not to mention, my record isn't clean."

"You've got a point there, my friend." Richie snorted.

"And, I'm sure that, by now, the two people I didn't want to know that I was here are well aware that I'm in this dump." Collins took a deep breath and balled his hands into fists. "This whole thing has turned into a fucking train wreck."

"Well, I guess that's what you get for going out and looking for some strange."

Collins stood up. "You know, I'm paying you to be here. You're working for me."

"And?" Richie shrugged.

Collins felt his face turn red. "And, if you don't have anything helpful to say, then you should shut your damned pie hole."

"Whoa!" Richie raised his left hand. "I didn't realize you were so sensitive. I was only joking."

"Well, knock it off! We don't have time for it!" Collins pivoted away from Richie. He stared at the blank TV as he contemplated throwing in the towel.

Sure, he'd thought about this whole revenge plan for a while. Then again, he'd had nothing better to do in lockup. Still, now he feared that if he didn't get his head out of his ass and back on track, he might be headed right back there.

At the prospect of going back to prison, only one thought came to mind: *no fucking thanks.*

"You were kind of vague on the phone." The sound of the tab on Richie's beer can snapping open filled the small space. "How are you coming into all of this money?"

140

"Let's just say that a long time ago, I was wronged," Collins admitted. "And, now, I'm here to make sure that that wrong is righted. The best way it can be, anyway."

"Who wronged you?"

"Two women from my past."

Interestingly enough, he remembered that night almost perfectly now, even though it'd been fourteen years ago. Not to mention he'd most likely altered his brain with all of the drugs he'd put into his body over time.

Still, he'd gotten clean during his time spent in the Arizona Department of Corrections facility, and his mind had become clear. While he couldn't decide where to place blame for what had happened in the past, Collins had ultimately made a decision and assumed that decision had already created plenty of fear, confusion, and punishment among the guilty parties.

Maybe he'd run into a small snag with the whole Tara thing, and his face might have been splattered all over Perry's Creek in connection with her murder and the other strangulations, but that wasn't going to stop him. He'd come too far, waited too long, and he'd follow through with his revenge plan at any cost.

"Is that all you care to share?" Richie sounded confused.

"Yes, for now."

"Fine." Richie burped again loudly. "Then can you at least tell me about my part? What I'll be doing to help the cause?"

"You'll be doing whatever I tell you to do." Collins faced Richie. "Understand?"

Richie stood up. "Look, I'm sorry for whatever shitty thing happened to you. Seriously, I am. But, that doesn't give you the right to treat me like I'm some worthless nobody. I know you're paying me, but I didn't have to come here. We used to be friends, Collins. I deserve to be treated with respect."

Collins didn't say anything, because, if he did, he'd have to admit that Richie was right. Collins was being a prick, and his friend didn't deserve it, but the last thing he was going to do was apologize for his behavior. That wasn't happening. Collins wasn't about to show weakness, not in front of Richie, anyway. It would give the other man the upper hand, and Collins had to stay in control. He *wanted* to stay in control.

Instead, Collins simply said, "I'm stressed." He shrugged, but added, "Honestly, this whole scheme hasn't been as easy as I thought it was going to be."

Richie returned Collins's gesture. "That's why I'm here, to help you. So, let me help you."

Richie was right...again. Collins had called the man for help, and it was time to let him help, but to properly do that, Collins knew he needed to fill Richie in on what was going to happen. Not just bits and pieces, but everything—every single part of the plan. Richie had a right to know. There was also the chance that the more he knew, the more helpful he could be.

Collins decided then that it was high time to stop being so damn antagonistic. Not only was it exhausting to keep up the act, but it could also make Richie turn on him. At the end of the day, he needed the other man. There was no way he was going to be able to pull anything off without him.

"First, I need you to deliver a note."

Richie resumed his seat on the bed. "Okay, seems pretty doable."

"It should be. I've done it twice now, and without getting caught. But, the note you will be delivering will be the most important one yet. It will say when, where, and how we want the money."

Richie leaned back against the cheap headboard of the bed. "That is pretty important."

Collins wasn't sure how Georgia was going to come up with the money but knew she'd find a way. When they'd been in each other's lives, she'd always seemed to be so resourceful. He assumed—or hoped—that she still possessed that quality. After all, she wouldn't want to involve the police. Collins was sure of that. He was positive his threats had gotten his point across. Georgia knew what she'd done and had most likely put two and two together as to why she was being targeted.

The past always comes back to haunt you.

Therefore, she'd want to play it smart: No cops and she'd get the money no matter what it took. Collins was banking on it.

Ms. Georgia Olsen was in for a very rude awakening because what she didn't know was that this was going to be just the first of many payments to come. Collins planned on making her suffer. As soon as she thought her troubles were all over and she was in the clear, he'd be back, delivering another note.

The woman's life would become one big torture session. She'd be looking over her shoulder constantly, wondering where her blackmailer was, and when he'd strike again. She would eventually put herself—and, if he was lucky, Cate, too—into a state of financial ruin by trying to pay him off.

Then, finally, when she had nowhere else to turn and no one else to lean on or bleed dry, the woman would have absolutely no reason left to live. She'd either turn herself in for what she'd done, or she'd kill herself.

Either way, Georgia Olsen was going to self-destruct, and Collins didn't particularly care how it happened, just as long as it did. The bitch had it coming.

"And, we're only asking for ten grand, right?"

Collins felt his jaw tighten. He was getting annoyed again. Why had Richie asked the question when he already knew the answer? That was one of Collins's pet peeves. Whether the man was trying to be cute or funny or was just plain dumb, it didn't matter. Collins had a plan, a damned good one, and he wasn't going to change it because Richie didn't necessarily approve of it. The man needed to understand that being too greedy too fast could—and, most likely would—cause a messy explosion to occur, resulting in them ending up with no money at all.

"Yes, the first time," Collins answered finally. "There will be more later. But, for now, we need to start small. Asking for more than ten grand will only draw attention to us. And, trust me, that's the last thing we want to do."

"Okay. I guess that makes sense."

Good, Collins thought. He was already getting tired of explaining every last detail to Richie. His friend was going to make an easy five thousand dollars, and that should have been the man's only concern.

"Is there a specific way I should deliver the note? Put it in the mailbox? Tape it to the front door? The windshield of a car? What's your preference?"

At the moment, Collin's only preference was for Richie to shut the fuck up. Was the man really that dense? Wasn't it more than obvious that Collins just wanted some peace and quiet?

Perhaps he had chosen the wrong person to assist him with this task.

Then again, it wasn't like Collins had a list of friends to choose from to ask for help. Richie had been the lucky one, because, quite frankly, he'd been the only one. Due to both burnt bridges and having "convicted felon" listed at the top of his resume, people from his past now seemed to steer clear of him.

Did Collins blame them for that? Not necessarily. He knew what kind of person he was—not the easiest to get along with. Well, now he was paying for that with Richie.

Oh, well. At the moment, there was nothing he could do about it, but, moving forward, he knew he'd have to be more mindful of how he treated people, just in case he ever had to call on them for help. Otherwise, he'd be left with slim pickings and end up with someone like…like…Richie.

Collins stared at the man now. Short, dark hair, pale skin. Nothing was intimidating about Richie's height. However, his tight, muscular build made people think about what they said in his presence.

He had a habit of wearing tank tops, even in colder weather. Collins wasn't sure if it was because his body temperature ran naturally hot or if he just liked showing off his biceps. Either way, most people didn't mess with him.

Except for Collins. Collins didn't even find his dark, soulless eyes that haunting. Richie was just a man, and Collins knew how to handle him: show no fear. In his experience, that was the fuel that most hotheaded thugs—or thug wannabes—ran on: other people's fear. So, if you didn't have any fear—or, at least, pretended not to—then guys like Richie came up empty.

Besides, nine out of ten times, the tank-top-wearing, muscle-bearing, soulless guys who tried to be scary couldn't even throw a decent punch. It was all an act.

"You trying to start a staring contest or something? You're cute and all, but I don't really feel like sharing a bed with you."

Shit, Collins thought. He didn't have enough money to get Richie his own room. Furthermore, the fewer people who saw Richie, the better. That meant the two were stuck sharing a single room that offered a queen-sized bed, a two-drawer nightstand, a dresser, a TV, and a bathroom.

Collins didn't believe Scott's Inn was the type of place to offer a cot, but, even if it did, there was nowhere to put it. Hell, the room had felt too cramped as soon as Richie walked in with his bag and the case of beer.

Collins wasn't sure which option was worse: spooning with an old junkie or lying on the shag carpet that probably hadn't seen a decent shampooing since being laid.

"You can have the bed. I'll sleep on the floor." Collins took a deep breath. He reminded himself that this would all be over soon enough. He planned on being out of Perry's Creek in a couple of days—max.

There was only one possible flaw in his scheme: the motel clerk who had checked him in a few days ago. However, Collins doubted the old man would remember him, anyway. He'd looked on the verge of senile, but, just in case, Collins would be prepared for the worst.

That was what separated the boys from the men—preparation—and Collins was all man. Preparation really did make the world go round.

"Suit yourself." Richie reached behind his back for a pillow and tossed it to the floor. "Hey, you never answered me from before. How do you want me to deliver—?"

Collins raised his hand. "I'll let you know in a minute. I need to think it all through, decide how I want to play it."

Richie shrugged. "Fine, but can you at least tell me *when* I'll be making this delivery?"

"Yes," Collins answered, "tonight."

They would be taking action and moving forward with the revenge plan tonight. Collins knew his dad would be very, very proud.

23

Today was the day. She wasn't going to take any more. She couldn't. When Cate got out of bed, she made a conscious decision to be strong—and that's exactly what she planned on doing.

Cate was familiar with how people went crazy: they focused on too much at one time. Sure, she had a lot going on in her life at the moment. So much, that if she stopped and took a second to consider it all, her head would likely explode.

It wasn't enough that she had a husband who got off on beating her. Now, there was also her issue with Matt, whatever that was. Then there were the problems with her mom and Collins, who was obviously in Perry's Creek. And, to add to the never-ending pile of heartache, pain, and bad luck that had somehow become her entire life, she also had Jerry from work to worry about.

And, that wasn't even all of it.

She was going to go mad if she dwelled on all of her problems and tried to fix every single one of them at once. She knew the best thing she could do was breathe, and, of course, be strong. It was definitely time to be strong.

Joshua had been in a hurry this morning. He'd wanted to get to the police department early. He'd stayed to gulp down a cup of coffee but refused egg whites and the handful of other options she'd offered to whip up.

While Cate knew quite well that her Joshua situation was far from being over or even remotely solved, she took the brief encounter for what it was. Her husband hadn't hit her this morning, hadn't even yelled at her.

The only real thing Joshua said to her was, "Don't forget to cover up your face today."

Still, she'd considered it a win. It was a good start, and because Joshua wasn't a current problem she needed to deal with, she was moving on—for the time being. Choosing her battles was a skill she was determined to perfect.

As for Matt, well, that was a landmine she had no interest in getting close to. Not now, and maybe not ever. He'd never called her back last night, which had probably been a good thing since she'd spent most of her evening in bed with Joshua.

Cate wasn't stupid. Matt hadn't talked to her on the phone or bothered to call her back for a reason, and that reason was painfully obvious: Kathy. Matt had clearly been with her the entire night. Although she couldn't quite explain it, just the image of the two of them together made her skin feel as if it was burning from the inside out, and in such a way that the idea of relief wasn't even plausible.

Okay, maybe Cate could explain it. Maybe she did have a small crush on her husband's best friend and partner. Maybe she had hoped that he would save her, or, at least, offer some sort of comfort. But, it hadn't happened, and it was probably smart to assume that it never would. It seemed that Matt had tried but failed in the end.

For the time being, she couldn't act on her feelings for Matt, and Matt couldn't rescue her. So, again, she was moving on.

As for her mother, Georgia was meeting her on her break to discuss the blackmail threats and Collins, who had obviously been the one to deliver them. The front page of last night's paper had made that more than clear.

Most importantly, she and her mom had to discuss how they were going to come up with ten thousand dollars. Sure, Georgia had an idea, but if Cate went along with it, she would likely end up dead. Literally.

Still, that conversation wasn't happening for at least another hour or so. Her mother had wanted to talk about Collins and his messages this morning, but Cate had flat-out refused. For one thing, she hadn't had enough time for a full-fledged discussion on the matter. For another, in an attempt to avoid going crazy, she was only focusing on one problem at a time.

With Joshua out of the house earlier than expected, Matt no longer on her radar, and her lunch with her mom scheduled for later, Cate had been left with plenty of time and energy to focus on her most recent crisis: Jerry.

Things with Jerry hadn't ended on a good note, and ever since their impromptu backroom chitchat, a part of Cate's mind had been dedicated to trying to figure out what she was up against.

Everyone had an agenda, even Jerry. Cate couldn't help but believe that unmasking him was a life-and-death type of predicament, and it just so happened that Cate wanted to live.

As a result, thoughts of Jerry filled her entire morning. She'd seen his once-comforting-and-now-almost-threatening smile in her head while trying to enjoy her first cup of dark roast coffee. She'd even smelled his signature odor of sweat and Old Spice while in the shower. The scent had somehow managed to overpower her own vanilla body wash.

However, the real clincher was when Cate heard his soft, flat voice while getting dressed in her usual work garb: jeans, a white T-shirt, and comfortable shoes.

Cate had made a point of only focusing on one of life's major problems, but whether or not Jerry knew it, he had her full attention.

Cate stood behind the counter at the Brim, trying to decide if she should say something to Jerry or wait for him to address the issue. Then again, in a few days, he'd be on vacation, and she'd be left detangled from the web he'd spun.

So, did she wait? Bide her time and just let the whole storm blow over? That seemed to be her MO these past ten months: do nothing, sit back, and wait for the puzzle to solve itself. Well, where, exactly, had that gotten her?

Unfortunately, she was all too familiar with how doing nothing worked: it didn't. She had the marks to prove it. In her experience, problems didn't just solve themselves. You had to take a stance, face the situation head on, tackle it, and then bury it as if it had never existed.

And, even then, those same problems had a way of resurfacing. Cate considered last night's newspaper. It was the circle of life. Or, more importantly, the circle of *her* life.

Cate's mind was starting to spin, so she reminded herself to zero in on the complication at hand: Her boss had made a pass at her and knew about her abuse. Right now, that was the only place her head needed to be.

"Doing okay, Cate?"

She turned at the sound of her name. Jerry was standing behind her, balancing a stack of white Styrofoam lids. He wore a wide grin that made the tiny hairs on both of her arms stand straight up. Cate had seen the same expression on Jerry many times before, but it no longer meant what it used to.

In the beginning, Jerry's smile had been warm, comforting, even sweet. There was a time when Cate first started working at the Brim when she had looked forward to seeing her boss *and* his smile. Oddly, it had relaxed her and made her feel safe.

Of course, that was no longer the case, not after Jerry's big revelation. Now, the smile seemed to seep evil. Cate felt like she was in danger when she was in Jerry's presence. It was almost as if she was being threatened, and she kind of was. He was dangling a secret over her head, trapping her. The very notion of it made Cate want to claw at her dry skin.

Then her morning mantra snapped back into sight: *Be strong.*

"I'm fine," Cate answered finally.

Cate would need to find common ground between being strong and being professional. She still enjoyed her job, and she didn't want to sacrifice it. Not yet, anyway. Not until she had no other choice but to give it up and avoid Jerry altogether.

That would be Plan B, Cate thought.

"Good to hear." Jerry placed the lids on the top shelf under the counter. "Looks like the morning rush has come and gone. Hopefully, the Creek will need an afternoon pick-me-up."

Cate shrugged. "I guess we'll see."

If he was trying to be cute, he was failing at record speed. Not to mention, his attempt at small talk was like listening to a child scraping a fork across the surface of a plate. The noise was nauseating.

"Have you given any more thought to our discussion?" Jerry leaned in closer to her.

She took a step away from him. She tried not to gag. Cate could smell the maple syrup that lingered on his breath. He'd probably had pancakes for breakfast.

"Because I've been thinking about it," he continued, "and—"

"Please, Jerry," she cut him off. "I'd prefer it if we just forgot about what was said the other day, okay? It was inappropriate and uncomfortable. Let's move past it."

"You know, Cate, if there's one thing I've learned from watching my wife die, it's this: Life is really short. Don't you want to be happy for whatever amount of time you have left here?"

"I am happy, Jerry." But, even Cate didn't believe the weak lie that had fallen out of her mouth. Maybe some things in life couldn't be hidden with a lie.

"You're not a very good liar, Cate." Jerry smiled again. "I've been watching you. I know you. And, now that I've had time to grieve for Sarah, I think I'm ready to—"

"Move on?" she asked. "Move on to a married woman who also happens to be your employee?"

"I wasn't going to say that." Jerry shook his head. "I'm ready to help someone else. I'm ready to help you. I wasn't in the right mindset before, but now I am. And, you need me, Cate."

"You're still not in the right mindset, Jerry," Cate argued. Her tone rose and became thicker. "I mean, listen to yourself. What happened to you? We were fine, even friends, before all of this..."

"I've been watching you closely, Cate," Jerry admitted. "Over the past few weeks, something has changed. You haven't been yourself. And now that I've seen the marks, the bruises—"

"I don't know what you're talking about," she lied again. "I'm f-f-fine. My marriage is fine. It's solid."

Cate turned her back to him and closed her eyes, and then she counted to three silently. She refused to break. Not now, not here. She couldn't let Jerry do this to her.

Be strong. The words echoed in her ears suddenly.

"I can help you, Cate. I can save you."

"Except I don't need help, and I don't need to be saved." She didn't bother to turn back around. "I'm sorry about Sarah. Watching the person you love suffer can't be easy. But, you're still in mourning, clearly, and latching onto me isn't going to do you any good."

"It's more than that, Cate. Since the day you started working here, even when Sarah was still alive, I had these feelings for you," he admitted softly. "Now that she's gone, I think I know what those feelings are, and I'd like to explore them further."

"I'm married!" Cate roared. Her jaw tightened. "You're my boss! Not to mention, you're also quite a bit older than me."

"Those are minor factors we can get around, Cate. And, as for Joshua, well, he doesn't love you. Look at yourself. Look at what he does to you."

"You're wrong, Jerry," she argued. "Joshua doesn't hurt me." He was getting closer to her. She could feel his hot breath on the back of her neck.

"Stop lying to me, Cate. Stop lying to yourself," Jerry pleaded. "I would never treat you like that. You're so special, Cate. I want you. Let me be with you." He placed his right hand on her shoulder and then gave it a light squeeze.

"Don't touch me!" She spun around finally and faced him. "What more do you want from me, Jerry? I've told you no!' You have to stop this. Now!"

"But—"

"No, Jerry!" Cate cut him off completely. She surprised even herself at how steady her voice sounded. This was much easier than she'd thought it was going to be.

Be strong.

"I've asked you to stop repeatedly," she continued. "I'm married, and my husband doesn't beat me."

"You're making a scene, Cate," Jerry muttered.

Cate looked around the shop. It was empty. "Are you kidding me? There's no one in here."

"Well…"

"Besides, I don't care who sees or hears me. I thought we were friends, Jerry. I wanted to be friends. But, that isn't an option anymore."

He frowned. "What does that mean?"

"From now on, we are nothing more than boss and employee. Understand? I don't want you to mention my personal life again. All of our conversations will be work-related."

"You're overreacting, Cate."

"I don't think so," she fired back. "I'm warning you. Stay out of my business!"

"And, if I don't?" he mocked. "What do you think you're going to do?" His signature grin was back, but, this time, it appeared with an agenda. Jerry flashed his teeth. He was out for blood. Even his eyes had gone dark.

"You don't know what I'm capable of."

"And, you just made a very big mistake, little girl." He edged past her, turned the corner, and headed for the back of the shop.

For the first time since their conversation had grown heated, Cate realized her hands had balled into fists, her stomach had knotted up, and she felt tears forming at the corners of her eyes.

Be strong.

She'd wanted to be strong; she'd tried. For a split second, Cate even thought she had succeeded, but, at the moment, she couldn't have felt weaker. She suspected she might crumple to the black-and-white tiled floor, fold into a ball, and start sobbing.

And, somehow, Cate was perfectly okay with that.

* * *

"You don't look so good."

"Thanks, Mom. You're too kind to me."

"Oh, Catie." Georgia waved her hand. "You know I didn't mean anything by that. You just look upset. Is something wrong?"

"Seriously?" Cate raised her eyebrows. "Is something wrong? Let's see: My husband beats me, all the while trying to get me pregnant; I may be in love with his best friend and partner but can't really do anything about it; my deranged stepbrother is in town and blackmailing me into giving him money; and now, it turns out my boss has a huge crush on me and just so happens to have threatened me."

"I'm sorry, Cate. I shouldn't have—"

"It's fine." Cate took a deep breath. "I'm fine. I'm trying this new thing where I only focus on one problem at a time. You came to talk about Collins, so…"

"Are you sure?" Georgia asked. "I mean, with everything you just listed, maybe you'd prefer to talk about Matt? Or even Jerry? I had no idea that either—"

"No, I can't." She shook her head. "I'll go crazy. I have to forget about Matt for now, and I'll deal with Jerry later when I absolutely have to."

"Okay."

"Besides, I'd rather think about the one issue I can fix—or, at least, make somewhat better." She reached for her glass of water that was now sweating. "Let's decide what we're going to do about Collins."

"Sure."

"Honestly, I'm surprised you're not more upset. Collins *is* in Perry's Creek. Don't you want to say, 'I told you so?'"

Georgia took a sip of her own water. "Well, last night's paper was an unpleasant surprise."

"Most surprises are."

"No kidding." Georgia nodded.

Cate returned the glass to the red surface of the metal table. The cool drink helped with the blazing heat, but not much. She knew they should have chosen a spot inside the restaurant where the air conditioner was just as friendly as the smiling teenage hostess, but there was too long of a wait. Cate wanted to make sure there was a decent amount of time to have a conversation with her mother and come up with a plan that would officially settle the predicament of the threatening notes. Now, they not only had the time but the privacy, too.

Cate looked around the empty back patio. It was obvious she and her mom were the only ones brave enough to test the June heat. It was almost amusing to think the gray umbrellas above them could provide a hint of shade.

The concrete beneath their feet felt like tiny hot coals burning small holes into the soles of their shoes, but, somehow, the worst part of their seating arrangement was the view—or lack thereof.

The back patio of the popular diner faced the parking lot, which had never made any sense to Cate. Instead of being blessed with the surroundings that the front of the restaurant offered—planted flowers and near-perfect landscaping, local shops, other eateries, and even the town fountain if you were able to crane your neck to the left far enough—they got to stare at a full parking lot mixed with cars, trucks, and jeeps, with more than half overdue for a good scrubbing.

At least they were sitting down. They also had plenty of privacy, cold water to drink, and were told their salads wouldn't take too long.

The silver lining to this already rotten day, Cate thought. At least she wouldn't be late going back to work. The last thing she wanted to do was give Jerry ammo. It was hard predicting what he'd do with it.

"Well, first things first," Cate said finally, "I think I owe you an apology."

"An apology?" The words came out of Georgia's mouth as if she didn't quite know their meaning.

"Yes." Cate nodded. "I was the one who got it in your head that Collins was in town and responsible for the original threat. Then I turned you off of the idea. But, lo and behold, he is in Perry's Creek. Therefore, he has to be the one who delivers the messages. I'm surprised I haven't given you whiplash with all of my back and forth."

"Don't worry about it. Believe me, I didn't want to think Collins had tracked us down, either. But, now that we know for certain he has, well, I'm not sure if I'm more terrified or relieved."

"Relieved?" It was Cate's turn to be confused. "Why in hell would you be relieved to learn that your stepson is in town, and, most likely, tormenting us?"

Georgia shrugged. "Because I, at least, know *who* is tormenting us, and *why.* That solves one mystery."

Cate hadn't considered that. However, she had to admit that her mom did make a good point. With all of the other uncertainties currently plaguing her life, it was refreshing to have an answer to something.

"By the way," Georgia added, "do you believe what the paper implied? Do you think Collins could have had anything to do with that bartender's murder? Or even the other two girls' deaths? I know a direct connection hasn't been made between the victims, but it's pretty obvious that whoever strangled one most likely strangled all three, right?"

"That would make sense," Cate agreed. "But, as far as Collins being involved? No, I honestly don't think he has anything to do with those crimes." She didn't bother sharing with Georgia her own theory of who she wanted the killer to be.

"Then why wouldn't he turn himself in? Clear his name, if he really has nothing to hide?"

Cate sighed. "I don't know, Mom. I've never understood Collins, not even when we were younger. But, I don't care about any of that. I want to know what our plan is. I want to know what *we're* going to do with Collins."

"I think there's only one way, Cate."

"Please, don't say pay him."

Georgia threw her hands into the air. "Then what's your solution? We can't go to the cops. No one is going to help us. We don't even know how to get a hold of Collins to maybe try and—"

"What?" Cate smacked her open palm down on the table. "You want to negotiate with him? I'm not negotiating with a man like that, not when he's blackmailing us. Collins is more of a coward than I thought he was, dropping off those stupid little notes. Besides, paying him will only lead to more trouble."

"What do you mean?"

"Think about it." Cate folded her hands into a bridge. "If we pay him off now, what's to stop him from coming back and asking for more money in the future?"

Georgia frowned. "I hadn't thought about that."

"Well, I have," Cate said. "I've been thinking about a lot of things— most importantly, we don't have ten thousand dollars to just hand over to him. Therefore, I say we call his bluff."

"Excuse me?"

"We don't know what kind of evidence he has—*if* he even has any. You really think he's going to go to the cops and report a crime that happened fourteen years ago? Let him! Not to mention, his record. Seriously, who's going to believe anything an addict has to say?"

"I'm not willing to take that chance, Cate. We're talking about the possibility of going to prison."

"Fine." She tossed her hands up again. "Then, I guess you need to find a way to come up with ten grand and fast because I'm vetoing your *other* suggestion."

"Cate…"

"No, Mom! How could you even ask me to take money from that joint account? Ten thousand dollars? Don't you think Joshua would notice if a huge chunk of the inheritance from his grandfather went missing?"

"Listen to me, Cate…"

"He'd kill me. Without a doubt, Joshua would kill me if I stole from him. I'd rather risk prison."

"Please, Cate. I'm trying to tell you something." Georgia's voice thickened. "I found another note this morning. This time, it was taped to the mirror in my bathroom."

"O-o-okay," Cate stuttered. She tried to swallow the lump that had formed in her throat. "What did it say?"

Georgia was quiet for a moment. She looked down at the table, then back up at Cate. "Collins doesn't want ten thousand dollars anymore. He wants twenty."

"What? Collins wants t-t-twenty…" Cate couldn't finish the rest of her thought. Her words trailed off.

This couldn't be happening, could it? Cate was sure that her head was going to explode. She didn't know if she needed to scream or cry. Perhaps standing up and running away was her best bet, just taking off in a quick sprint.

Somehow, that seemed wise: Leaving all of her troubles in the dust, forgetting they even existed, and getting the hell out of Dodge. She could start over again: a new town, a new name this time, a new life where no one could find her.

Then Cate was hit with the cold, ugly truth: You couldn't escape your past. No one could. She'd tried, and she'd failed. Now, she had to face the consequences.

"Say something, Cate," Georgia ordered.

"I don't know what to say."

Her past seemed like some disgusting beetle that could survive anything. It didn't suffocate and die when more dirt was thrown on top of it. It thrived, becoming stronger and stronger…impossible to kill.

"Well, we still have enough money to pay—"

"No, we don't!" Cate screeched. "*We* don't have any money to pay Collins. That's Joshua's inheritance, and we're not touching it."

"There's no other way out of this, Cate," Georgia argued. "We don't have a choice."

"Did you not hear me mention that Joshua will kill me? Twenty thousand dollars? That's almost everything! Why would Collins assume you even had that much money?"

"I don't know, but—"

"I say we ignore the threat. Collins isn't going to do anything if we don't pay up. He has nothing on us."

"You don't know that, Cate."

"There's only one way to find out." Cate took a deep breath. "These notes or messages—they're all empty threats. He's using this false fear to try and get to you."

"And, it's working! I'm scared, Cate!"

Cate shook her head. "We can't give in, Mom. Collins is banking on that. We need to stick together and just wait this whole thing out."

"That's easy for you to say." Georgia sat up taller in her chair. "You're not the one who keeps getting threats. Collins has been in my house at least three different times now, and twice while I've been asleep. It's hard to tell what he'll do if he doesn't get—"

"He's not going to do anything," Cate interrupted. "You really think he's going to go from delivering mail to…what? Killing you in your sleep?" She tried to laugh, but the gesture felt too fake. Nothing about this situation was comical.

"Like I told you, I don't know what that man is capable of. But, if he's looking for revenge and hoping to settle the score—"

"Once he realizes we're not giving in, he'll leave us alone. We have to show him that we're strong and not going to roll over so easily no matter how many messages he types up and delivers."

"You're taking twenty thousand dollars out of that joint account, Cate," Georgia demanded. "I'm not asking. We're not risking our lives or our freedom for money."

Cate's eyes narrowed. Everything around her became quiet. She didn't even hear the hostess walk out and seat the group of young boys two tables over. It was as if she was trapped in a tightly vacuumed bubble. She was perfectly familiar with her surroundings and could see it all, but had lost all control as to what was actually happening. Cate wasn't going to be able to stop the events that were falling into motion, and she knew that. Her mother's crisp command had paralyzed her.

"And, what am I supposed to tell Joshua?" she asked finally. "You know his temper. You know what he'll do to me."

"We'll think of something. We always do."

The waitress dropped off their salads, but Cate pushed her plate away almost immediately. The last thing on her mind was food. Her stomach ached, but not because she was hungry. The strong, tangy scent of the honey mustard salad dressing was almost nauseating.

"Besides," Georgia picked up her fork, "when you think about it, Collins is blackmailing the wrong woman. It makes no sense that he delivered the notes to me and expects me to pay for what *you* did."

Cate's jaw fell open. While her throat felt as if she'd just swallowed a bag of sand, she managed to get out in a brittle tone, "You can't be serious, Mother. That's not fair. We were both there that night, and we're both responsible for what happened."

"We were both there," Georgia agreed. She stabbed her fork into the bed of lettuce and green peppers. "But, only one of us committed murder."

"You were there." Cate stomped her foot on the ground. "You helped me…"

"I didn't help you kill anybody," Georgia snapped. "I may have assisted you afterward, but killing Mark…that was all you."

"Please, Mom," Cate begged, "don't say it like that. You know it's not that cut and dried. It was an accident. And, Mark was a horrible man. He was—"

"Yes, he was awful, Cate." Georgia nodded. "But, you were the one who killed him, not me." She took a bite, chewed for a few moments, and then swallowed. "*You* were the one who killed Collins' father, Cate. And, don't ever forget it."

157

He didn't believe in having regrets, because, quite honestly, what was the point? Why break your neck trying to change the inevitable? What was done was done, and moving forward was your only option…if you planned on staying sane, of course.

Sure, there were things in Beau's life that he would have liked to have happened differently, a long list of difficult courses and outcomes that had been created mostly by poor judgment and foolish acts on his part. After all, the ex-detective's past was as damp and muddy as a dirt-covered road after a bad rainstorm.

However, there was nothing he could do about that now, so he tried not to dwell on it.

The same could be said for the conversation he'd had with Diane. Beau knew calling the woman a bitch hadn't been his wisest move, but it was done and over with. It was all in the past, and there was no way to take it back. Therefore, he didn't regret the argument. He was glad it had happened. Beau felt like it had been a long time coming.

Unfortunately, he was now getting the silent treatment from Shannon, so maybe he should have at least tried to hold his tongue.

Beau sat in the sheriff's office and stared down at the blank screen of his cell phone. He'd called Shannon twice and had sent three text messages. No response. It wasn't like Shannon to come into work late. And not return a call or text? Well, that was out of character, too.

So, Shannon was either pissed off, or some sort of emergency had happened. Beau was about one hundred percent certain it was the former, which was why he wasn't going to worry. Not yet. He and Shannon would battle it out later. Right now, he needed to catch a killer.

He made himself comfortable behind Shannon's desk. He leaned back in the sheriff's chair and placed his bridged hands at the base of his neck. Beau closed his eyes. For the moment, he only wanted to see darkness.

If he was being true to himself, then he had to admit he didn't think Collins was the killer, and, while he was well aware of how important it was to find the man and question him, Beau's gut told him point-blank that the man hadn't strangled any of the women in Perry's Creek.

He didn't have concrete evidence that Collins was innocent, but, then again, there was no proof the man was guilty, either. This fun fact, Beau knew, only added to the magnitude of why Collins needed to be brought in, and pronto.

What Beau did have were reasons, good instinctive rationalities, as to why Collins wasn't a killer—or the killer *he* was searching for, anyway.

To begin with, Beau didn't believe the real killer would be careless enough to be seen outside one of the victims' homes. However, if a mistake had been made, if Collins was the one strangling women and had slipped up, allowing Jed to see him, wouldn't he have chosen someone other than Tara Burns to be next on his chopping block? The Creek had to be filled with plenty of other young, blonde-haired, blue-eyed options. It didn't make any sense to go back to that apartment after his cover had "supposedly" been blown.

Beau had said it plenty of times this week, and he was sticking to his guns. The strangler was smart, very smart. He'd killed multiple women without leaving any sort of trace behind, and he'd followed one of the cardinal rules to becoming a successful serial killer: Never murder someone you know.

Unfortunately, linking the three victims together had proven to be useless. Although Beau had entertained the notion that the strangler earned the women's trust before gaining access to their homes and offing them, he was no longer buying it. He knew the real reason why there was no sign of forced entry found at any of the crime scenes, and it was simple: Every single person living in Perry's Creek, California, was too stupid to lock their doors. Hell, even after a second girl had been found dead, Tara still hadn't bothered to secure her home.

Beau was a lot of things, but a scientific man wasn't one of them. However, he couldn't help but wonder if Tara being killed was in some weird, twisted way natural selection at its best. Not that he believed all stupid people deserved to die, but not dead-bolting your front door when a

159

killer was on the loose was just asking for trouble.

Although Beau didn't agree with the ignorance, he happened to understand a fraction of it: No one wanted to believe that the nightmare could happen to them.

The good-looking pedophile who lives across the street and uses candy to attract children; the lonely and tortured kid who brings a shotgun to school to solve his bullying problems; the unstable mother who drowns her newborn baby because it won't stop crying—no one was ever prepared to deal with these sorts of uncomfortable issues when they snuck in through the white picket fence and landed so close to home.

Beau shook his head. In this particular case, ignorance wasn't bliss; it was a motive for murder.

He stole another glance at his phone—nothing—then shifted focus. He took in the pictures of Collins that littered Shannon's desk.

The man certainly looked the part: low brow, dark eyes that appeared deep enough to sink in, and skin that had to be the same texture as a burlap sack. In a word, Collins was rough, but that didn't make him a killer, and, while his stiff body language seemed to imply that he was hiding something, Beau highly doubted it had anything to do with the strangled women.

"Damn this case to hell," he muttered through a heavy breath. He closed his eyes again and lowered his forehead to the surface of the desk.

The killer wasn't Jed; his alibi had checked out. And, Beau was willing to bet his entire pension that it wasn't Collins.

So, who was the damn killer, then?

Maybe the third time around would be the charm. That's the idea he was clinging to, anyway. Beau knew how a murder investigation went: lots of touch and go, lots of questions and headaches and sleepless nights, and not many answers. Still, Beau wasn't giving up. He'd made Shannon a promise, and he was pulling out his hair trying to keep that promise.

Beau stood up suddenly. His legs felt like anchors. He'd been sitting for too long. He rounded the corner of Shannon's desk and began pacing the length of the small office.

What were they missing?

His mind raced back to the first two victims: Stephanie Karr and Shelly Marthers. Could they have been regulars at Tammi's Pub? Is that how all three victims were tied together? Had the killer chosen his prey via the local bar?

Beau shook the idea away. No one who had been questioned had mentioned the pub as a link between the three girls. If Beau remembered correctly, the second vic, Marthers, didn't even drink. She'd gotten a DUI a month or so back, and, according to friends, having felt lucky to not have lost her nursing license, had quit alcohol cold turkey.

That was one thing that didn't make sense to Beau. A young woman changes her ways and tries to better herself, and what happens? She gets murdered. Where in hell was the fairness in that?

He leaned over the front of the desk and looked down at his cell again. Nothing. Shannon must truly be upset. Or perhaps...

The phone started buzzing.

Beau didn't wait a second. He grabbed the phone, hit a button, and shoved the device to his ear. "Shannon?"

"Yeah, it's me," the sheriff answered. His voice was dry, almost unrecognizable. "I got your voicemails and texts."

"Good," Beau said. "I was starting to worry that something might be wrong."

"Well, something is."

Beau's stomach clenched. He held onto the edge of the desk for support. He'd known that a discussion was coming, but this seemed worse than he'd been expecting. Arguing with Diane hadn't been his finest moment. Maybe he *did* believe in regrets, after all.

"You still there, Beau?"

"Yeah," he choked out, "I'm here. So, w-w-what's going on? If something's wrong, then—"

"I'd rather talk about it in person," Shannon cut him off. "I just called to let you know I'm on my way in. I'll be there soon. And, please let O.J. and Matt know that I want an update on Collins ASAP."

The update was that Collins was still missing. That was it.

"Beau?"

"Yeah, I heard you. I'll see you when you get here." He clicked off, then tossed his phone back onto the desk.

So, Shannon was upset, more than what Beau had planned on him being. Okay, he could deal with that. So, what would be the best way to tackle the issue?

He resumed his seat. He knew he could always apologize to Diane. That was one way of breaking the ice.

Beau rolled his eyes. He'd rather eat hot coals and take a Tabasco shot chaser. Besides, the old bat was too soulless to accept an apology. He'd have to try something else.

He inhaled slowly, pushed out the heavy breath, and then pinched the bridge of his nose. This was ridiculous. Why should he be the one to apologize? Diane had ambushed him with insults so he'd hardly had time to swat them away. She'd even threatened to kill him. Did Shannon know all of that?

Beau shrugged and folded his hands in his lap. It probably didn't matter that much. Shannon wouldn't care that Diane had called Beau "grotesque." She was the sheriff's wife, and she'd been disrespected.

But, she'd definitely deserved it. Diane had never been nice to him. Hell, the woman didn't even know how to fake being civil, and Beau knew why.

The reason brought another impromptu smile to his face. She felt threatened by him. The woman was extremely insecure, and the collar she'd placed around Shannon's neck wasn't nearly as tight as she'd hoped it was. Diane was afraid of losing, and that fear was definitely warranted.

Without a doubt, Diane had given Shannon a completely different version of their encounter, one where she was one hundred percent innocent and had the privilege of playing the victim.

Well, Beau didn't care. He'd talk to Shannon, and he'd get everything straightened out. He'd tell the sheriff the truth about Diane. She had no idea just how "grotesque" Beau could truly be, and if she wanted a war, then . . .

Grotesque. The ugly word filled Beau's head. He frowned. He, too, had used the word to describe someone recently: Jed.

He'd spoken with Jed only once when they'd been in the interrogation room. Jed had been talking about Tara, describing his relationship with her. Dammit! His hands balled into fists. How was it going to help...?

Beau had it! He jumped out of the chair.

Tara Burns. Jed said Tara was only good for two things: giving head and collecting parking tickets.

The parking tickets.

The DUI.

Holy shit!

Beau planted himself back in the chair. He reached for the thin file to his left and began digging through it. He already knew what he was going to find, but he needed confirmation.

It didn't take him long: pictures of the very first crime scene, and pictures of Stephanie Karr's home.

There it was, in the third picture he flipped to: a faint image of an unpaid speeding ticket.

Speeding ticket.

DUI.

Parking tickets.

Had he just found a connection to all three victims?

Stephanie Karr had gotten a speeding ticket right before she died. Shelly Marthers had been given a DUI. And, according to Jed, Tara had a collection of parking tickets.

Eyes wide and body stiff, Beau couldn't breathe. He became as still as a statue as his tired, overworked brain attempted to process this new development.

There was a soft knock at the door. Beau looked up just as it was pushed open.

"Oh, sorry. I was searching for Sheriff Sutton."

Beau managed to find his voice. "No worries, Deputy Benson. The sheriff should be in shortly."

"Okay, thanks."

"Wait!" Beau got to his feet again. "Before you go, I need your help with something."

"Sure," Benson agreed. He stepped into the office. "What's up?"

"I have a handful of traffic cases here: speeding ticket, DUI, and parking violations. I need you to see if the same deputy was involved in all three incidences."

"That's easy enough."

"And, I also need you to be discrete," Beau warned. "I know you haven't been with the department long, and the last thing I want to do is create trouble for you. But, this is very important."

"I understand, sir. I'm willing to help out with whatever you need me to."

"I appreciate that, Deputy Benson."

As the young man stepped forward, smiling and eager to assist, Beau realized that he, too, wanted to smile, but he just couldn't force himself to. Because, if he was right—if this little hunch panned out—then he might have just found the killer.

And, how was he possibly going to tell Shannon that the killer was a deputy at the Perry's Creek Police Department?

e was ready to be back at his happy place, sitting in his backyard, looking over the manicured lawn he'd poured blood, sweat, and tears into. He wanted to listen to the calming chirping of the crickets because that was the only thing he could think of that might make this morning a little more tolerable.

If he closed his eyes, it was almost as if he was there. Matt could see the wide gravel path he'd dug out by hand and the rose bushes that were just starting to bloom and reveal a touch of wild color. He thought about the small lemon tree he'd planted by the edge of the porch. If he tried hard enough, Matt could smell the potent sweetness the entire area had to offer.

He spent a lot of his time in that yard. He took pride in it, and the hours of hard work had paid off beautifully. But, it went so much deeper than that. He had a happy place, a *safe* place, a place where he could do whatever his heart desired—laugh, cry, scream, be silent and still—and no one would be the wiser, because his backyard never told a soul.

Matt had had friends over for BBQs in the yard and for beers after work, but he mostly enjoyed the space when he got to be in it alone. There was just something special about the solitude. Maybe that made him selfish because he wanted the entire yard to himself, but he didn't really care.

He'd gone there the night things had ended with *her*. There'd been so much crying and yelling and feelings of guilt. He'd had to get away, and he'd had to clear his head. So he'd gone to his backyard, sat in his rocking chair, and waited for peace to engulf him. His own slice of paradise helped to make the dark, violent world a little less depressing.

Matt opened his eyes. He found himself back at the Perry's Creek Police Department—and the smell was nowhere near as sweet.

The past few days, *weeks*, had been rough, and it wasn't one of those adjustment phases where there was a light at the end of the tunnel and things were bound to get better. This was a growing rough patch that Matt feared would only get worse. There was no light at the end of the tunnel. That light had burned out...for good.

As far back as Matt could remember, he'd always wanted to be a police deputy. Most little boys talked about being a cop or firefighter when they were little but then replaced that desire with something a little more nine-to-five-ish: banker, something with sales, maybe even a teacher.

Not Matt. He'd dreamt of being a cop, held onto that dream, and then made it come true. Now, he couldn't help but wonder if he'd made a mistake.

Over the years, he'd gotten comfortable knowing he could clock in and the worst scenario he'd encounter would be a bad traffic accident. His shifts mostly consisted of writing speeding tickets and administering sobriety tests, and Matt was perfectly okay with that. He still put on his uniform and badge each day, and he still protected his hometown, but from a different type of crime. Instead of keeping Perry's Creek safe from murderers and drug lords that didn't exist, he'd kept the town safe from drunk drivers and the occasional petty theft.

Matt's dream had expanded to getting married one day, even having kids—a boy and a girl, if he was lucky. It was easy to want these things when the place you lived in was a carbon copy of Mayberry. Hell, Matt had even played with the idea that he could one day be the sheriff of the Creek.

However, that all seemed completely farfetched now like a little boy wanting to be an award-winning movie star or bestselling author. Because Perry's Creek had been plagued with a monster, and his dream had been crushed. Mayberry didn't exist. He couldn't have the woman he was in love with, and, as for murder investigations and chasing down suspects, well, Matt wasn't quite made for that kind of lifestyle.

Perhaps it was time to start over.

"Don't look so sad, my friend. People get in trouble with their bosses every single day. We'll survive."

Matt looked up. O.J. had taken a seat at the edge of his desk. Body slumped, arms folded loosely, he didn't seem to have a care in the world. Typical O.J. Show no fear.

"He's not even here," O.J. said. "That's how serious Sheriff Sutton is taking this investigation."

"He probably had another meeting with Mayor Jackson," Matt suggested.

"Whatever." O.J. shrugged. "Listen, you need to stop beating yourself up for what happened yesterday. We made a couple of mistakes. It happens. No big deal. We'll catch Collins."

"And, if we don't? He could kill someone else."

"He won't," O.J. argued. "His face is plastered all over town. He's not going to be able to take a shit without someone knowing how much toilet paper he uses. He'd be downright stupid to try and strangle someone else. Trust me. We'll get him, Matt."

"How can you be so sure?"

"Positive attitude?" O.J. shrugged again. "Hell if I know, but I do know one thing: Sitting around here and looking like someone ran over your puppy won't accomplish anything."

Matt nodded. "I guess you're right."

"Of course I'm right. We'll get another chance to prove our worth. And, if the sheriff's that upset, well, he should have been here yesterday. Or, at least, reachable."

"Are you scared, O.J.?"

"Scared?" O.J. frowned. "Scared of what, Matt? Losing our badges? You can't possibly think—?"

"No." Matt shook his head. "Scared of what's going on here? Scared of what's happening to Perry's Creek. I mean, we grew up here. This isn't normal. This isn't a place for a serial killer to hunt down women. What *is* this?"

"It's life." O.J. stood up suddenly. "No, it's not normal, and it's definitely not ideal, but it happens."

"Not in Perry's Creek."

"Well, it looks like it does, Matt. And, pouting over it won't change a damned thing."

He knew his friend and partner was right, but that didn't make it any easier to hear. Bad things happened everywhere, that was a fact, but Matt still didn't want to accept it.

He glanced around his surroundings. The whiteboard was still in its place, but new images and stats had been added to it to accompany the latest victim.

Matt saw that Deputy Benson was also on duty. He sat hunched over his computer, most likely in the middle of a difficult game of solitaire.

166

Other than that, the room was quiet. Desks sat unorganized and empty, and the stench of stale coffee filled the entire building. Through the streaked glass door of the sheriff's office, Matt noticed that Reynolds had taken up residence at Shannon's desk and was currently going over what looked like a case file.

O.J. had a point. Where *was* Sheriff Sutton? It wasn't like the man to be a no-show, especially now with everything that had happened. Matt didn't want to be at the department, either, and just looking at the dull walls and stained floor made him want to sprint to the nearest exit and never look back.

Still, he'd managed to fight off temptation and show up to work. After all, he had a job to do. Didn't the sheriff feel the same way? So much for leadership.

"You going to ignore me now?"

Matt blinked. He brought himself back to the conversation. "No, of course not. I was just thinking."

"About?"

"The case," Matt answered. "Collins, the victims, the crime scenes. Don't you think it's strange the killer takes an earring from each girl?"

O.J. nodded. "It's sick. I don't get it."

"I just can't wrap my head around—"

"Because you're not a killer, Matt. You don't think that way, and neither do I. It's fucked up. Hell, I didn't even share that detail with Cate, and I usually tell her most stuff about work. I like keeping her on her toes."

"Why not tell her about the earrings? It's not gruesome. It's just—"

"Because she'd get *too* scared, and knowing her, she'll probably never wear jewelry again."

Matt shrugged. "Well, I guess you know her better than I do." He didn't realize it would hurt to say those words, but it did. Just like that, Matt found himself in a new state of depression.

"Are you sure that's the only thing bugging you? The case?" O.J. asked. "I don't want you to get the wrong idea. I mean, we're not girlfriends chatting over cocktails, but if something is wrong, you can tell me."

"I know."

"Okay, so tell me, then. What's wrong?"

"Nothing," Matt lied.

"Come on, Matt. Quit insulting me. I've known you forever, and I know when something is eating you. Stop acting like a little bitch and tell me what's going on."

"Kathy and I broke up."

"When? What happened?"

Matt shook his head. "Last night. We've been having problems for a while, and I guess we just got to that point where enough was enough."

"Wow, man. I'm really sorry."

Matt waved his hand. "It's fine. It's for the best. Kathy loved me, but I didn't feel the same way about her."

He flashed back to last night in her dining room: the ultimatum. He still couldn't believe she'd made him choose between her and Cate.

"Come on! That's not fair," he'd fired back at her. "How am I supposed to stay away from my best friend's wife? I'm bound to cross paths with her."

"Well, if O.J. knew how you felt about Cate, I highly doubt he'd let you see her."

"Is that a threat?" he'd yelled.

Kathy rolled her eyes then. "Oh, just admit it already. You have feelings for Cate. You're in love with her!"

"Fine!" He banged both of his fists against the table, and the dishes had rattled noisily. "You want me to say it? You really want to hear it? Fine! I love Cate. I'm *in* love with Cate! Is that what you needed to hear? Do you feel better now?"

"You're pathetic."

"Me? Look how insecure you are! I wanted to make this work. I tried. But, then you expected me to choose—"

"Oh, you made your decision," she interrupted him. "I was right about you all along. No one stands a chance with you. You're too obsessed with Cate. And, the sad thing is, you'll never have her."

"And, you'll never have me."

"Get out of my house!" She started crying, then, but Matt had followed her order.

"So, what are you going to do now?"

Matt was thrust back into the present. O.J. was sitting on the edge of his desk, Benson was even more engrossed in his computer game, and Reynolds was flipping through pages of a file in the sheriff's office.

"I'm not sure," Matt answered finally. "She told me she was going to San Diego for a few days for work and warned me not to bother her."

"That helps," O.J. said. "At least you don't run the risk of bumping into her."

"Silver lining," Matt muttered. "She doesn't have to worry about me contacting her. I don't love her. I was willing to try, but…"

"But, what?"

"She freaked out, thought I was in love with someone else, and ended it."

"Well, are you?" O.J. leaned in closer.

Matt had just entered dangerous waters. A few more feet out, and he was going to sink right down into the dark abyss.

"You are, aren't you?" O.J. smiled. "You dog!"

Maybe it was already too late. "No," Matt tried. "It's not like that…"

"Who is it?" O.J. slapped him on the shoulder. "You have to tell me."

"It's no one. Seriously."

"Oh, come on," O.J. begged. "Why won't you tell me?"

"What happened to us not being girlfriends who chat over cocktails?"

"Shit, Matt! You have a crush on someone. I want to know who she is. Don't you want to brag about how hot she is? God knows you weren't able to do that with Kathy."

"That's just mean. Kathy was—"

"Is it Deputy Deeds? Because she's single and so sexy."

"Stop, O.J.! Pease."

"I don't know who else it could be. You hardly go out, and you're never around any women. Deputy Deeds and maybe Cate, but…" His words trailed off. O.J. jumped back to his feet.

Matt stood, too. "Please, O.J. Let me explain."

"Oh, my God!" O.J. shook his head. "You son of a bitch!"

"Calm down, O.J." Matt took a step toward his friend, his partner. "It's not what you think."

"Everything makes sense now. Why you're always asking about Cate. Why you assumed I was beating her."

"That's not—"

"You want to be her knight in shining armor. You want to save her. Is that it?" O.J. balled his hands into tight fists. "Well, guess what, pal? Cate doesn't need to be saved."

"Can we please talk about this?" Matt asked.

"What's there to talk about? You're my best friend, my partner, and you're trying to steal my wife."

Matt pinched the bridge of his nose. "No one's stealing your wife, O.J. You need to calm down."

169

"And, you need to stop fucking telling me what to do!"

"Is there a problem, deputies?" Benson had come over, officially making the conversation a three-ringed circus.

"No," Matt answered first. "We're fine. Just a little argument."

"Deputy Abbott?"

"It's true, Benson," O.J. sighed. "We're fine."

Benson nodded and walked away.

O.J. stepped up to Matt. "You know, if we weren't under a microscope right now, you'd be in pain."

Matt frowned. "What's that supposed to mean?"

"It means we're done. You and me. We're over."

Matt rolled his eyes. "Don't be so dramatic, O.J. I've never acted on my feelings for Cate, and I'm not going to. Can we please be adults about this?"

"You stab me in the back, and then have the audacity to imply *I'm* the one behaving like a child? You've lost it!"

"You're acting like I did this on purpose. It just happened."

"Then why didn't you come to me, huh?" O.J. crossed his arms. "As soon as you realized you were developing feelings for my wife, why didn't you let me know? We're brothers, Matt."

He shrugged. "I don't know. I guess—"

"Because you're a rat. You preferred sneaking around behind my back and lying to my face. Why? So you could eventually try and steal Cate from me?" He shook his head. "Go to hell."

O.J. walked away.

Matt was left standing alone.

He looked down at the floor and bit his lower lip. He knew he'd messed up big time, but he also knew this battle wasn't over, not by a long shot. O.J. would want revenge. He usually did.

And, O.J. always got what he wanted.

26

"We need to talk."

"I know," Beau agreed. "But, before you say anything, I have something to tell you about the case."

"Collins. You found Collins?"

"No," Beau answered. "I found another angle, actually."

The sheriff's face dropped, and then he frowned. Beau wasn't sure if this gesture was better than the one the man had sported when he'd first walked into the office—a crinkled brow and pursed lips.

Beau decided he liked his chances better with the frown.

"Okay, well, spit it out," Shannon ordered.

Beau nodded. They did have a problem, and it was much bigger than he'd thought it was, but they would just have to cross that unsteady bridge later. The investigation needed to come first.

"I may have found a new suspect, but I wanted to run it by you before I shared it with anyone else. It's kind of complicated."

"Well," Shannon sighed, "make it as uncomplicated as possible. It's been a rough morning. I'm not in the mood to clean up another mess."

"Right," Beau said. Shannon was in full cop mode, one hundred percent business. Beau had to respect that.

He rounded the corner of the sheriff's desk and gave Shannon plenty of room to slide through. Once the man had taken his seat, Beau contemplated sitting as well but then realized he preferred to stand. He'd been on his ass practically all morning.

He took a deep breath. "I discovered that all three victims do, in fact, have a connection."

Shannon seemed to sit up straighter in his chair. "Go on."

"The first victim was recently caught speeding and had gotten a ticket.

The second girl, the nurse, had been issued a DUI. And, the bartender, Tara Burns, had lots of unpaid parking tickets."

Shannon shrugged. "I guess no one's perfect. But, what do these girls' traffic records have to do with them being strangled?"

The rhythm of Beau's heartbeat picked up speed. He was trying to be patient, to give his friend the benefit of the doubt, but he knew he was close to losing it. Shannon needed to give him something. This song and dance was getting old, and fast.

"Look, Beau," Shannon broke the silence. "You said you found a new suspect, so just tell me who—"

"What's your problem?" Beau crossed his arms. "You ignored me all morning, went so far as to avoid me, and now you're acting this way? It's like you have some big chip on your shoulder. If you have something you want to say to me, then just say it. Enough of this passive-aggressive bullshit."

"I talked to Diane. She told me what you said."

"I figured," Beau admitted. "And, out of curiosity, did she bother to tell you what *she* said?"

"I don't care what she said!" Shannon hit the desk with his fists. "Did you really call her a 'big bitch?'"

Beau wasn't sure how to respond, so he didn't say anything. He put his hands on his hips and looked down at the floor. A coward's move, he knew, but he felt stuck. No matter what he said next, it wouldn't help the situation. The damage had already been done, and now it was time to pay the consequences.

"Your silence speaks volumes, Beau."

"Look—"

"No, you look. I know you don't like Diane. That's fine. I get it. But, you had no right to disrespect her—and in my office, to boot. We just had this fight. It feels like we *keep* having this fight. And, I can't deal with it anymore."

"I think one of your deputies is the killer."

"Excuse me?"

Beau hadn't meant to just blurt out the words, but he'd been unable to stop them.

"Are you serious, Beau? Because if this is just some ploy to—?"

"It's not," Beau interrupted, "I'm serious. And, I know we've been putting off this conversation for a while, but now the time has come where we can't avoid it any longer. I get that. But, first, let's talk shop. Please."

Shannon nodded. "All right, what do you have?"

Beau took a seat, finally. "So, the three victims all had some sort of traffic violation."

"So you've said. Speeding ticket, DUI, and parking tickets."

"Correct," Beau said. "Well, I did some digging, and with a little bit of help, I discovered that one deputy was involved with all three victims' violations."

"You're kidding me?"

Beau shook his head. "Unfortunately, I'm not. I'm pretty sure I found the link." He was back on his feet, pacing in front of the sheriff's desk. "One deputy is connected to all three victims prior to their murders. This could actually be how the killer chose the women he strangled."

"Holy shit, Beau!" Shannon's eyebrows shot up. "And, no one else knows about this?"

"No," Beau answered. "Well, Deputy Benson, but only because I needed his help. I don't know if he followed the trail, but I told him to be discrete."

"Okay, good."

"Like I said, it's complicated. I wanted you to be the first one to know about the discovery so you could handle it as you saw fit."

"Yes, of course," the sheriff agreed. "So, who is it? What's the deputy's name?"

Beau took a deep breath and then exhaled slowly. He gripped the front of Shannon's desk and then stared into the man's eyes. He didn't blink.

"Beau?"

"It's Deputy Matt Combs."

* * *

"Is this really necessary, Sheriff Sutton?"

"This won't take long, Matt," Shannon answered. "We just want to ask you a few questions."

"Okay, but why aren't we in your office? Why are we back here?"

"Never mind that. Let's get started."

They were back in the interrogation room. Beau stood in the doorway just like last time. The place remained the same: water-stained boxes in the corner, mildew stench, a small table with mismatched chairs, and a brown linoleum floor.

Only one thing had changed this time: the suspect. Instead of looking down at Jed Turner, Beau saw Deputy Matt Combs. Beau was almost positive he was the killer.

"Is this about O.J.?" Matt asked. "I can explain…"

"This has nothing to do with Collins and what happened at the pub," Shannon said.

"Well, O.J. and I—"

"This has nothing to do with Deputy Abbot," Beau spoke up finally. "We're here to talk about you."

"Fine," Matt said dryly. "What do you want to talk about?"

Shannon paused for a moment, then took the time to clear his throat. The loud, rough grumble filled the tight space. Another second passed, and then he said, "What can you tell me about Stephanie Karr?"

"Are you serious?"

"Yes," the sheriff confirmed. "Please answer the question."

A crease appeared in the center of Matt's forehead. "She was murdered about two weeks ago. Strangled. The first of three women."

"Okay." Shannon nodded. "And Shelly Marthers?"

"The second victim, also strangled."

"And Tara—?"

"Tara Burns was the third victim, strangled a couple of days ago," Matt interrupted. "What's your point, Sheriff? Where is all of this going?"

Shannon didn't answer the question. Instead, he folded his hands on top of the table. "And, do you know what Karr, Marthers, and Burns all had in common?"

"I just told you." Matt's voice rose. "They were all strangled. What is going on here?"

"They had something else in common," Shannon said calmly. "Karr had a speeding ticket, Marthers had a DUI, and Burns had parking tickets."

Matt shrugged. "Okay, their driving records were shit. Do you think that's why someone decided to strangle them?"

Beau noticed it immediately. Matt had fallen into the same pattern as so many suspects before him. He'd gotten defensive.

"There's no reason to be smart, Matt," Shannon continued. "We're just talking."

"Can we hurry up, please? I'd like to get back to work. I feel bad about losing Collins, and—"

"Do you?" Beau asked. "Do you *really* feel bad about losing Collins?"

"What's that supposed to mean?" Matt crossed his arms.

Beau shrugged. "Well, if all of our resources are being used to try to find Collins, then it's not likely we'll pursue the other angles of the case or look for another individual who could be the killer."

"You've officially lost me."

"One particular deputy in the department was involved with all three victims before they were murdered."

Shannon started again. "Do you know who?"

"No."

"You," he answered.

"What?" Matt pinched the bridge of his nose. "What are you talking about? I-I-I don't understand."

Beau took a step forward. He flipped open the manila folder he'd been holding. "You issued Stephanie Karr a speeding ticket, you cited Shelly Marthers with a DUI, and you wrote Tara Burns three parking tickets."

"Wait a second!" Matt leaned back, eyes wide. "Are you saying...you think I had something to do with their murders?"

"On Friday, June 3, where were you between the hours of—?"

"Sheriff!" Matt turned to Shannon. "You can't honestly believe I'm involved in this. You know me. You know I'm not capable of murder."

Shannon sighed. "Look, Matt, we don't have a choice. Sure, these questions are uncomfortable, but we have to get to the bottom of this. So far, you're the only connection to all three victims."

"You know me, Sheriff!" Matt shouted. "You know I'm not capable of murder!"

"It's rough, I know. And, it doesn't seem right, but..."

"Really? You know? Because I don't think you do. You're not the one who's being branded a serial killer! Do you know how humiliating this is?"

"Just answer Beau's questions," Shannon ordered. "The faster we get this over with, the faster we can put this mess behind us."

"And, if I want a lawyer?"

"You haven't been charged with anything, Matt. Like I said, we're just talking. Cooperate, and we'll be done in five minutes."

Matt turned to Beau. "Fine. What do you want to know?"

Beau scanned the file again. "Stephanie Karr was the first victim, murdered on Friday, June 3. Where were you on that night between the hours of midnight and 2:00 a.m.?"

Matt closed his eyes and tilted his head to the right. He was either concentrating, or this was his way of signaling that he wasn't going to answer the question.

Beau gave him a nudge. "Matt?"

"I'm thinking," Matt fired back. "Two weeks ago, Friday night…I was probably with my girlfriend. Ex-girlfriend," he corrected. "And, between the hours of midnight and 2:00, we were most likely sleeping."

"Will your ex-girlfriend verify that?"

"I don't know," Matt admitted. "I'd like to think so, but we broke up last night. It was messy, and now she wants nothing to do with me. As far as I know, she left for San Diego this morning."

Messy breakup, Beau noted. *Interesting*. He wondered if this ex-girlfriend of Matt's happened to have blonde hair and blue eyes like all of the victims. He made a mental note to check that later.

"We'll need her name and number," Shannon said.

"Sure," Matt mumbled.

"Shelly Marthers was strangled on Monday, June 13. Again, this happened between the hours of midnight and 2:00 a.m.," Beau continued. "Do you recall your whereabouts that evening?"

"A Monday night? I was probably sleeping."

"With your ex-girlfriend?" Beau asked.

"I don't fucking know," Matt said.

There it was again: Deputy Matt Combs had a nasty temper. Beau had purposely pressed the man's buttons to see how he would react, and Beau had hit pay dirt. Matt was an angry person, but was he angry enough to kill? Perhaps. Beau had seen it plenty of times before. Some people really did believe the best therapy was squeezing the life out of another human being.

"And Tara Burns was strangled on——"

"Tuesday, June 21," Matt finished. "Was I at home? Yes. Was I with Kathy? I think so." He threw his hands up. "This is bullshit. A complete waste of time."

Beau closed the file and threw it down on the table. It landed between Shannon and Matt. "So, that's it? That's your alibi for all three murders? You were with your ex-girlfriend, and the two of you were sleeping?"

Matt shrugged. "I guess so."

Beau wrinkled his nose. "Seems kind of weak to me."

"I don't give a fuck what you think! You're not even a cop. You have no

SLAGLE

right to even be here, accusing me of anything."

Beau took a step back. He smiled. "Sounds like you're upset I found your connection to all of the victims. Word to the wise: Next time you decide to go on a killing spree, cover your tracks a little better."

"Go fuck yourself!"

"Spoken like a guilty man."

"Stop!" Shannon ordered. He stood up. His chair made a *screeching* sound against the linoleum. "I've had enough of this back and forth."

"Well, that's what you get for accusing one of your own of being a killer."

"Watch it!" Shannon snapped. "I'm trying to give you the benefit of the doubt, Matt, but I'm still your superior. You *will* treat me with respect. Understand?"

"Yes, sir," Matt mumbled.

"And, Beau?" The sheriff turned. "Matt isn't a *normal* suspect, so quit setting him up. Ask him the damn questions and move on."

Beau felt his jaw fall open. *What in the hell was Shannon doing?* This wasn't the time to walk on eggshells. They were in the middle of a murder investigation, and Beau was positive he'd scored the case's first big break. This wasn't some dead-end find like Jed or Collins. This was legit, and now the sheriff was worried about hurting the suspect's feelings just because he was a police deputy?

Bullshit!

"If there are no other questions, then I'd—"

"I'm not done," Beau informed him.

"Fine," Shannon said. He fell back into his chair. "Let's make it quick, hmm? Matt has given us his alibi. I want to check it out and then clear him of this once and for all."

Beau turned his back to the table. He ran his fingers through his hair and left them resting at the base of his neck. Another moment passed before he faced Shannon and Matt again. They both stared at him blankly.

"We're waiting, Beau."

"I've noticed you don't wear a ring, Matt."

He nodded. "Most single people don't. What's your point?"

"According to the strangulation marks, it's likely the killer doesn't wear a ring."

"You mean, before putting on gloves and strangling the victims, the killer could have removed his ring? Great catch, ex-detective. I see you're

177

not wearing a ring, either. Care to explain that?"

It was weak, Beau admitted. He moved on.

"I have a hard time believing that when these women turned up dead, you didn't recognize them. Not even their names seemed familiar to you?"

Matt shook his head. "You expect me to remember every single ticket I hand out? Everyone I've ever pulled over?"

"I've been here less than a week. Do you know how often I've heard how small Perry's Creek is? How safe Perry's Creek is? How everyone pretty much knows everyone at the Creek?"

A brief silence filled the room. Beau could even hear the soft ticking of his watch. It reminded him annoyingly of the fact that he hadn't gotten the suspect to admit guilt yet.

Matt spoke up finally. "Did you expect me to answer that? You want me to give you a rough estimate?"

"My point," Beau added sharply, "is how could you *not* remember citing those girls? Maybe you wouldn't have thought anything of it after the first victim," he offered. "I'll give you that one. Small town girl ends up dead that you just happened to issue a speeding ticket to a few weeks prior. No big deal. But then, victim two turns along. That didn't sound some kind of alarm? And then, by the time victim three rolled around, you didn't start panicking? You're not just connected to all three victims; you're *recently* connected to them. And, still, you decided to say nothing, sit back, and wait it all out. What? Hoping and praying that no one would catch on?"

"I told you already: I don't remember those girls. I didn't realize I was connected to all of them."

"I think you're lying," Beau said.

"Well, that's your prerogative," Matt replied.

"You expect me to believe that your connection to all three victims is purely coincidental?"

"I can't believe you're dumb enough to think that that's how I'd choose my prey—women I've previously given citations to. That'd be pretty stupid on my part, having a direct tie to the women I strangled."

Beau shrugged. "You'd be surprised how common criminals slip up. They all think they're so smart, can outwit anyone. The truth of the matter is there's no such thing as the 'perfect murder.' Sooner or later, it all catches up with you."

"I didn't kill anybody," Matt said.

"Keep lying," Beau suggested, "because I'm not even close to—"

"Stop!" Shannon slammed his fist on the table. "You two are right back where you started."

"He's lying, Shannon! He's—"

Shannon lifted his hand. "Are you lying, Matt? At any point in this investigation did you realize you were connected to all three victims?"

Matt didn't answer at first. He looked down at the floor.

"Matt?" the sheriff pressed on. "Answer my question. Did you know?"

Matt sighed. "Fine. Yes, I knew."

Beau bit the inside of his cheek to keep from smiling. He was getting closer.

"But, I didn't kill those girls. I swear it!"

"Then why did you lie?" Shannon asked. "And, why didn't you say something when you realized you'd been in contact with them before their murders?"

"Because of this!" Matt admitted. "I figured that you'd think I did it."

"Well, now you look even guiltier for trying to hide it," Beau said.

"After Marthers' murder, it caught my attention. I realized that I'd been in contact with both victims before they'd been strangled. Then, once the bartender was killed, I started panicking. I wasn't sure what to do."

"You should have come to me, Matt."

"I know, Sheriff, I know. But, then there was Jed and the tip about Collins. I just assumed it was all a coincidence. I figured Collins was the killer, and my connection to the victims was moot."

Shannon turned to Beau. "Well, what do you think? Seems like the explanation you were looking for."

"Wait!" Beau ordered. "Just wait a damn second. I don't believe in coincidences, so someone is either setting you up or you're still lying to us."

"I'm not lying," Matt pleaded. "Give me a polygraph test. Search my house for the missing earrings."

Beau waved off the suggestions. "Please, you could have buried those earrings, for all we know."

"I didn't kill anybody," Matt tried again. "Call Kathy. Get my alibi."

The tables had turned suddenly. Matt's demeanor had changed once again. Caught in a lie, he was now ready to be as helpful as possible. This wasn't new for Beau, and it in no way supported the suspect's innocence.

"I think that's a good idea, Beau," Shannon said. "We should make a call and see if Matt's alibi checks out." He handed Matt a legal tablet and pen. "Write down the best way to get a hold of your ex-girlfriend."

Beau nodded. "Fine." He walked to the door and opened it. "We'll be right back, Matt," he called over his shoulder.

"Hang tight, Matt."

Beau waited until they were back in the sheriff's office behind the closed door before he said, "Do you coddle all of your suspects like that?"

"Excuse me?"

"'Hang tight?' Not to mention, you chastised me in there. You were supposed to have my back. But, instead, you attacked me. You made me look crazy for questioning the suspect."

"That's ridiculous, Beau!"

"Is it?"

"Yes. And, Matt isn't a suspect. He's my deputy, and his connection to all of this is purely circumstantial."

"So, you believe him?"

"Of course I believe him. Why wouldn't I?"

"Wow." Beau placed his hands on his hips. For the first time in his life, he was becoming familiar with his friend's incompetence, and it made his stomach ache.

"We made a mistake, Beau. Your discovery was relevant, and I understand why we needed to question Matt, but we handled that the wrong way."

"And, how should we have handled it?"

"I should have talked to Matt myself, one-on-one," Shannon said. He took his seat behind his desk. "And, in my office. It would have been more respectful."

"More respectful?" Beau shoved his hands into his pockets to stop himself from hitting something. "Are you listening to yourself right now? We're talking about a suspect who could be responsible for murdering three women. And, you're worried about disrespecting him?"

"I told you already: Matt didn't kill any of those girls. There was a misunderstanding, but we've cleared it up."

"Nothing has been cleared up!" Beau argued. "You're too close to this, Shannon. You don't want to admit that one of your own is most likely the killer. We already caught Matt in one lie."

"Oh, come off it, Beau! He was scared. That's why he lied to us. *You* scared him. Besides, I've known that kid for quite a while, and he's not capable of strangling three women. You'll see. I'll get in touch with his ex-

180

girlfriend."

"That still won't mean he isn't involved. Even if he alibis out, he could be picking the women for the actual killer. That could be his part in all of this."

"So, now *two* people are responsible for the murders, huh? One does the choosing, and one does the strangling?"

Beau's hands slipped out of his pockets. He crossed his arms firmly. "Maybe. Why not?"

"And, I'm the one who's seen too many movies?" Shannon rolled his eyes. "Have you been drinking this morning, Beau? Because you sound like you're not all here."

"For your information, I haven't had a drink in days. I've been focusing on this case, and, thank God, because I seem to be the only one who isn't too biased to do his damned job."

Shannon shook his head. "I'm calling this woman. I'm verifying Matt's alibi, and then I'm putting everything I have into finding Collins. *He's* the killer."

"And, you're just going to chalk up Matt's connection to all three victims as a—?"

"Fucking coincidence! If you were sober, Beau, you would have gotten that through your thick skull by now!"

Shannon reached for the large, box-shaped phone on his desk. Beau immediately turned his back to the man. He couldn't bear to watch his friend be played a fool. Listening to it would be rough enough.

It was as if he'd fallen down the rabbit hole. Perry's Creek wasn't just a place off the beaten path; it was a place of ruins. No one wanted to see what was right in front of them, staring them in the face. This went so much deeper than residents failing to lock their doors. Shannon believed the only way the Creek could be plagued with a serial killer was if one was visiting from out of town. Perry's Creek was a freak show, a place that catered to those who believed the world was made up of rainbows and butterflies. It was Stepford, and the longer Beau was here, spending time in East County, the more he was faced with the cold, hard truth: His best friend fit right in.

"Well, that doesn't help much."

Beau turned back around. "What?"

Shannon replaced the receiver in the black cradle. "The number Matt gave me has been disconnected. It's no longer in service."

Beau threw his hands up. "Okay. *Now* do you believe me?"

"No," Shannon said, "I don't. You heard Matt. He and the girl just broke up. It was messy. She most likely changed her number."

"This guy has you eating out of the palm of his hand. Wake up, Shannon! Be the sheriff of this damned town!"

Shannon didn't speak. He stood up, rounded his desk, and started for the door.

"Where are you going?" Beau asked.

"To talk to Matt, but I want you to stay here."

"What are you going to do?"

"I'm going to apologize, and then I'm going to tell him that he can get back to work."

"Back to work?" Beau repeated. "You can't be serious! He shouldn't be anywhere near this case, not until his alibi checks out. And, even then…"

"That's not your call, Beau."

"You're making a mistake, Shannon. You should at least leave Matt sitting in that room until you personally talk to the girlfriend and get her to confirm his alibis for all three murders."

Shannon stopped. He turned and stared at Beau. Eyes wide, he said, "I'm well aware of the mistake I made, and, trust me, I won't make it again."

Shannon left the office but returned in less than a minute.

"That was fast," Beau said. He took a seat on the edge of the sheriff's desk. "I guess it doesn't take long to kiss your employee's—"

"Matt's gone."

"What?"

"He's gone, Beau," Shannon whispered. "Deputy Benson saw him leave. He got in his car and drove off."

27

"So, that's what twenty thousand dollars in cash looks like."

"I guess so," Cate said. "The first and probably last time I'll ever see that much money at one time in my life."

"Oh, Catie Cat, don't be so negative. You're young. You still have plenty of time to become rich."

"I don't care about being rich, Mom. I want to be happy. But, even that doesn't matter, because as soon as Joshua gets wind of this, I'll be dead."

"What are you going to tell him?"

Cate shrugged. "I'm not sure yet. I've been playing around with a few different ideas, but he's going to see through them all. No matter what I say, he's going to think I stole his money, and he's going to want to hurt me for it badly. I don't know if I'll be able to survive him this time."

"That makes me sick to hear! Why don't you stay with me tonight?" Georgia suggested. "Maybe even for a few days, or until Joshua has a chance to cool off?"

"Have you not been paying attention to my marriage these past ten months, Mom?" Cate's temperature rose immediately. She reminded herself to calm down. "Joshua doesn't cool off." Cate took a deep breath. "When he's angry, nothing satisfies him until he hits something, or until he hits me."

Georgia responded by picking up her coffee mug and taking a slow sip.

Cate knew she needed to adjust her attitude. This situation wasn't her mom's fault—well, not entirely—but being bitter wasn't going to change anything. She'd made her decision, and she'd gotten the money. They were going to pay Collins off, and then, hopefully, move on. She needed to live with that decision now…if Joshua allowed her to.

Cate picked up her own coffee mug. She hadn't slept much the night before, and the rich caffeine was the only thing keeping her eyes open. She couldn't help but wonder if she'd ever sleep again—comfortably, anyway, and without assistance. In her current state, she wasn't betting on it.

"How long do you think you have until Joshua figures out you took the money?"

Cate returned her coffee mug to the glass table. "It's Saturday, so the bank will close at noon. If Joshua *is* alerted, I'm hoping it doesn't happen until Monday. But, my name is on the account, so, technically, I didn't do anything wrong. I'm praying the bank doesn't call Joshua, and he just randomly finds out on his own."

Georgia nodded. "Well, getting the money wasn't too difficult. The bank didn't give you any sort of hassle?"

Cate shook her head. "That's the way banks work. They hold onto your money until you ask for it back. After our lunch yesterday, I called to get the paperwork started, and when I went there this morning, everything was ready to go."

Georgia traded her mug for the envelope of cash. She folded down the thin white flap, making sure all of the one-hundred-dollar bills that made up the twenty-grand total were secure. She tossed the package down in front of her, where it landed on the glass with a soft *thud*.

"Look, Cate, I know you're upset, and you have every reason to be. What I said yesterday wasn't fair. But, I was scared. I've *been* scared. And, as for the money, well, I honestly don't know what else to do. If there was some other way out of this—"

"There is," Cate interrupted.

"Okay, what is it, then? I'm listening."

"Don't give Collins the money. Don't feed his extortion."

Georgia rolled her eyes. "Be serious, Cate."

"I am, Mother." Cate tried to flatten her tone. It didn't work. She was too upset. "Nothing good is going to come of this. Giving him exactly what he wants is only going to make us sink. We're admitting guilt, and now he can come back for more money any time he wants to."

"We are guilty, Cate. I don't know how that keeps slipping your mind."

"It doesn't! You remind me of it every five minutes: We killed Collins' father. Or, *I* did."

"Giving Collins the money will make me feel safe. Ignoring him and hoping he goes away on his own isn't a realistic solution to the problem."

"Then I hope you're prepared for the next time he comes around and demands another twenty thousand dollars because I won't have it. And, I may be six feet under, so I won't even be able to help you get it."

"What happened to dealing with only one problem at a time?"

Cate leaned back in her chair. She closed her eyes, took a deep breath, and then exhaled. She hoped that by sitting still and silently, her head would stop pounding all on its own. It didn't. In fact, the pounding picked up its pace. It was like she was at a bad heavy metal concert that just wouldn't end. The pressure refused to go away.

Yes, for her sanity's sake, she'd tried to focus on one problem at a time, and the method had worked for a day. However, now that she had the money and was moving forward with that plan, it was hard not to think about all of the consequences that would follow, and how the events would play out next with both Collins and Joshua. Not to mention, she had to be at work in an hour, so she'd have to deal with Jerry, too.

And, even though she knew it was for the best, she hadn't talked to Matt since he'd hung up on her the other night. It was her own fault. Cate had allowed Matt to become her rock, and now that rock had crumbled and disappeared. She was sad, but even more so, she felt alone.

Just like that, Cate was overwhelmed again. Her heart was racing, and sweat had formed at the base of her neck. She was going to lose it. She was going to go completely crazy. She could feel it. Cate was standing on the edge, looking down, and she was more than ready to jump. She was even looking forward to it.

"Are you all right, Cate?"

"I just need a minute, Mom." Cate opened her eyes. They were watering.

"Can I get you anything?" Georgia tried. "A glass of water?"

"Sure," Cate nodded. "That would be great."

"You got it."

Cate watched as her mom stood, turned, and walked to the wooden cabinet. She grabbed a small glass, filled it from the faucet, and walked back to the table.

Cate accepted the drink and took a long swallow. The cool water felt refreshing against her burning throat. She chugged the remainder of the glass and then handed it back to her mom.

"More?"

"No, thank you," she answered. "I'm fine now."

Cate stared across the table at her mother. Dressed in the same silk robe she always wore when lounging around the house in the mornings, the woman seemed oddly relaxed. Her body appeared to be at ease. She was slouched in the chair almost as if her toughest task of the day would be deciding where to eat lunch, not pay off a dangerous blackmailer who had emerged from their recent past.

Cate tilted her body forward. For the first time since she'd arrived at the house, she noticed that her mother's hair looked as if it had been styled. Not just brushed quickly after getting out of bed, but Georgia had used product…and was that eyeliner, too?

"Are you wearing makeup, Mom?"

"Oh." Georgia blinked. "A little bit. I couldn't sleep last night, woke up early, and had to keep myself busy somehow."

Cate nodded. "Well, you never did like mopping the floor." She smiled finally.

Georgia returned the gesture, but it only lasted a split second before she replaced it with a frown. "I feel strange being here. I feel strange being in my own home. It's like I'm being watched or something."

"I'm sure," Cate agreed.

"As soon as you leave, I'm getting dressed and getting out of here."

"Where are you going?"

Georgia shrugged. "I don't know. Maybe take a long drive, or go to the beach. I don't want to risk being here when he…"

"When is Collins coming to pick up the money? What did the last note say?"

"It said to have the money here and ready by 1:00 p.m. But, I want to be gone just in case he gets a hankering to come early."

"It's kind of interesting," Cate noted. "I mean, why would he want to come here in broad daylight and risk being seen?"

"I don't know," Georgia answered. "Most of his notes came in the middle of the night. I'm not sure why he's changed his pattern all of a sudden. Maybe he's anxious to get the cash and get out of town."

"Part of me would like to be here when he shows up so I can actually *see* him and not just his typing skills."

"Why?"

Cate didn't have the answer to the question. She didn't know why she wanted to see Collins, but she did. She couldn't remember the last time she'd laid eyes on her stepbrother, but it had definitely been years ago. Well, besides the side of his face at the Brim earlier in the week, if that counted.

She probably hadn't *really* seen Collins since right around the time of the "accident," fourteen years ago. According to the picture in the paper, he hadn't changed much. Still, Cate would have liked to have seen for herself, in person. Maybe even confront him and find out what he knew about that night. Or, what he thought he knew.

"What if you told Joshua you're pregnant?"

"Excuse me?" Cate's vision went blurry for a moment. "You're going to have to explain that, because—"

"You're worried Joshua is going to hurt you—more so than usual—when he finds out you nearly drained the joint account."

"Yes," Cate confirmed. "He will. What's your point?"

"Well, if you tell him you're pregnant, then won't he be less likely to beat you? If he really wants a baby…"

"He does want a baby, but there's a flaw in your plan, Mom: It requires me getting pregnant, and soon."

"Aren't you going to have to eventually? How much longer do you think you can keep on fooling Joshua? He's going to find out you're on birth control, and that that's why you haven't gotten pregnant yet."

"I don't want to have a baby," Cate said. "Not with Joshua. I refuse. And, until I come up with another way around it, I'm going to keep on taking the pill."

"But—"

"No! I can't raise a baby with that man. He's a monster. It's impossible to tell how he'd react if the baby woke him up in the middle of the night, or, God forbid, spit up on him. I won't take that risk. I won't bring a baby into our toxic environment."

"You're right," Georgia agreed. "It was a dumb idea. I was just looking out for you. I don't want to see you get hurt over this."

Cate shrugged. "I think it's inevitable. Joshua is going to hurt me, but I'd rather him hurt me than a hypothetical baby." She ran her fingers through her hair and then folded her hands in her lap. "I'll come up with something. I always do."

"Try pushing him down the stairs. That worked out perfectly last time."

"Don't joke about that, Mom. Please. And, as you can see from the mess we're currently in, *that* didn't work out perfectly last time. Look around at the pile of shit we're standing in."

"Work on executing the plan better this time," Georgia suggested. "It's just the two of you in that house. Wait till he starts up the stairs for bed, make sure no one is at your front door, and…"

"You can't be serious."

"Why not?" Georgia asked innocently. "It's a good plan. Figure out the kinks from last time…"

"It was an accident!" Cate yelled. She jumped to her feet. "I've been telling you that since the beginning, since the night it happened. Why won't you believe me?"

"Mark was a horrible man."

"Yes, he was," Cate agreed. She crossed her arms. "He beat you regularly, and he beat me. Hell, the only person he didn't beat was his pride and joy—Collins. But, that doesn't mean I set out to kill him."

"It's fine, Cate. Our lives got better the day he died."

"For the last time, it *was* an accident. I was thirteen! I didn't…I didn't…" She lowered her face into the smooth skin of her palms. After a moment, she looked at her mom. She whispered, "I wanted him dead. I wished it all the time. But, I never once planned to kill him."

"Okay," Georgia said. Her voice was flat. "Okay, honey. I believe you."

"He came after me that night," Cate continued. "I'm not even sure why now." Her forehead creased as she tried to remember. "I'd probably been playing my music too loud. That was always one of his favorite excuses for attacking me.

"He came into my room, yelling at me, threatening me. He raised his fist, but I'd managed to sidestep him somehow. I ran out the door. He followed me."

"You don't have to do this, Cate. You don't have to go back there."

"He caught up to me right as I reached the stairs. That's when he grabbed for my arm. But, he missed. He missed, and I-I-I pushed him."

"Stop, Cate!"

"It seemed like it took him forever to reach the bottom landing. He just kept rolling, hitting every hardwood step, crying out the whole way down, *begging* for help. But, I just stood there and watched. I didn't do anything."

"What could you have possibly done?"

"And, then he hit the tile floor, finally. I heard the *crack*, like I'd dropped an entire carton of eggs or something. I knew he was dead. I knew Mark was dead, and that I had killed him." Cate stopped. She expected her face to be soaked with tears, but it was completely dry.

"You're forgetting one thing," Georgia said.

"What's that?"

"He deserved to die, Cate. Mark deserved to die, and in a much worse way than he did."

She shook her head. "That wasn't our decision to make."

"The hell it wasn't," Georgia argued. "He made our lives miserable. Why else do you think I helped cover it all up? Helped make sure it looked like an accident, like Mark had fallen on his own?"

"You were protecting me."

"Yes, I was." Georgia took a step forward. "And, it kills me that I can't protect you now. It literally eats me alive." She wrapped her arms firmly around her daughter and squeezed.

Cate embraced the hug. She held onto her mother and didn't plan on letting go any time soon. She inhaled her mother's clean scent, and, for a moment, allowed herself to believe that she was a child and that everything would be okay.

After a couple of minutes, Cate parted from her mother. She found the tears she'd been missing earlier. Her face felt warm, blotchy, and irritated, but she'd gotten the release she needed.

"I believe you, Cate," Georgia said. She held onto Cate's arms. "I believe you. It was an accident, and I'm so sorry you've had to live with the guilt all these years. It's not fair."

"I think it is," Cate argued. "It's my punishment."

"Look at me, Cate." Georgia grabbed her chin and forced it downward. "It was an accident. You didn't mean to kill Mark, but he most definitely deserved to die. You *have* to understand that."

Cate shrugged but then nodded almost immediately. "Okay, Mom. I'll try to believe you. I really will."

Georgia smiled, and Cate couldn't help but notice that the gesture came off a little weak. Did her mother truly believe Mark's death had been an accident? It was more than obvious that the woman blamed Cate for Collins' threats and blackmail demands. After all, Georgia was making her pay him off.

And, maybe that's only fair. Cate was responsible for the disaster they were currently in. She'd been the one to deliver that fatal push, but did her mother still think it was planned? Or was she only saying what Cate wanted to hear?

Cate didn't know the truth, and, she figured, she probably never would.

"What do we do now?" Georgia returned to her seat.

Cate remained standing. She wiped at her face and tried to clear the

189

mascara that had undoubtedly smeared. "I guess it's a waiting game. We leave the money for Collins and then wait for him to take it. We wait to see if he contacts us again."

"Right."

"Not that we've ever been religious, but praying probably wouldn't hurt, either," Cate suggested. "We pray that Collins doesn't contact us again. We pray that he takes the twenty grand and leaves us the hell alone. And, we pray that when Joshua finds out what I did, he doesn't kill me."

"You're not even going to consider—?"

"I'm not pushing my husband down the stairs, Mom," Cate interrupted. "I can't."

"Just be careful, Cate. I'm worried about you. And, no matter what happens, I hope you know that I love you. I've never stopped loving you. Not even once."

"I love you, too," Cate said. "But, you don't need to worry about me. I'll be fine."

"How can you be so sure?"

Cate stared at her mom. Eyes wide, she didn't blink. Her face was as solid as stone. "Because I'm a survivor."

28

He'd always thought his name was ironic, maybe even a cruel example of the fact that God really did have a sense of humor: Richie. Yet, he'd never once in his entire life had two pennies to rub together.

Well, that was all about to change, and, when it did, Richie knew he'd have the last laugh. It was about damned time.

Though his high school teachers would have probably said differently, he wasn't a complete moron. Richie knew that five thousand dollars was a far cry from rich. Hell, in today's world, a million dollars wasn't even a big deal anymore, just pocket change to some. Still, Richie was all about opportunity and taking advantage of that opportunity when it came a-knockin'.

Collins hadn't just been an opportunity that knocked—it had pounded full force, nearly breaking down the door.

The truth was pretty simple: Richie was in a bad place, a place where five big ones did make him rich, and if he had even the slightest chance of making more in the future, well, damn, that was just gravy.

Initially, he'd needed to make sure that Collins' offer was worth the trouble. After all, he was risking prison if he got caught. His friend never seemed to do anything legal, and his new blackmail scheme was no exception.

The more Richie had spoken to Collins about this particular "job," the more he'd realized what a cash cow it truly was. Riche wasn't the type of man who knew how to earn an honest living, so this deal couldn't have come at a better time.

Come to think of it, maybe God didn't have a sense of humor. Maybe he just worked in mysterious ways, and maybe one of those ways was granting Richie exactly what he needed. *Finally*.

Before all of the details had been discussed, Richie had considered biting off the hand that was going to feed him. Still, before he had time to conceive a plan in which he got away with all of the money, Collins offered him a tidbit: There would be no time-out in this little game of extortion. Collins planned on making it a monthly ritual.

Just like that, Richie had been back to feeling rich. Not rich *rich*, like being able to afford a luxury car, a trip to Europe, or a suit made with material that wouldn't make his skin itch, but white trash rich, where he could buy steak dinners, plenty of cold beer, and lap dances with the hot stripper instead of the one with the lazy eye.

The only problem with the whole arrangement was that Richie was taking orders, not giving them. He wasn't used to being told what to do, and he didn't care for it. But, ultimately, he and Collins needed each other. It was that simple, yet that complicated. Richie was desperate for work, and Collins required someone to do his bidding around town without raising any eyebrows.

They were stuck together, a classic *Odd Couple*-type relationship.

It was then that Richie made a big decision: God *did* have a sense of humor.

"So, ten grand this time. How much do you think we can demand next month? And, when, exactly?" Richie asked last night. "Maybe at the beginning of each month like rent?"

"We've already talked about the consequences of being too greedy," Collins warned. "Let's get through tomorrow, and then we'll go from there."

"Yeah, okay," Richie agreed. "I'm just ready for more."

"Everybody wants more. That's what's wrong with this world. Now, there were no issues delivering the note tonight, right?"

"Right." Richie nodded. "I put it right where it couldn't be missed. And, by tomorrow afternoon, we'll each have five thousand dollars to our name."

"Here's hoping."

Richie had been too excited to sleep. It certainly hadn't been nerves. Over the years, he'd done a lot worse for a lot less. All he had to do was pick up a bag full of cash. This was kid's stuff. Easy peasy.

Richie couldn't stop thinking about the first thing he planned on doing with the money.

Well, the first thing he planned on doing was smelling it. That distinctive, crisp smell was almost foreign to him, and the ink, especially if any of the bills were printed recently, would feel silky and smooth to the touch.

As for new purchases, Richie figured food topped his list. Good food, like lobster, and then maybe a massage, or a few nights in a decent hotel so he could get some rest, finally.

That's all the time he would be giving himself—three days, max—and then he'd have to go back to work. For the most part, Richie was a cheap, simple man, but, even so, five thousand dollars wouldn't last long, and until Collins got his head out of his ass and designed a decent plan of action for the future, he'd be back on the hunt for employment.

He was resourceful. Someone always needed a driver to get behind the wheel of a getaway car or smack around an unruly prostitute for a pimp who didn't want to get his hands dirty. Another gig might even pop up like his latest one: delivering threatening notes and collecting blackmail cash.

"Don't draw attention to yourself," Collins demanded that morning over instant coffee and stale donuts. "And, make sure no one sees you when you go into the house. Everyone seems to be particularly cautious with a killer on the loose."

"Yeah," Richie agreed. "But, everyone's looking for you, not me. I'll be fine."

"You'll be fine if you drop the cocky attitude. We're so close, there's no reason to fuck it up now."

"This whole thing isn't about the money for you, is it?" Richie asked. "You just want to torture someone, make them suffer."

"You're my employee, Richie, not my friend. So, you can drop the therapy act. I'm not interested in sharing."

Richie had considered telling Collins off but had ultimately bit his tongue. After all, Collins was right: They weren't friends—not anymore. A strictly professional relationship was probably for the best—and, Collins, well, he'd get what was coming to him soon enough. Whether it took a day, a week, a month, or a year, karma always had a way of dealing with the assholes of the world.

Besides, being treated like shit was one of the setbacks of his career choice, and he'd grown accustomed to it. There wasn't an HR department to file a complaint. You took the good with the bad, and you learned not to take anything too personally.

He'd been watching the house for at least twenty minutes before he'd decided to make a move. No one had come, and no one had gone. It appeared to be empty. While Richie didn't personally know the woman he was collecting the money from, he did assume she was smart enough to not be home when a blackmailer was scheduled to stop by.

Once he'd decided the coast was clear, he parked Collins's Honda two streets over and started out on foot. An inexperienced man might have parked right in the driveway with the car running, or even on the street where nosy neighbors could get an easy view of the license plate.

Not Richie. He knew better.

He didn't know what he was walking into. He hoped for the best but expected the worst. It was a valuable life lesson he'd familiarized himself with a long time ago and still used on a daily basis. Just because he hoped the money was waiting for him inside the front door didn't mean he expected it to be there.

He'd already accepted that he didn't know this woman. For all Richie knew, she could be waiting for him with a shotgun.

So, Richie sure his own gun was loaded and ready for business before tucking it into the back waistband of his pants.

He headed toward the brick house. Dressed in dark jeans, boots, and a T-shirt that had a small stain on the left sleeve, Richie silently prayed he didn't stand out too much.

Luck appeared to be on his side. The neighborhood, small and a little too "green" for his tastes, was empty. Whether families had taken shelter from the blazing sun inside their little boxes with air conditioners or outback with swimming pools, Richie didn't know or particularly care. The coast was clear. He was going in.

Richie climbed the concrete stairs that led to the small porch. At the door, he grabbed the knob and twisted it. It was unlocked. Whoever lived here was making his job a lot easier.

He stood in the foyer and scanned the lower level of the house. He expected to see the cash but didn't. Instead, he was greeted with the same tacky knickknacks and furniture he'd seen the night before when he'd been in the house. He saw rustic picture frames holding images of a woman, and, he assumed, her daughter; dull, gray walls that created a feeling of claustrophobia; a long, braided rug that was splattered with stars and stripes; and a few end tables, cloth chairs, and a stiff couch that looked as comfortable as a wooden board.

But, no cash.

So it was going to be a scavenger hunt. That was just fine. He could do that. No problem.

Next on Richie's list: the kitchen. Yet, it proved to be empty, too. No money, and no one. Just two lone coffee mugs sitting on the table.

He walked to the counter where the coffee pot sat. It still held some liquid. He used the palm of his right hand to touch the glass. Cold.

Richie turned around. The back door was unlocked and the deadbolt wasn't in place. He zeroed in on the checkered curtain beside the door. Someone liked their country-style décor a little too much.

One more quick look around the kitchen. Nothing out of the ordinary, but also nothing he'd come to collect. He kept going.

Back in the hallway, Richie found the stairs. He started up them slowly. He wasn't scared, not even a little bit, but the *creaking* sound added a sort of eeriness to his surroundings. The rest of the house was silent.

Less than sixty seconds later, his suspicions were confirmed: The rest of the upstairs, just like the downstairs, was empty.

No money. No one.

Richie pulled his cell phone from his front pocket and stabbed in a number. He waited.

"Well? Are we each five thousand dollars richer?"

"Not exactly." Richie frowned.

"What do you mean? Do you have the money or not?"

"No. It's not here."

"Fuck!" Collins screamed on the other end. "She decided not to pay. She's testing me."

"There's more," Richie said. "The master bedroom—it looks like someone packed up some clothes and left in a hurry."

"Huh?"

"Whoever lives here, well, I think they left. Permanently. The closet is a mess, and the dresser drawers are open and empty."

"Wait!" Collins ordered. "Are you saying…?"

"I'm pretty sure this bitch left town," Richie interrupted. "And, she left with our money!"

"I can't believe you're letting a murderer roam the streets! I mean, what if he decides to strangle another girl, huh? That death will be on you."

"Stop it, Beau! I've told you enough times: Matt isn't the killer. So, drop it!"

"You don't know that, Shannon. There's no evidence that proves he's innocent."

"And, there's no evidence that proves he's guilty."

"Which is exactly why we should be talking to him, asking him questions about those girls. Hell, we still haven't been able to track down his ex-girlfriend. Matt has no alibi for any of the murders. But, instead of trying to lean on him a little bit, you let him walk right out of here yesterday and take a damn sabbatical."

"You know that's not what happened," Shannon argued. "Yes, he left without permission. But, it wasn't like we were holding him officially. We have nothing to hold him on. If he doesn't want to cooperate with us, he doesn't have to."

"You could have threatened him. Told him his job was on the line, something to make him want to cooperate."

Shannon shook his head. "You have the audacity to question my skills as a cop, yet you stand there pissed off because I didn't do something unethical, not to mention, illegal?"

"Oh, please," Beau fired back. "It's not like I wanted you to plant evidence."

"You know I talked to Matt. He asked for a couple of days to clear his head and sort some stuff out."

"I know what he asked for. What I don't know is why you agreed to it."

Shannon sighed. "Well, for starters, he just went through a bad breakup. Then, to add insult to injury, I—with your lead, of course—implied that he could be a cold-blooded killer."

Beau shrugged. "And?"

"And, he's family. I feel bad for my mistake. I want to make it right. I don't know why I considered even for a moment that Matt could—"

"Because facts don't lie," Beau interrupted, "and killers do. And, the fact remains that Matt is connected to all three victims, and he lied to our faces about knowing it."

"It's just two days, Beau. Matt will be back in the office on Monday. Who knows? By then, maybe this ex-girlfriend will turn up, confirm Matt's alibis, and make this whole conversation meaningless."

"Yeah." Beau nodded. "Or maybe Matt will kill some other defenseless girl, steal her earring, and then skip town."

"I'm not kidding, Beau," Shannon warned. "Knock it off. As far as I'm concerned, Matt is innocent, and this Collins guy is our prime suspect. Understand?"

Beau didn't answer the sheriff. Instead, he bit his lower lip to stop himself from speaking his mind. Once the moment had passed, Beau dropped into the chair in front of Shannon's desk, rested his elbows on his knees, and stared down at the floor.

What a fucking rotten day. Except, in all reality, it had been a fucking rotten week.

As far as Beau was concerned, he'd kept his end of the bargain. He'd been in Perry's Creek a little over a week, and he'd single-handedly delivered the best suspect the investigation had yet to see. Sure, eyewitnesses put that Collins guy at a victim's apartment, but that had been hours before her death. Plus, she had only been one of the strangled girls. Beau's suspect was connected to all three. Matt was a police deputy working the case, so he was close to it, able to cover his tracks and keep a watchful eye out for any leads or developments that might implicate him.

Then there was the *coup de grâce*, the factor that had Beau believing Matt was the killer: He'd let Collins get away.

With Collins still in the wind, Matt was free to continue his little strangulation spree, all the while keeping the finger pointed at someone else. Furthermore, if Collins wasn't in custody, then Collins couldn't talk.

Beau was familiar with the one minor snag in his theory about Matt allowing Collins to escape: O.J.

Matt hadn't been alone at the pub when Collins "evaded" capture. O.J. had been at the scene, too, and had eagerly backed up Matt's story. Then again, from what Beau had heard, Matt and O.J. were close—closer than close. Friends, partners, pretty much brothers, and they had each other's backs. They respected one another, and, in some sense, whether they were man enough to admit it or not, probably even loved each other.

If there was one thing Beau had come to learn the hard way throughout his career—and life—it was that the feeling of love made you do crazy, stupid, downright fucked-up things before ultimately leaving you confused, bruised, and completely alone.

In the end, love didn't conquer all. Being able to survive was the only thing that mattered. O.J. would find that out soon enough.

One thing Beau hadn't been able to figure out in the past twenty-four hours was Matt's motive. Why would he want to strangle young women and take their jewelry? This wasn't about sex. None of the victims had been touched *that* way before or after they were murdered. So, what did Matt get out of the killings?

Maybe the actual killing was what got Matt off, the power play, the squeezing of the life out of another human being.

Dammit! He needed to talk to Matt, pick his brain, try and get him to slip up and reveal something useful or concrete, but Beau knew that would have to wait until Monday, and without Shannon knowing about it. The thin ice that currently surrounded their relationship had already started to crack; there was no way it could take much more strain.

"We still need to talk about what you said to Diane."

Yes, Beau thought, *there was still that.* He couldn't get around the issue. He'd been foolish to even assume that the conversation could be avoided.

Shannon felt the need to duke it out, to defend his wife. Although Beau wasn't in the mood to fight, he knew he'd have no choice but to shove his hands into his boxing gloves and defend himself. After all, no one was going to do it for him.

"Okay," Beau said finally. "What do you want to discuss?"

"You called my wife a bitch, Beau."

"Yeah, I did," Beau admitted. "What's your point?"

Shannon folded his hands on his desk. "So, that's how you want to play this?"

"I'm not playing anything," Beau argued. "Diane came down to the department looking for you. We had words. That was pretty much it. I probably shouldn't have said what I did, but I was provoked. She made some nasty comments, too, and—"

"She's my wife, Beau, and you're my friend. You do understand how relationships rank, right?"

"What I understand is that you're the one playing make-believe or pretend or whatever you want to call it. Diane and I may have said some unflattering things to one another, but at least we were being honest."

"And, what in hell is that supposed to mean?"

"What do you think it means, Shannon?" Beau jumped to his feet. "It means that you're a coward *and* a liar. You've been lying for over thirty-five years."

"Are you implying I don't love my wife?"

Beau shook his head. "I'm sure you really do love Diane. But, I don't think it's the type of love you make it out to be. You've got everyone fooled: Diane, co-workers, maybe even yourself. You're not being true—"

"You wanted to see me?"

Beau turned to face O.J., who was standing in the doorway.

"I didn't," Shannon said.

"Deputy Benson told me—"

"That was me," Beau interrupted. "And, it was earlier this morning. What took you so long?"

O.J. shrugged. "I've been busy. You know, trying to solve a string of murders."

"Right." Beau nodded.

"So, did you still need to talk? Or..."

Beau glanced at Shannon, and the sheriff frowned. He was confused. "I was hoping to discuss Deputy Combs with you."

"What about Matt?" O.J. asked.

"Jesus, Beau!" Shannon yelled.

Beau ignored the sheriff's outburst. "Just some routine questions about his personality and your experience with being his partner. Those sorts of things." Then Beau added, "Oh, I was also hoping to get another statement about that day at the pub, and what happened with Collins."

"It sounds like you need to talk to Matt," O.J. offered, "not me."

"Well, I can't really do that, now, can I? In case you haven't noticed, Matt's not here today. By the way, you haven't talked to him recently, have you?"

"What in hell is going on, Sheriff?" O.J. crossed his arms.

"Dammit, Beau! Why can't you ever fucking listen to anybody?" Shannon stood. "It's nothing, O.J., honestly. Just Beau, here, has this wild notion that Matt is the killer we've all been looking for. And, he won't drop it."

"Seriously?" O.J. mocked.

"Let me guess," Beau stated, "you don't think your life-long buddy is capable of strangling three women?"

"No, I don't. Matt's a lot of things, some I'm just now realizing for the first time. But, he's no killer."

"How can you be so sure?"

O.J. sighed. "Because if Matt was a killer, believe me, I'd know it."

"I don't think so," Beau argued. "Check your voice, son. There's some hesitation there."

"Is there anything else you need from me, Sheriff? Or can I go back to my desk?"

"Yes, O.J., please. You can go," Shannon answered. "And, I apologize for what just happened here."

O.J. nodded. He closed the door and walked away from the office.

"You know what your problem is, Beau?" Shannon returned to his seat. "Authority. You can never let someone else be in charge. You can never take a damn order."

"I followed your orders, Shannon." Beau remained standing. He put his hands on his hips. "You wanted me to find your killer, and I did. I'm the only one who—"

"That's right," Shannon interrupted. "You're the great and powerful Beau Reynolds. No one else holds a candle to the best detective in all of Southern California."

"What the hell are you talking about?"

"You, Beau! You're so damned stubborn and full of yourself, you can't even see when you're wrong."

"You don't know that I'm wrong. You won't even give me a proper chance to further prove I'm right. You're too embarrassed to—"

"It doesn't matter! I'm in charge. I gave you an order, and you keep on refusing to accept it!" Shannon took a deep breath and then exhaled slowly. "No. That's my final answer. The sooner you get that through your head—"

"We're not talking about Matt and the case anymore, are we?" Beau fell

200

into the chair. He placed his face in the palms of his hands and became still.

"I guess not," Shannon whispered. "Looks like you're getting what you wanted. We're talking about it, finally."

Beau looked up suddenly. He stared wide-eyed at Shannon. He opened his mouth but no words came out. He wasn't sure if he was stunned or hurt. Maybe both.

"What?"

"You think this is really what I want, Shannon? You think this is why I came to Perry's Creek?"

"Why did you come here, Beau?"

"Why did you ask me to come here?"

"You know why. I needed your help.."

"Bullshit!" Beau countered. "If you're going to do this, then do it right. That's only fair."

Shannon leaned back. He looked up at the ceiling, no doubt to avoid eye contact. "What happened between us, Beau, it was a long time ago. We were young. We were stupid kids who were just having fun. Messing around, nothing more."

"I don't believe you." Beau felt tears forming at the corners of his eyes. They begged to be released, but he refused to let them fall. He'd die first.

"It's true," Shannon continued. "And, I'm sorry if you thought I had an ulterior motive for asking you to come here. I didn't. I just wanted your help with my case."

"Why'd you tell Diane about us? My first night here, when you came to my motel room, you said—"

"I told Diane because keeping a secret like that from my wife was eating me alive. And then, having you here, working side by side, I couldn't help but feel guilty. So, I told her. And, after a couple of days, she came around. She's fine with it, understands it was only in college, and—"

"She's not 'fine' with it," Beau snapped. "If she was, she wouldn't have verbally attacked me the other day. She blames me, and she's in denial. Just like you."

"Excuse me?"

Beau reached for the knot of his tie. It was suffocating him. He loosened it and could breathe, finally, for the first time in a long time. "You invited me here, pretty much begged me to come, and then felt guilty about it. Why do you think you felt guilty, Shannon?"

Shannon blinked. "I-I-I…"

"And, why do you think Diane felt the need to tell me how disgusting and grotesque she finds me? Could it be that she's threatened by me? Threatened by my relationship with you?"

Shannon shook his head. "Why can't you just let it go, Beau? You're wasting your life. Look at yourself. All the drinking, the booze. You're miserable. Accept that what happened between us is history. It's in the past. It didn't mean anything."

"I can't accept that," Beau choked out in a thick voice. The tears started to fall now. He didn't stop them.

"Why not?" Shannon asked. His tone was soft, almost unrecognizable.

"Because it meant something to me." Beau stood. He turned his back to Shannon.

It was then that Beau realized he had something in common with both Shannon and Diane: denial. He had been in denial for the past thirty-five years. He'd always thought that staying in that dark, secluded place would allow him to survive, but, in the end, it had done the complete opposite. It had destroyed him.

The tears kept coming. They burned down both sides of his face, and for the first time in his life, Beau wasn't ashamed to be a grown man who cried.

He tried to dry swallow the pit that had formed in his throat. He couldn't. It was almost as if the pain of it was his punishment, his sentence for being such a fool all of these years. On some level, Beau was okay with that. He understood it.

His heart began pounding faster than ever like it had grown fists and was trying to punch its way right out of Beau's chest. He knew what was coming next, what Shannon was going to say, and he still couldn't prepare for it. Beau suspected hearing the words might even make him drop to his knees.

Still, he managed to take his own advice from earlier. He manned up. No more running. No more hiding. No more lying to himself. He was way overdue to face the truth even though it was bound to feel like getting kicked in the gut.

Beau pivoted around and looked at Shannon. The sheriff's entire complexion had faded to ghost white. Beau had never seen his friend look so pale.

"I doubt this will come as much of a surprise, Beau," Shannon began quietly, "but I think it will be best if you leave and go back to San Diego. I know who the killer is. I just have to catch him. I can do that without your help."

"All right," Beau whispered. He had no more strength left to argue about the case. Frankly, he didn't even give a damn about it anymore. There were more important things in life than climbing the career ladder, and he was ready to win at something else for a change.

Beau was well aware that he was about to lose what mattered most to him...again.

Still, he asked because he had no choice. "And, us? What's going to happen to us?"

Shannon shook his head. "There is no 'us,' Beau. There never was. And, now, well, it's more obvious than ever that we can't even be friends."

"That's it, then?" Beau bit his lower lip and instantly tasted coppery blood, but the gesture had worked. It had stopped him from sobbing. After a few moments, he was able to continue. "We're just going to go our separate ways and never see each other again? Never talk?"

"That's right." Shannon nodded. "I'm sorry, but there's no other way. This is goodbye, Beau."

I t was after one. Collins had to have the money by now, but as much as Cate wanted to call her mom to check in and make sure everything was okay, she couldn't. Jerry had personally seen to that. The man had made good on his threat from the other day, and then some.

As soon as Cate arrived for her Saturday shift, Jerry cracked the whip. He'd more than proven that he was the boss, that he was one hundred percent in charge. He'd begun by assigning her meaningless tasks that were usually reserved for lower-ranking employees, and he hadn't stopped there.

Cate had spent most of the late morning scrubbing the floor in the back, washing the glass door at the front of the shop—twice—and re-stocking lids, straws, stirrers, and anything else Jerry happened to think was running low.

Still, one good thing had come from his stubborn, childish behavior: She hadn't had a split second to sit and dwell on Collins and the blackmail exchange.

Until now—and, now, well, she was starting to worry.

Cate was well aware that she spent most of her time these days worrying about men and their power. As she wiped at a dark coffee ring on the front counter, her mind seemed to zero in on that idea. The truth was that her life was full of examples of men who thrived on power…more than her fair share.

First, of course, there was Joshua. He'd never come right out and said it, but Cate was willing to bet her life that power had a lot to do with the way her husband chose to treat her. He liked being in control. He liked that he made the rules and then got to hand out the punishments when those rules were broken.

Their relationship had been different in the beginning, but weren't most relationships in the early stages?

Then there was Collins, whom Cate had thought she'd never see again. Technically, she still hadn't seen him, though just his presence had proven to be quite powerful. He'd weaseled his way back into her life and had forced her to give him twenty thousand dollars.

Hell, even her stepdad had shown strength from beyond the grave. Collins had used the man as a meal ticket. She couldn't even properly fight a man of flesh and blood. How was she supposed to fight a ghost?

She couldn't forget about Jerry being in the mix. He'd shown his true, dark, and very ugly colors, but his power was the least of Cate's worries because she knew that she could walk away from it at any time. If Jerry didn't have a change of attitude and quickly, then she'd quit, and Cate knew for certain she'd have her husband's support.

The power that surprised Cate the most, the man in her life who definitely had the most control over her and her emotions, was Matt. She couldn't explain it, and she didn't fully understand it, but she knew it was true. Matt hadn't called her back since he'd hung up on her...and it was now driving her crazy. Crazy enough that she wanted to run right out into the middle of the street and scream.

But, what would that accomplish?

She wondered if she'd ever talk to Matt again. Cate wanted to. She *needed* to, but that, too, would be a pointless act. Her non-existent relationship with Matt was officially over.

She'd lost. It was time to accept that.

Right now, she needed to move on and consider more pressing issues, like what she was going to tell Joshua about the missing money.

Cate knew she still had one option left, and, while she hadn't wanted to resort to it just yet, with everything that had happened recently, she figured there was no reason to wait.

"Daydreaming about the wonderful life you could have if you were with me?"

He'd snuck up behind her again. Jerry reminded her of Joshua in that respect. He was fast, quiet, and could appear randomly. It seemed the two men shared a lot of qualities, and neither of them was worth a damn.

"No new bruises today," Jerry whispered. "Did Joshua find a new hobby? You know, one that doesn't include beating his wife?"

"We're not doing this, Jerry," Cate warned. "I'm just not in the mood, and we have customers."

"What's the matter?" he taunted. "Don't want the whole town to know one of its finest men in blue beats his wife? Or are you just worried that the Creek might find out you're a victim?"

She spun around to face him. "I'm not a victim! I may be a lot of things, but a victim is not one of them!"

"Oh, Cate. Did I hit a nerve?"

"Why are you doing this, Jerry?" She angled herself to make sure her back was to the half a dozen customers flooding the shop. "What happened to you? Why the sudden change?"

He shrugged. "You'd be surprised by what love can do to a person. And, rejection, well, that doesn't look good on anyone."

She agreed with the explanation—only a naïve fool wouldn't—but it still didn't fit.

"You don't love me, Jerry. You're not *in* love with me."

"No?" He tilted his head to the side. "What would you call it?"

She sighed. "You watched your wife die. You never grieved her death, and you're lonely. After working side by side with me, you think—"

"I appreciate your analysis, Cate, but have you ever considered that I'm just into blonde-haired, blue-eyed women? That that's how my attraction for you started? And, then, when I noticed Joshua was hurting you, well..." He paused. "I couldn't save Sarah, but I knew I could save you. And, I wanted to. That's love, Cate."

She shook her head. "You're not getting it, Jerry."

"Quit rejecting me, Cate. Everything would be so much easier if you'd just give me a chance."

"Can you come here, Chrissy?" Cate called to the back of the shop.

A twenty-something girl immediately appeared. Her long, light hair was styled in a messy bun and her leaf-shaped earrings almost touched her shoulders. She wore the same green apron as Cate.

"Yes?" she asked.

"I need to talk to Jerry about something in the back. Can you watch the register for a few minutes, please?"

"Sure," Chrissy answered.

Cate smiled at the girl and then grabbed Jerry's arm and pulled him into the back. She couldn't describe her frustration with the man. Cate wanted to hate him, and though she was angry with him for violating whatever friendly boss-employee relationship they'd once shared, she couldn't help but feel sorry for the man.

Whether he wanted to admit it or not, Jerry was still in mourning—yet another dangerous emotion that could cause someone to do crazy, stupid things.

Like Collins. Was it possible her stepbrother was still mourning the death of his father, even all these years later? Did grief have an expiration date?

"You have something you need to share with me in private?"

"This is it, Jerry. I'm going to give you the benefit of the doubt one last time."

"I wish you'd give me more than that, Cate." He winked and then took a small step toward her.

"Stop, Jerry. Please. You don't want me." She pointed to his ring finger. "Look. You still wear your wedding band. You're trying to replace me with Sarah because you don't want to be alone."

"You couldn't be more off base, Cate."

She tossed her hands in the air. "You need to get help, Jerry. I can't keep having this same argument."

"Good news. You don't have to." He took another step toward her. In one swift motion, he bent down and pushed his lips against hers.

Cate pulled back. "Jerry!" she screamed. "No!" Then she raised her right hand and smacked him across the face. Cate hadn't planned the hit. She'd just reacted. It was almost as if someone else had been in control of her body for a minute.

"What the hell do you think you're doing, Cate?" Jerry's entire face had turned bright red. His fingers grazed the spot she'd connected with. "That was a big mistake."

"I quit, Jerry." She reached around for the knot of her apron. "I told you I don't need you. I can save my damned self."

* * *

On the way home, Cate tried to get a hold of her mom at least three different times. No answer, and, as if on cue, her stomach had started doing somersaults. Something was wrong. Cate could feel it in her bones. Her skin began to burn like someone had struck her with a match.

Now, she was forced to make a decision. Did she go to her mom's house? Or did she go home and wait for a phone call?

Cate chose the latter. She needed more time to prepare herself for the worst. She wasn't sure she could handle finding…

No! She pushed the thought out of her head. She wouldn't think like that, not yet. There was no reason to. There could be a million reasons why Georgia wasn't answering her phone. She'd mentioned going to the beach. Maybe she'd left her cell in the car. Or just didn't have any service.

Cate would get a hold of her mother. She'd keep trying until she succeeded.

The next ten minutes passed in a blur. Cate had pulled out of the Brim's parking lot, gotten onto Main Street, and eventually found her driveway without even remembering to put the key in the ignition.

She gripped the strap of her purse and headed toward the front door. She wasn't sure what she'd do inside. Pour a glass of wine? Try her mom's cell again? Fall to the floor and cry? It didn't matter. Cate just knew she had to keep moving. She feared that if she stopped even for a moment, she'd fall over dead.

Cate opened the door and darted through the entrance. It wasn't until she was standing in the kitchen that she sensed his presence.

She turned around slowly. As soon as she saw him, she dropped the wine glass. It hit the floor and shattered.

"Hello, Cate."

"W-w-what are you doing here? Where's my mom?"

"You don't sound too welcoming," he said. "After fourteen years, that's how you treat family?" He shook his head. "Don't worry. We'll get to your mom. But, first, come over here and give your stepbrother a big hug."

* * *

"Is she dead? Did you kill her?"

Collins laughed. "Of course not. Though, come to think of it, I probably should have." He shrugged. "Hell, I still might."

"Then where is she? Why hasn't she returned any of my calls?"

"Actually, Cate, that's why I'm here. I thought you could help me find your mom."

"What?" She crossed her arms. "I don't understand. You have the money, right? Why do you care where my mom is?"

"That's where you're wrong, Cate. I *don't* have the money, but I'm willing to bet Georgia does. Which would also explain why she's missing."

"You don't have the money?" She heard the thick confusion in her own voice. "But, you were—"

"Supposed to pick it up at one this afternoon at your mom's house?" he finished. "Yeah, I'm aware of what was *supposed* to happen. My associate went to Georgia's to get the cash. Only, it wasn't there. And, that wasn't the only thing not there."

"Huh?"

"About half of your mom's clothes were gone, too. Looks like she left in a hurry."

Cate's eyes went wide. "You honestly expect me to believe that, Collins? You think my own mother would double-cross me? Take the twenty thousand dollars I put together for you and just bail?"

"I don't care what you choose to believe. I'm telling you…" Collins stopped. "Did you say twenty thousand dollars?"

"Yes," Cate nodded. "You demanded twenty grand, and I found a way to get it."

"Oh, my God!" Collins burst into a dry laugh. The screeching sound made her want to cover her ears. He didn't stop.

After a few moments, Cate finally asked, "What's so damned funny?"

"Your mom has got some big brass balls. I'll give her that."

"I'm not following."

"I didn't ask for twenty grand, Cate. I asked for ten."

"What? No."

"She played you. Georgia used my scam to scam you, her own daughter. I mean, it's kind of genius, if you think about it. Sick and twisted, but genius, nonetheless."

"No," Cate repeated. She shook her head. "There's no way. That didn't happen. M-m-my mom wouldn't do that to me."

"I'm thinking she would, Catie. And, she did."

"Don't call me that!" she ordered. "I'm telling you. My mom wouldn't have betrayed me like that. You said you have an associate. He could have—"

"Nope. Sorry, Catie. I know for a fact that my guy expected to snag only ten grand today, not twenty. Your mom is a liar, and she's also a thief."

"But, why? I don't…" Cate couldn't believe it. She didn't *want* to believe it.

Maybe her mom had had second thoughts about paying off Collins. Maybe she'd taken the money and hid it and was now lying low until…

Cate didn't bother finishing the thought. The excuse was too weak for even her to believe it. She knew Collins was right. Her own mother had stabbed her in the back and robbed her blind. That was crystal clear now. The woman's makeup and hair being done up...Georgia had been ready to flee this morning, and she probably had as soon as Cate had left.

What Cate didn't understand was why. Why had her mom done this? The woman had abandoned her and left her with a big mess to clean up.

Perhaps this was payback. She'd changed the course of her mom's life all those years ago. Maybe Georgia had lied. Maybe she'd never been fully okay with what happened that night, and, now, her mother had made a clean break and was getting a new start...twenty thousand new starts.

Was this her mother's revenge?

Cate looked at Collins. He sat on a barstool. His face was blank like he didn't have a care in the world. Like he hadn't threatened her and blackmailed her. Like he hadn't just lost the ten grand he'd been expecting all week. His body was relaxed, even slumped, as if he was visiting a friend for coffee.

Why was he still here? What in hell did he want?

"I don't know what else to tell you, Collins." She folded her hands on the counter. Just standing across from him was too much. Cate was angry. She was scared. Mostly, though, she was confused. "I don't have any more money to give you. Honestly. And, I don't know where my mom is, so..."

"Yeah, I believe you," he said. "However, I think you can help me find her. And, I think you're going to *want* to help me find her."

"That doesn't make any sense," she argued. "I'm upset, of course, but I'm not going to put my mom in danger. I'd rather she have the money than you, anyway. And, you can go to the police. You can tell them I killed your father. I don't care. I doubt they'll even believe you."

He raised his hands. "You caught me. I'm not going to the police. I never was. Like they'd really believe some ex-junkie who just got out of prison."

Dammit! her mind screamed. Why hadn't her mother listened to her? They could have avoided this whole...

Wait! Had this been Georgia's plan the entire time? Ever since she'd received the note demanding money, had her mother decided to hang her out to dry like this? To increase the blackmail payment so she could get away with more money?

"Georgia couldn't have gotten too far and—"

"I'm not helping you," Cate said. She took a step back from the counter. "My mom may have screwed me over, but I won't do the same thing to her."

"Cate…"

"No," Cate refused. "She must have her reasons for doing what she did. And, maybe someday I'll understand those reasons. But, I'm not going to help you, Collins. You still threatened my mom, and you put me in danger with my husband. I'm glad you're not getting a dime."

"I need to explain something to you, Cate."

"Go to hell, Collins!"

"You're right. Your mother *does* have a reason for running off, and I know what that reason is."

Cate rolled her eyes. "You're pathetic. Get out!"

"That's not very nice, Catie." He frowned. "I went to a lot of trouble to come and see you today. I risked a lot. Now, don't you want to know a family secret? It's a juicy one."

She sighed. "If you have something to say, then just say it. Otherwise, get out."

"Oh, don't you worry your pretty little head, Catie. I'm going to share with you, but you may want to pour that glass of wine before I do." Collins stretched his arms over his head. "Come to think of it, I'd love a beer. Your husband drinks beer, doesn't he, Catie?"

"Please, Collins…"

"Get the drinks, Cate. You'll need the alcohol to soften the blow."

She wasn't sure why, but she listened to him. Cate stepped over the broken shards of glass that littered the floor. She grabbed a cold beer bottle from the top shelf of the fridge and handed it to Collins, then she set out for her own vice.

It wasn't until after she'd taken a long, slow sip of the smoky merlot that she said, "Talk."

"Growing up, were you always this bossy? I don't remember."

"Collins."

"Fine, fine." He took a swig from his beer. "I'm not sure how to say this, exactly. What I'm about to tell you is going to be hard to hear. So, I guess that *does* make it easier for me to tell you, but…"

"Spit it out!" she ordered.

"You didn't kill my father. Your mother did."

Her hold on the stem of her glass became tighter. "Get out!"

"What? I'm telling you the truth."

"How stupid do you think I am?" she asked. "I pushed Mark down the stairs that night. Were you even there?"

"Oh, I was there, Cate. I was high as hell, but I was there. I saw everything."

"Then you know it was me who killed your father."

He shook his head. "No, you didn't. You pushed him down the stairs, but that's not what killed him."

"You're not making any sense, Collins."

"You pushed my dad down the stairs, and then your mom told you to go to your room, that she would take care of it."

"Yes." Cate nodded.

"And, she did. Georgia took care of it, all right. When she went to move my father's body, he was still breathing—barely—but he was alive. That is, until she smothered him."

Cate stared down into her wine. The thick maroon color reminded her of blood. Collins was lying. He had to be. This was all some ploy to get her to help him, to get her to turn on her own mother.

She'd killed Mark, not Georgia. Why would her mom have lied to her all this time? She wouldn't have. That didn't add up. It would mean her mother had let her take the blame for something she didn't do, let the guilt eat away at her insides for fourteen years.

Was her mother that diabolical? That malicious? But, why?

Then the answer came smashing into Cate full force. She backed up against the dishwasher to stop herself from falling over. She set her wine glass down beside her and placed her face in the palms of her hands. Sweat had formed at the back of her neck, but she ignored it. Her focus was on one thing only—her mother.

Her mother had lied to her to get away with murder. It was so obvious now, and Cate hated herself for not seeing it sooner. Sure, she'd only been thirteen at the time, but, even then, how could she have been so dense?

She hadn't wanted her mother to be such a monster. She'd denied it, and, in the process, her mother had gained complete control over her.

Could someone really be that selfish? Her mother was a snake, and by running off with that money, she'd set Cate up…for everything. Georgia had abandoned her, broken her, and now Cate was left all alone to deal with the thorny consequences.

"What do you think of Mommy Dearest now?"

"Why didn't you ever say anything, Collins? All these years, all this time, I thought…"

"I was too busy getting high, self-medicating my pain. Even if I had said something at the time, no one would have believed me. Besides, you weren't completely innocent in the whole ordeal. You deserved to suffer."

"I did suffer!" she yelled. "I suffered every single time your father put his hands on me. I was only thirteen, and—"

"Don't you dare trash my father!" Collins jumped to his feet. "He may not have been perfect, but he was a good man."

"Okay." Cate lifted her hands like a shield. "I won't talk about Mark."

"Great idea." Collins sat back down. He took another quick drink of his beer and then began peeling at the label. "The truth is that it took me going to prison and getting clean to remember everything about that night. It was only then that I decided to get revenge. I didn't initially know if I wanted to go after you or your mom."

"Well, you ultimately made a decision."

"I figured Georgia would rope you in somehow, and then you'd both get tangled up in my plan. 'Two birds one stone' sort of shit."

"It worked."

"Almost," he corrected her. "I don't have my money. I also don't understand something. Why did it take you so long to leave Arizona? I figured you two would have moved right away, not waited all of those years."

"That was all Georgia," Cate answered. "She wanted to stay put, keep up appearances. 'Only the guilty run,' she said."

"Well, look who's running now."

"Ironic, huh?"

"I will find your mom, Cate. I found her in Perry's Creek. I'll find her again. She's not great at disappearing. And, it doesn't matter if she changes her name, her car, or her appearance this time around. I swear, I'll find her."

"And then what will you do?"

Collins shrugged. "That depends on you. The longer she's out there, the more money she's spending. My money. And my associate has a short temper, Catie. If he doesn't collect a big payday, it's hard to predict how he'll react."

Cate thought for a second. She bit her lower lip. The pressure didn't sting. It felt nice, oddly comforting. She knew what she had to do. It's what she should have done a long time ago.

She had to be strong. She had to save herself.

"If I help you, Collins, then we're square. Okay?" she asked. "You won't threaten me, and you won't ask for more money. You'll forget I exist. If I hand my mom over to you, then I never want to hear from you again, and I never want to see you again. Do we have a deal?"

"Well, what makes you so sure you'll be able to find Georgia? Like you said, she's not answering her phone, so..."

"I don't need her to answer it," Cate interrupted. "I just need it to be on. I'm going to track it."

"Ah." Collins nodded. "Technology is grand."

"Do we have a deal, then?"

"We have a deal, sister. But, I do have one last question—a courtesy question, I guess. When I catch up to your mom, what do you want me to do with her?"

Cate hadn't expected Collins to ask that, but she didn't need any time to think about it. When she answered her stepbrother, she didn't blink. Her expression was completely flat.

"You'll be face to face with the woman who murdered your father. You do what you think is fair."

He knew he shouldn't have been there, that it was a mistake, but he'd come this far, and now he needed to follow through with his plan. So, he raised his right fist, gently tapped on the door, and waited.

Seconds later, the door swung open.

"What are you doing here, Matt?"

"Hi, Cate."

"Joshua isn't home. He's at work. Actually, I'm surprised you're not down at the police department with him. Is everything okay?"

He nodded. "Yeah, everything's great. I came to see you. I know I should have called first, but…" He stopped. Matt frowned. "Have you been crying, Cate?"

"Oh." Her hand shot up to graze her cheek. "It's been a long day."

"I'm sorry to hear that."

She shrugged. "It's fine. I'll be fine. What did you need?"

"Can I come in? It's kind of hot out here. I'm starting to sweat."

"Sure." Cate opened the door wider. "Can I get you something to drink?"

"No, thank you." Matt entered the house. "I just want to talk."

"Okay, then, let's talk."

Matt followed Cate into the front living room and took a seat beside her on the couch. He leaned back into the soft cushion and crossed his right leg over his left. Although his body language suggested otherwise, Matt wasn't comfortable. A deep tension surrounded him. His throat was suddenly dry. He wasn't sure he was going to be able to get the words out.

"So, why aren't you at work?" Cate asked. "Hell of a time to take a day off."

"Right." Matt nodded. "I-I-I guess I'm trying to figure that out."

Cate frowned. "What does that mean?"

"Some stuff is going on at the department, and, honestly, I don't know if I'm going back."

"You're not going back?" Cate crossed her arms. "What are you talking about? You don't want to be a deputy anymore?"

"I don't know what I want." Matt's voice deepened. "Yesterday, I was questioning my career choice, and then Sheriff Sutton and his friend basically accused me of strangling those three women…"

"They think you're the killer?"

"I don't know. I guess. Well, that ex-detective more so than the sheriff. Sutton apologized, but still. It all kind of got me thinking: What *am* I doing?"

"I don't understand. How can they think you're the killer?"

"I'm connected to all of the victims." He briefly explained how he was loosely tied to Stephanie Karr, Shelly Marthers, and Tara Burns.

"Well, that doesn't mean anything," Cate said. "And, I'm sure it will all blow over soon enough. Besides, don't you have an alibi for those nights?"

"My alibi is Kathy, but she's not talking to me. We broke up, and now she's ignoring me. She even changed her number."

"You and Kathy broke up?"

"Yes." Matt stared at Cate. "She thinks I'm in love with you."

Silence immediately filled the room. The atmosphere between them grew rigid. Cate's eyes went down to the floor. Matt shifted his body. He looked out the large window behind him.

The yard needed to be watered. That was the first thing he noticed. The heat hadn't destroyed it completely, not yet, but it had left its mark in the form of dry, brown patches.

"You know, Matt," Cate said, standing, "I should get dinner started. I'm going to make Joshua's favorite…"

"I owe you an apology, Cate. A couple of them."

"We don't have to do this, Matt. Not now."

"If not now, then when?"

Cate sat back down on the charcoal couch, but she didn't say anything.

"I'm not sure where to begin." Matt spoke truthfully. There was so much he wanted to say to Cate, and so much he needed to say. But, how? How could he possibly put into words everything that had happened recently? Everything he felt?

"You don't owe me anything, Matt. I'm the one who should apologize. This is all my fault. I should have never gotten you involved in my marital problems. And then, to come between you and…"

"The first time you told me about O.J.'s abuse, the first time I saw it firsthand, I should have done something about it."

"No, Matt—"

"Please, let me finish." Matt reached for her hand. He held it limply. "I didn't want to believe O.J. was capable of something so terrible. So…even after I saw the bruises, I still didn't want to accept the fact that my best friend, my *oldest* friend, could be abusing his wife."

"Don't beat yourself up, Matt. It was never your job to save me. I need to save myself."

"But, I could have helped you," he argued. "I could have been there for you." He squeezed her hand. She was crying. "I want to be here for you, Cate. I want to be here for you now, from this point forward."

"It means a lot to hear you say that," she choked out, "but I'm fine."

"You're not, Cate. But you will be. I promise."

Her eyes narrowed, and she shook her head. "How can you promise something like that?"

"I don't know if O.J. is the killer. I don't know if he strangled all of those women. But, I know he has a temper. And, I know he's never going to hurt you again."

"Stop, Matt." She pulled away. "I already told you. You don't have to save me."

He nodded. "I know I don't, but I want to."

The silence returned, but just for a moment. Matt looked at Cate and smiled. She returned his gesture immediately. She took his hand again, her grasp tight. He couldn't help but notice how large her hands were, much larger than Kathy's. He used his left thumb to blot at her tears. He breathed in her wildflower scent. It was almost like he was seeing her for the first time: white T-shirt, jeans, no makeup, hair down. She was so beautifully plain, but what Matt found most attractive about her was how vulnerable she appeared to be.

"I'm sorry about Kathy," Cate whispered. "I know how much you wanted to make it work with her."

"I'm not sorry," Matt said. He edged closer to her. "The truth is, Kathy's right. I am in love with you, Cate." He lowered his face. He touched his lips to hers. He kissed her, and he didn't stop kissing her.

* * *

"I think you should stay at my house tonight. Pack a bag, enough things for a few days, and—"

"You're not serious, Matt." Cate's head rested on his bare chest, and she could feel his heart beating. The rhythm was a soft, even sound. "I can't just leave Joshua like that. He'll come looking for me, and do you know what he'll do if he finds me with you?"

"I don't care, Cate," Matt stated. "I don't want you to be alone with him. Not anymore."

"You don't have anything to worry about, Matt," Cate lied. "I can take care of Joshua. You should go to the pub, maybe see if they're having a poker night or something. Try and have some fun."

"I don't care about a damn poker night, Cate. I want to be with you."

"Well, we've got to think about this. Do what's smart here." She pulled the sheet up to cover her naked body. It was different, sharing her bed with someone she truly liked, someone she loved. Cate knew she could get used to the feeling.

"I'm not going to let him hurt you again."

"He won't," Cate said. "But, I need to make sure Joshua—"

"What? Has another opportunity to beat you? Or worse?"

"No, Matt, of course not."

"I love you, Cate. Now that I have you, I'm not letting you go. Please, let me save you."

"I love you, too, Matt." Cate had thought about the words many times before, but this was the first time she'd spoken them out loud. And, as soon as she'd whispered them, it was as if her life had started all over again. *Finally.*

She closed her eyes, and then said the words again, "I love you, Matt."

ife was all about surviving disappointment. He'd found that out the hard way.

He first discovered the fact to be true when he was a teenager and his parents had abandoned him. They'd packed a bag for him, given him a few bucks, and warned him not to come home ever again. They just couldn't stand to support his lifestyle. He was dead to them.

Then, there'd been the fallout at work, followed by the demise of his career. His superiors could have spun it however they wanted to, and they had. It was all about whatever looked best on paper, and, while he'd seen and heard the words "early retirement" at least a hundred times throughout the whole ordeal, Beau would always know the truth: He hadn't wanted to give up the badge. He'd been forced to.

Now, there was Shannon, probably the biggest disappointment he'd yet to meet in his life. His friend had given him false hope, and, on some level, that was so much worse than cold, blunt honesty. It was downright cruel.

Thankfully, with all of life's disappointments, there was one thing that never seemed to let him down: the bottle. The brown liquid splashed around as he lifted the whiskey bottle and took a long gulp.

The alcohol burned as it coursed down his throat, and, as it made its way into his gut, Beau only wanted more. So, he tilted the bottle back and took another drink. He'd worry about packing his suitcase tomorrow morning. Tonight, he had another agenda…getting sloshed.

Beau fell back onto the stiff bed, careful not to drop the bottle. He couldn't afford to waste any alcohol. He was already running low, and he was currently in no position to drive anywhere for a fresh supply.

When he'd agreed to come to Perry's Creek, he'd had high hopes. Realistic hopes, sure, but high ones, nonetheless. Now, instead of fulfilling those hopes, he'd be leaving town without seeing an arrest made in the case, and without having a best friend.

Wasn't that some shit?

Beau was sure that Matt was the killer. Handcuff him, lock him up, and throw away the key. Matt had done it. He'd strangled those three women and stolen an earring from each one, and even though Beau knew this, he also didn't give a rat's ass about it.

He'd tried. He'd more than done his part, and Matt would either slip up and be taken down eventually, or he'd just keep on killing and the world would continue to go round.

Beau only had enough room in him now to care about Shannon. He wanted to call his friend. He wanted to see him, but even with a whiskey-soaked brain, Beau knew that wouldn't be happening…ever again.

It seemed that some relationships were created just so they could end. He'd never expected that to happen between him and Shannon, but it had, and now it was time for Beau to move on. Or maybe start over.

But, the sharp pain that stabbed his gut warned him that the chances of that happening were non-existent.

At the moment, Beau didn't know what was worse: being flat-out rejected or learning that his friend of so many years had no backbone. Beau had always known that Shannon seemed to migrate toward the weaker side, and Beau had never had a problem with it. After all, the man had plenty of other great qualities. However, recent events proved that this went so much deeper than being weak or strong. Shannon was a complete coward. In life, in love, and, in the simple task of just being honest, Shannon Sutton was afraid.

Beau knew what it was like to be afraid. He'd spent most of his life too afraid to even look in the damned mirror, terrified of the stranger that was bound to stare back at him. He was well aware of what living in such fear got you: alone.

One of these days, Shannon would find that out. He'd wake up and realize he was all alone. Even with Diane lying next to him, he'd be alone. Probably even more alone, because Shannon might have a wife, but he'd never have a true confidante. Not with the smokescreen he insisted on putting up throughout his life.

Beau couldn't bear to think about Shannon anymore. It made his head pound. He'd done all he could do. He'd tried. He'd been honest. He'd told the truth and had expressed his real feelings. Well, look where that had gotten him. He'd still wound up alone.

Just another one of life's sick jokes, Beau thought. Because you couldn't curl up at night with honesty, and you couldn't take the truth out to dinner.

So, maybe Shannon had been right all along. Maybe compromising your real self wasn't such a bad thing. After all, Shannon was most likely lying next to a warm body right now, perhaps even cuddling, or whispering plans to her for Sunday brunch, while Beau was in a cheap motel room in a strange town, watching the ceiling spin and getting to second base with an almost empty bottle of whiskey.

Beau stood up, staggered, and the room danced around him. The bed, the dresser, the TV, his open suitcase, everything in sight kind of seeped together and became one big, long, misshapen object. He didn't know where one item ended and the other began. He couldn't even see color. The bedspread, the carpet and everything in the space around him had faded into a dark hue of gray.

His eyelids felt heavy, and it was a struggle to keep them open. It was almost as if he was trying to lift two buckets of water with just the tips of his fingers. He knew the smart thing would be to sit back down, but he remained standing.

Beau didn't need to see his reflection to know how he looked. At this sad point, it was always the same: dress shirt wrinkled and rolled up at the sleeves, tie hanging around his neck loosely and dangling down like the last tiny bit of his pride, messy hair, and the touch of a five o'clock shadow creeping in.

And, if his appearance was bad, his smell was ten times worse. The stench of warm, sour booze surrounded him. Not even a shower was going to help mask the stale odor. He'd have to bide his time and sweat it out.

He turned. There was a wall in front of him. He didn't think, just acted. In one motion, he lifted the bottle and launched it at the wall. The glass shattered on impact. The brown liquid dripped down the wall, staining it.

No more self-pity. He'd given himself enough time—*too much* time—to reflect and regret and regurgitate the past. It was impossible to drown your sorrows. They always seemed to float right back to the surface—and with a vengeance.

It hit him suddenly. He'd tried the pathetic "woe is me" lifestyle. It didn't work. It was exhausting. Beau was ready to try something new,

221

something different. Something positive. He realized then that he wanted to live. He wanted to survive. And so, he would.

He would pick up the pieces of his broken life, and he'd start by cleaning up the mess on the wall.

Beau took a small step forward, swaying slightly. He tried to keep his balance, but his foot became tangled in the thick end of the bedspread. He began to go down. On instinct, he thrust his hands out. He wanted to catch himself. Beau reached for his suitcase on the chair. The bag spilled open. He fell to the floor, his personal items joining him. That's when he heard it...the gunshot.

He immediately jumped to his feet. The alcohol-infused haze around him lifted, but an annoying ringing sound exploded in his ears. He did a quick body check: front, back, side. He wasn't hit. He was fine.

So, where in hell had the shot come from?

He bent down and examined his pile of clothes and other belongings on the floor. There, right in the middle of socks, underwear, and a pair of tennis shoes, was his gun. Safety off, like usual, it had been fired recently.

"Jesus, Beau!" He ran his fingers through his hair, but that didn't stop them from shaking.

A bad habit—just one of many on his long list—could have gotten him killed. He kicked the gun under the bed.

Beau closed his eyes. He took a deep breath. Yes, he wanted to live. He wanted to survive, and he knew that was only possible with change.

He walked to the small bathroom, splashed some cold water on his face, and, without hesitation, looked up and stared at himself in the square mirror. It would take a while, he knew, but, eventually, he would like what he saw.

Outside, Beau inhaled the fresh air. The summer heat had retired for the evening, and in its place was a light breeze that offered a much-needed change of pace. Standing on the walkway balcony with his head craned back far enough, Beau could even see stars scattered across the big, dark sky.

Change was definitely coming.

"She's close, Collins, and that means our money is close!"

"Keep your fucking voice down. The police are still looking for me. I got lucky once today, leaving our fleabag motel room. I don't need you ruining that by flapping your big gums."

"Sorry, but I'm excited."

Beau tilted his head to the left. He'd heard it all, every single word. Two men were heading his way, illuminated by the dirty yellow light from the motel's front marquee.

One of them was Collins.

Beau waited until the two men passed him. Then, he reached out, grabbed the one closest to him by the shoulder, and spun him around.

"What the fuck?"

"You're a hard man to track down, Collins." Beau tried to hold him in place, but he wouldn't stop moving.

"Who the hell are you? Get off of me!" Collins pushed.

Beau knew he didn't have many options. Two against one, he'd gone about this all wrong. He should have waited until the two men had entered their room. He should have grabbed his gun from under his bed. He should have called Sheriff Sutton.

There was no time for any of that now. Beau had made his decision, and he had to roll with it.

"Did you strangle those girls, Collins?" Beau tried to get a better grip on him. He wouldn't stay still.

"Get the fuck off of me!" Collins pushed. "Help me, Richie!"

Beau lifted his fist. He shoved it forward. It connected with the center of Collins's face. There was a loud *crack!*

"Motherfucker!"

Beau looked at Collins. Blood covered his face, but even through the thick curtain of scarlet and snot, Beau could see the man's dark eyes. They were filled with rage.

Beau raised his fist again. Collins's friend charged forward. Beau knocked him in the gut and he went down. Just for good measure, Beau drew his right leg back and gave the man a kick. He was pretty sure his foot hit his ribs. The man on the ground didn't move.

Then, once again, it was a fair fight: one on one.

"You're coming with me," Beau ordered.

"You're crazy! I'm not going anywhere, old man!" Collins took a step forward.

"This doesn't have to be difficult, Collins. I don't think you killed anyone, but—"

"You broke my fucking nose. We're way past this being difficult." Collins pounced.

Beau tried to plant his feet, but his left ankle rolled. A sharp pain shot up his entire leg. He lifted his hands to try and block Collins's blow. The motion was useless. The man dodged Beau's makeshift shield. They were now just inches apart.

Collins stretched his arms out. Beau knew what was coming next, but he was unsure how to stop it.

Both of Collins's hands pressed into the center of Beau's chest. The man pushed. The thrust was quick and powerful. Beau fell backward. He lost his balance. Before he could right himself, Collins was there, pushing again.

That's all it took.

One more push and Beau flipped over the short, rusty railing and fell all the way down.

"You have nothing to worry about, Mom. You're going to make yourself sick."

"I just want to know that you're safe, sweetie. I've seen pictures of the other girls, and you fit the type."

"Oh, please. There are hundreds of blonde-haired, blue-eyed girls in Perry's Creek. The killer isn't going to come after me."

"I bet that's what all the other girls said, too. You know, right before they were strangled in their own homes."

Chrissy sighed as she made her way up the walk to her apartment complex. Her mother was relentless, and it was probably going to be next to impossible to get her off the phone. She appreciated the sentiment, and she respected the worry, but she was also annoyed by the inconvenience of it all.

She was tired and hungry. She wanted to enjoy what was left of her Saturday night by eating whatever junk food she could scrounge up in her kitchen while sitting in front of the TV.

"You should come back home, stay with us for a few days. Or until—"

"Please, Mom," Chrissy begged. "There's a reason I moved out on my own. I like being alone. And, I'm almost twenty-six years old. I can take care of myself."

"Oh, okay. Then you don't need help paying next month's rent?"

"Wait! I didn't say that," Chrissy argued. "I meant...what are you even doing up? It's late." When in doubt, a change of topic was always best. Chrissy happened to be skilled in all things including avoiding her mother's lectures.

"I could ask you the same question."

"I went out with some friends after work. No biggie. And you?"

"Well, I can't sleep. And, I'm not going to be able to until—"

"Okay, okay," Chrissy said. "I have an idea. I'll keep you on the line and check out the apartment room by room. I'll make sure no one else is in here before I hang up. How does that sound?"

"It's not exactly what I had in mind when I called, but I guess it will do."

"Good. Now, hold on a sec. I have to get my key out of my purse."

"You lock your door? I'm impressed already."

"Of course I lock my door. There's a killer on the loose who strangles blondes with blue eyes. I don't want to be next."

"Is it necessary to torture your mother?"

"When she makes it so much fun, yes." Chrissy held her cell up to her ear with her shoulder. She dug around in her leather purse for a few moments, and then her hand emerged with the gold key. "Okay, I'm unlocking the door. I'm opening the door. I hope no one is waiting for me on the other side."

"Stop it, Chrissy! That's not funny!"

"Fine." Chrissy frowned. "Let's search the apartment."

It didn't take long. There were only so many places for a psychopath to hide in a five-hundred-square-foot studio apartment.

Chrissy didn't find anyone crouching behind the white refrigerator in the kitchen. No one was slouched underneath her wooden desk, and her small, beach-themed bathroom proved to be empty, too.

There was just one place left to look: underneath the bed.

She knelt, her bare knees hitting the hardwood floor. When this was all said and done, and her mother was satisfied, Chrissy was going to take two minutes and sweep. A young girl living in her own apartment was exciting, even empowering, but a young girl whose apartment was decorated with dust bunnies and what seemed to be pizza crust crumbs was just sad. Probably even pathetic.

Chrissy held her phone with her left hand and used her right to lift the light purple bed skirt. She pressed her face closer to the dark opening.

"Oh, my God!" she screamed.

"Chrissy? Are you there? What happened? Are you okay?"

Chrissy started laughing. She got back on her feet. "I'm fine, Mom. Calm down."

"Seriously, Chrissy? What the hell?"

"It was a joke," she stated. "You scare so easily." She kicked off her flip-flops.

"Do you want to give me a heart attack?"

She shrugged. "Not today."

"You're a brat. I'm going to bed. Deadbolt your door and call me first thing in the morning."

"Will do, Mom. Love you."

"Love you, too, sweetie."

Chrissy tossed her cell phone onto the cheap coffee table. It landed beside her purse and apartment key.

She turned and faced the door, reaching for the deadbolt. The soft knock stopped her.

Chrissy's stomach tightened immediately. It was past midnight. A late-night visitor didn't make sense.

"Hello?" she called out. "Who's there?"

No answer.

Sweat started dripping down the small of her back. Her gray T-shirt instantly felt damp.

Another knock.

Chrissy took a step toward the door.

"H-h-hello?"

Nothing. Just silence.

She pushed her body up against the door and peered out the tiny peephole. Her body relaxed, her shoulders dropped, and she exhaled. Chrissy swung the door open.

"Hi," she said. "You scared me."

"Didn't mean to do that."

"Don't worry about it." Chrissy waved off the apology. "Come on in." She opened the door wider and then closed it behind her guest. "What are you doing here?"

"I came to see you."

Chrissy looked down. For the first time, she noticed the other person was wearing plastic gloves. Her body stiffened and she couldn't move.

The clear plastic gloves reached for her neck. And then, the soft voice filled her ears. The last thing Chrissy heard was, "I'm so sorry."

34

She didn't have time for a flat tire. She was already way behind schedule. She regretted stopping for that cup of coffee, but she'd needed something to help keep her awake.

Well, she was fully awake now, just barely out of California, and stranded.

Georgia wasn't sure what she should do. She could call for help. Her Auto Club card was somewhere in her purse. Or, she could wait it out and hope that there was at least one person left on this planet with enough decency to stop and assist an older woman who was all alone and down on her luck.

Georgia was capable of a lot of things, like suffocating her abusive husband, making it look like a bad accident, and letting her daughter take the blame and carry the guilt. However, one skill she didn't have was the knowledge of how to change a flat tire.

Damn her luck right to hell!

Some would believe this was a basic example of karma. Georgia had manipulated her only daughter, basically robbed her, and then left her to deal with the consequences and whatever punishment Joshua had planned for her. As a result, she was stuck on the side of some dark, cold, unknown road to think about what she'd done, to learn her lesson.

Well, Georgia didn't believe in karma. Bad things happened, and good things happened. It was called life—and she was more than ready to move on with hers.

She opened the driver's side door and stepped out of the vehicle. The air had gotten much colder. She pulled the zipper of her jacket up to her neck. The light coat didn't provide much warmth, but it helped a little bit. She was glad she'd thrown it on, having decided at the last minute to pair it with her jeans and short boots.

Georgia would wait for help. She wasn't sure what deep lengths her daughter, or maybe even Collins, would go to try and track her down, but she didn't want to take any risks, and she didn't want to make anyone's job easier by leaving a trail.

So, no Auto Club. Someone would come. She'd just have to wait.

What bothered her most about waiting was that it led to thinking. The last thing Georgia wanted to do was think…especially about Cate.

Sure, she felt bad for what she'd done to her daughter. She wasn't completely heartless. Still, Georgia had been looking for a way out of Perry's Creek for quite a while, and she'd found it when the blackmail notes had started coming in.

Georgia may not have believed in karma, but she did believe in fate. It was fate that had educated her to the fact that her daughter had access to twenty-five thousand dollars on the same day she'd received the first threat.

She hadn't known then how everything was going to come together, just that it would, and she'd been right. She had an envelope full of cash and was ready for a new start.

Well, once she got her tire changed.

In the beginning, she'd gone back and forth with Cate, wondering if Collins really was the one behind the messages. Once they'd figured out it was, in fact, her stepson who was responsible, she'd grown a little worried. After all, she had no idea how much Collins knew about that night, and not knowing led to trouble.

Although she still didn't know if Collins was aware of the truth, it no longer mattered. Cate didn't know. She thought she had killed Mark and had felt guilty enough to pony up twenty grand, only ten of which had been demanded by Collins.

Georgia knew she'd pretty much ruined Cate's life the night she'd let her take the blame for Mark's death, but that had been the sacrifice that she was willing to make. He deserved to die, and when Georgia noticed he was still breathing, well, she'd made the rash decision to suffocate him. Just like that, all of her problems had seemed to have vanished.

Of course, she hadn't known that she'd had an audience that night, or that Collins would later resurface in her life. Then again, it had all worked out.

Fate.

The bottom line was that Cate couldn't be saved. As soon as Georgia recognized that, she knew it was time to let her go.

Cate had managed to find yet *another* abusive relationship and wasn't even trying to get out of it. Some people just refused to save themselves, and it was people like that, people like Cate, who didn't deserve to be saved by someone else.

So, Georgia had gotten away with murder, and now had more than enough money for a new life. How was that for karma?

Two dull headlights cut through the black night. A car was coming her way. She took a step toward the road and waved her hands. Just as she'd expected, someone was going to help her.

Bad things happened. Good things happened. Life.

The Honda came to a stop behind her car. Georgia started walking toward it. The passenger side door opened first. There was no interior light, and she only saw darkness. Georgia stood a couple of feet in front of the hood. She waited.

"Having some trouble?"

"Yes," she answered, "flat tire. Can you help me?"

"Sure," the voice stated. "That's an easy fix."

She moved toward the stranger standing by the passenger side of the car, and that's when she heard the driver's side door open and the driver got out. She glanced over her shoulder. He stepped closer to her and into the low glow of the headlights.

Georgia recognized him immediately from the paper, of course, but also because his features hadn't changed that much, even after all these years. He was harder looking, sure. He had more rough edges and lines on his forehead and cheeks than she'd remembered, but he still appeared pretty much the same. Only, now, he was almost the spitting image of his father.

"Hi, Mother."

Georgia froze. The stranger was in front of her. Collins was behind her. She didn't know what to do. She didn't know where to go. She was trapped.

"You don't look too happy to see me," Collins said. "And, after I came all this way to see you. I even went through the hassle of tracking you down after you tried to run away from me."

"H-h-how?"

"Your cell phone. Pretty nifty, huh? Obviously, I had Cate's help. Kind of convenient that she set up your phone and knows all of your passwords."

Georgia shook her head. "You're lying. Cate wouldn't betray me like that."

"Oh, she would, and she did," Collins argued. "You see, Catie and I had a little family reunion. She knows all about what happened that night. The truth."

"It was an accident. Mark fell and—"

"Don't embarrass yourself, Georgia. We all know what type of person you are."

"So, what now?" She shrugged. Her eyes bounced from Collins to the other man. "You came here to get your revenge? To kill me?"

"I'm not sure. I haven't decided yet. But, for starters, I want my money."

"That's Cate's money."

"Oh, I'm aware of whose money it is," Collins fired back. "And, by the way, Cate's aware that you greased her for an extra ten grand. You're really a natural at this parenting stuff."

"Screw you!"

"You know, Richie and I have already had a pretty rough night. If you could can all of the unnecessary drama, that'd be great."

"Take the money," Georgia ordered. "It's all there, twenty grand. It's in the envelope under the driver's seat. It's yours. Just don't hurt me."

"Do you think you hurt my father when you suffocated him?"

"Collins..."

"When you placed your hands over his mouth and nose and *physically* prevented him from breathing, do you think he felt much pain?"

"I'm sorry, Collins," Georgia tried. "Please..."

"Okay," Collins interrupted. "I promise that I won't hurt you."

"T-t-thank you," she stuttered.

"I'll try to make it fast. As pain-free as possible." He took a step toward her.

"No!"

She ran away from them. Both men were closing in on her. She shifted her body and started around the passenger side of her car. If she could just get in and lock the doors, maybe she could make it a few miles up the road with the flat tire.

However, Georgia went down suddenly. One of them had pushed her. She fell. Her body hit the hard, angry ground. She thought she heard something *snap*. Tears burned the corners of her eyes. Collins rolled her over. Flat on her back, Georgia knew this was it. She was going to die. It was all over.

He got on top of her. His full weight crushed her, and she could barely breathe. Georgia coughed and instantly tasted the thick, dry dirt.

"I should have done this a long time ago," Collins said. He lifted his hands.

"No! Please!" she begged.

Both of his bare, sweaty hands covered her nose and mouth. The heavy smell of gasoline made her want to gag, but she knew that if she puked, she'd choke on it. She managed to control her urge.

Georgia looked up at Collins. Even with what appeared to be a bloody, broken nose and dark circles under his eyes, he was a replica of Mark.

Then it dawned on Georgia: Collins wasn't suffocating her; her husband was, just like she'd done to him fourteen years ago.

Was this karma? Or fate?

Georgia would never know.

* * *

"Come on, Richie. We have to hurry!"

"I *am* hurrying!"

"We have to get out of here before another car comes," Collins ordered. "Did you get the money?"

"I got it," Richie answered. "All twenty thousand dollars of it."

"Good. Now we should…" Collins stopped and frowned.

Richie was leaning up against the backside of Georgia's car. He held a large envelope in one hand, and, in his other, a gun. It was pointed at Collins.

"What the fuck are you doing?"

"Twenty grand is a lot of money," Richie said. "In fact, it kind of makes me feel rich." He pulled the trigger. The *bang* echoed in the crisp air.

The bullet ripped into Collins's chest. He hit the cold earth and rolled onto his side. He could feel the warm, sticky blood pooling around him already. A metallic stench filled his nostrils.

He looked up, and his vision started to blur. The last thing he saw was his dead stepmother's gaze staring back at him.

35

"**A**re you okay, Sheriff Sutton?"

Shannon hated that question for many reasons, but mostly because Deputy Benson already knew the answer to it, and, if he didn't, then he was a complete fool.

How the hell could he possibly be okay?

First, there'd been another murder. A fourth girl had been strangled and her left earring stolen. No fingerprints, no evidence, and no clue as to who the real fucking killer was. Or, more importantly, why someone had chosen to off a handful of blonde-haired, blue-eyed girls in Perry's Creek.

Collins still hadn't been located, which caused Shannon to have doubts that he was even the killer. Maybe the guy really had been in the wrong place at the wrong time and had since skipped town to avoid further trouble and harassment.

It made sense, finally, and Shannon questioned why he'd been so reluctant to fight the notion to begin with. Except, of course, he knew why. Deep down, he knew why he'd been so damned stubborn. He just didn't want to face that fact now.

Sure, having Mayor Jackson breathing down his neck hadn't softened the situation, but, still, Shannon knew that as the sheriff of Perry's Creek, he should have had more faith in himself.

And, more faith in Beau.

He should have trusted his friend. He should have listened to him. Shannon figured that was one of the main reasons he'd decided to check up on Matt: out of respect for Beau.

However, according to half a dozen people, Deputy Matt Combs wasn't the killer, either. He'd been at the pub, drinking draft beer and playing poker till just after 2:00 a.m., the same time someone had wrapped their hands around Chrissy Miller's neck and squeezed the life out of her.

In the past forty-eight hours, the investigation—not to mention, the sheriff's life—had been turned upside down, and Shannon couldn't help but figure that if Beau were here now, he'd...

Stop! the sheriff's mind demanded. Finishing the thought was too damned painful.

"Would you give me a couple of minutes, Deputy Benson?"

"Sure, Sheriff, no problem." The deputy stood. "Is everything okay?"

That damned question again. "Everything is fine, Deputy. I just need a minute alone. And, for God's sake, please stop asking me that!"

"Oh." Benson frowned. "Okay, I'm sorry. Is there anything I can get you while—?"

"Yes," Shannon interrupted. "Find out where Deputy Abbott is. He should have been here by now."

"You got it, sir." Deputy Benson left the office and shut the door behind him.

What was the Perry's Creek Police Department coming to? When had *his* deputies decided they could run the show?

Combs had taken time off right in the middle of a murder investigation to "find himself" and was wondering if he even wanted to be a police deputy anymore. Although Abbott hadn't been scheduled to come in today, when a serial killer strikes for the fourth time, Sunday Funday plans had a tendency to get tossed by the wayside. Only, now, the deputy was taking his sweet time in reporting for duty.

Then there was Deputy Benson, who didn't know his own asshole from a hole in the ground.

Shannon's life legacy was starting to resemble a bad comic strip.

If only Beau hadn't...

"Dammit!" the sheriff muttered. He hadn't cried, not yet, but it was only a matter of time before he did. When that happened, Shannon predicted there'd be no way to stop the flood.

Suicide attempt.

Just holding the words in his mouth evoked the taste of vinegar. It didn't add up. Only, it added up perfectly, and Shannon was fighting with every bone in his body to not give in and accept that reality.

He wasn't sure if he was rebutting the facts because he didn't want to believe his friend was cowardly enough to take the easy way out, or if he didn't want to personally accept the blame for Beau having a reason to take his own life.

The facts were as simple to follow as a grade school math equation.

Fact: Beau had gotten his heart broken yesterday.

Fact: Beau had drunk almost a fifth of whiskey before smashing the glass bottle against a wall in his motel room.

Fact: Beau had fired his weapon, most likely in an attempt to shoot himself, but had backed out at the last minute.

Fact: Beau had jumped off the second-floor balcony of the Scott's Inn motel—again, most likely in an attempt to kill himself. But, thankfully, his attempt hadn't been successful.

Fact: Beau was alive—for now, anyway. Or, at least until Shannon could get to him.

Because as soon as Beau got out of surgery, Shannon was going to kick the man's ass. Until then, though, he had a murder investigation to solve and a wife to admit the cold, hard truth to, finally. At the moment, Shannon wasn't sure which task was more terrifying.

It was interesting how death, or even the idea of death, could change a person. Or maybe it wasn't interesting at all. Maybe it was just plain sad that it took losing someone or something for a person to open their eyes.

Shannon shrugged and leaned back into his chair. He didn't have all of the answers, but he was somehow all right with that. Because his eyes *had* been pried open, and now he would get a second chance at life, a true life. And, hopefully, love, too.

That would all come later, though. Much later. Right now, he needed to focus and keep his mind on the case. If Shannon wanted to prove his worth and save even a sliver of his reputation as a sheriff—a *good* sheriff—then he'd have to work hard, and that's exactly what he planned to do.

He took a deep breath and then exhaled slowly. The relaxation technique didn't calm him. Shannon still felt on edge. He contemplated more coffee, but how was another jolt of caffeine going to help him make an arrest, or, at the very least, point him in the right direction?

All four victims flashed before his eyes, and then the suspects:

Jed.

Collins.

Matt.

Who was the damned killer?

36

"Didn't you get called into work, Joshua?"

"I did," he said. "But, before I go, there's something I need to ask you."

Cate felt a cold sweat break out over her entire body. It started at the small of her back and then shot up and down her spine. She didn't know where Joshua's question was going to lead, and that made her catch her breath.

She had a guess, though. Cate figured this was it.

"Can't it wait?" she tried. "I don't want you to get in trouble with—"

"It will only take a minute," Joshua interrupted.

"Sure, okay. What's on your mind?"

"Well," he started, "did you really think you could steal twenty thousand dollars from me and get away with it?"

If Cate had been holding something, she was positive she would have dropped it. For a moment, she became dizzy. She thought she might fall. She grabbed for the kitchen counter in front of her to keep her balance.

"You're either really stupid, Cate, or you think I am. And, quite honestly, I don't think there's room for that much stupid in our marriage."

"I can explain, Joshua. I just…"

"Can you, Cate? Do you have an explanation for why you lied to me, betrayed me, *stole* from me? Because I'm dying to hear it."

Joshua stood by the dining room table. He was as still as a statue. His blue uniform was pressed perfectly, and it hugged his body in all of the right places. His dark hair was swept back, and he'd even taken the time to shave this morning. As a result, Joshua's face was completely smooth. He didn't have one unwelcomed nick hiding anywhere.

Her husband stood so tall, so proud. Once again, he was ready to save the day. Or maybe ruin hers.

Cate didn't have many moves to choose from…except fight. There was a counter between them, but Joshua was quick and steady. He could be on her in seconds.

She scanned the white kitchen sink for a rogue knife or fork, any sort of weapon that could help protect her from him. Then Cate remembered that she'd loaded the dishwasher last night before going to bed. The sink and its surrounding area were both empty.

Cate glanced down at herself. Not exactly dressed for battle, her bare feet, black sweats, and plain T-shirt would just have to do. At least she'd had the good sense to brush her hair back into a ponytail when she'd gotten out of bed this morning. It wouldn't be in her face, but Joshua could attempt to pull it and yank her down to the floor. He knew she hated that the most.

"That's what I thought, Catie. You're silent, fresh out of excuses."

"No, you don't understand, Joshua. I—"

"Are you planning on leaving me, Cate? Is that why you took my money? You want a new start, a new life? Maybe even a new husband? Is that it?"

"No," she choked out. "Not at all." Cate felt the tears form. She didn't know if they were there out of fear or anger. Perhaps both. Still, when he took a step toward her, she wanted to scream.

"And here, I thought you loved me, Catie," he taunted. "I mean, you made my favorite dinner last night, and…"

"I do love you," she lied.

"But, I guess it was all just a ruse to throw me off, huh? You figured if my belly was full, then I wouldn't notice you sneaking behind my back." He took another step.

Cate wasn't ready. Her head bobbed from side to side. She needed something, anything that would allow her to dodge around Joshua and get upstairs.

"Well, your little plan didn't work, honey. Clearly." One more step. He'd almost reached the kitchen tile. "I ran into Eric this morning on my run. You know Eric, right? The manager down at the bank? He asked me what we were doing with all of that cash. If we were planning on leaving Perry's Creek, making a lavish purchase of some kind, or maybe involved in any illegal activity."

"I took the money, but only because—"

"I played along, of course." He entered the kitchen. "I didn't want him to think I had a reason to be mad at you." Joshua shook his head. "No witnesses. You know how much I hate people around town to know my business."

"Please, Joshua," she begged. "D-d-don't hurt me."

"I told him that you and I were going to do something extra special together." He shrugged. "I guess that's not a total lie. Depends on how you look at the situation. I mean, I think this is going to be special. I'm pretty excited about it."

"Stop, Joshua!" Cate exploded. She couldn't take it anymore. He was teasing her, and he was enjoying it.

Joshua was attempting to create a thick atmosphere of fear with every small step he took, and with his slow, drawn-out words, he was succeeding.

"Don't be like that, Catie." He frowned. "We're just talking, a simple conversation between husband and wife. Why are you getting so upset?"

"Look, I gave the money to my mom. It was an emergency. I'm sorry."

"Well, if it was an emergency," he mocked her, "then I guess it's okay. Besides, your mom is family, and that's what families do for one another, right? Families help each other out during times of need."

"You're scaring me, Joshua."

"You don't need to be scared of me, Cate. I'm your husband. I love you. 'Til death do us part, remember?"

"Y-y-yes."

"And, there's still five thousand dollars in our joint account. We're going to be just fine."

"Really?"

"Of course." A smile stretched across his face. It kept getting wider. "Now, give me a big hug, Catie."

"But..."

"Oh, come on. Give your husband a hug before he goes off to work. Please?"

"Sure." She tried to swallow, but her throat was too dry. Cate opened her arms. They trembled.

"Good girl." His pose matched hers. With his arms outstretched, Joshua took a step forward. Right before he grabbed her, his smile faded. His eyes got darker, almost black. The rest of his face went blank.

Her body stiffened. "Joshua?"

He had her. He wrapped his arms around her. He pressed his body flat against hers and tightened his hold. He was like a snake squeezing its prey.

"I warned you, Catie," he whispered. "There's no room in this marriage for stupid."

"You're hurting me, Joshua."

"Oh, I'm sorry. Here, I'll let you go." He swung her around and threw her across the kitchen.

She smashed into the refrigerator. Her forehead hit the handle of the door. She bounced off and fell to the floor.

"Honey, let me help you up." He grabbed her right arm and pulled her to her feet.

As soon as Cate was standing, she felt the blow of his backhand. She went down on the tile again.

"You're just a stupid little bitch, aren't you?" He kicked her. His boot met her gut.

She thought she was going to be sick. "Please, J-J-Joshua! Stop!"

"You're a whore, too! Getting knocked up before marriage, trapping me! Who the fuck do you think you are, Cate?" He extended his boot back and then shot it forward. It connected with her gut again.

"Ahhh!" Cate twisted and writhed on the cold floor. With each fresh strike, her entire body exploded with white-hot pain. Her hands shook uncontrollably. She used them to cover her face. They became a shield, blocking her view of Joshua. At least she didn't have to see her husband attacking her. She just had to feel it.

Blood dripped from the corner of her mouth and seeped into her palm. From where he'd backhanded her, she knew. That was the only upside to the kicking: Cate could hide a bruised abdomen a lot easier than a bruised face.

But, this time, she wasn't sure it would be much matter. Joshua now had a rage in him she'd never seen before. It was almost as if he was someone else, a different type of beast, unnerving and detached.

This beast didn't show signs of stopping. This beast was moving in for the kill.

"Um, Catie," Joshua said softly. "I have something else to ask you: Why the hell aren't you wearing your wedding ring?"

"R-r-ring?"

"What? Now you're hard of hearing?" He pulled her up to her feet again. He grabbed her left hand and pulled it toward him. "Your ring, Cate. Why did you take off your wedding ring?"

"I-I-I…"

"You *are* trying to leave me, aren't you?"

"No! I swear it!"

"The money…the ring," he spat out. "You really think you can leave me, Cate? Make a fool out of me?"

"No, I-I-I…"

"You're right," he said through clenched teeth. "You can't leave me. I'll kill you first."

For the first time, she caught a wave of his heavy musk scent; it was nauseating. Cate tried to break free, but he wouldn't let her. He still held onto her left hand. He began bending it back. He was going to break it. She swore she could almost hear the *snap*.

"Don't do this, Joshua!"

"It's too late. *You've* already done it, Catie."

She had to be strong.

She had to survive.

She had to save herself.

Cate wasn't sure what happened next, exactly. Her body was somehow filled with strength. She felt capable. She felt alive. She knew she could take care of herself. She didn't have a choice.

It was time to get out of her own head. It was time to stop thinking so damned much and just react. And, that's what she did.

Cate drew her foot back. In one swift motion, she brought it up. It connected with Joshua's groin.

"Ahhh!" He released his hold on her immediately. Joshua doubled over, and both of his hands went to his crotch.

Cate didn't waste a beat.

With everything she had left, she pushed him. Her hands pressed into his hard shoulders and she shoved. He flew backward. Joshua hit the lower cabinets and rolled into a ball on the tile floor.

Interesting, she thought. In the past five minutes, they'd changed places.

Cate spun around. She started running.

"Get back here! I'm going to kill you!"

She didn't have much time. Joshua didn't like to lose. He'd be back on his feet in seconds.

Cate ran through the hallway, past the front door, and bounded up the stairs. This was her plan, her way to survive. She had to get to the bedroom. Everything would come together if she could just keep moving. Keep moving. She had to keep moving…

Cate reached the landing. She darted into her room, the room she shared with her husband. She slammed the door and made sure it was locked. Then she rounded the queen-sized bed and immediately crossed to Joshua's side. His nightstand dresser, the spare gun: It became her vision. It filled her mind. Only after she'd wrapped her hands around the cool, metal weapon would she feel safe again, safe in her own home. Finally.

She gripped the brass handle of the dresser drawer and flung it open. Four earrings stared back at her. They weren't a set. They were lone, single pieces.

A round opal earring.

A diamond stud earring.

A gold hoop earring.

A long, leaf-shaped earring.

They weren't hers.

Cate scooped them up. She looked at them in the palm of her hand, and then she tossed them onto the soft comforter that covered the bed. She went back to the drawer. She grabbed for the gun.

Cate heard Joshua stomp up the stairs, and then, just like that, he was at the door. His first pounded against it. The whole door shook in its frame.

"Open the door, Cate!" he ordered. "Now!"

She didn't have a chance to respond. He pounded on the door again, and then he kicked it. He kept kicking it. The sound grew louder. This time, the floorboards shook. The edge of the door started to splinter.

This was it! He was coming in. He was coming for her!

Cate planted her feet shoulder-wide. She raised the gun. She was ready.

The door split open. Joshua stepped into the bedroom. A smirk spread across his face, but then his gaze went from the gun in her hand to the earrings on the bed. His smirk faded into a frown.

"Cate?"

"Don't move, Joshua!"

"What the hell is that?" He nodded toward the jewelry. "Is that…how did you…?" His words trailed off, and his eyes widened.

"It's like you've always said, Joshua: 'Til death do us part."

"Whatever you're thinking about doing, don't—"

"Fuck you!" Cate pulled the trigger. Nothing happened. She tried again. Still nothing.

Joshua's high-pitched laugh filled the room. He took a step toward her.

"I warned you about being stupid. Here's a little tip: The gun works better when the safety's off."

Cate looked down at the gun in her hands, then back up at Joshua. He was moving, and fast. Soon, he was just feet away from her.

Cate's fingers skated around the gun. She thought she'd found the safety. She released it. Cate tried the trigger once more. The *bang* exploded in the room.

Cate hit the trigger three more times. Each bullet tore into her husband's flesh: shoulder, neck, and then cheek. He fell to the floor. Eyes open, he didn't move.

She dropped the gun. She dug into the front pocket of her sweatpants and dragged out her cell phone. Cate punched in the number she'd memorized a long time ago. She waited.

After three rings, he answered finally. "Hello?"

"I need you, Matt. Now."

And then, she breathed.

37

She heard the front door open and then immediately snap shut. He was here.

"I'm upstairs, Matt."

It didn't take him long to appear in the smashed doorway. Sweat dripped from his forehead. His black hair looked damp, and his white T-shirt was stuck to his body like paste.

But, those blue eyes. His bright blue eyes burned into hers, and Cate somehow knew everything was going to be okay.

Her plan had worked out perfectly. It had always been about execution, and she was pretty sure she'd nailed it.

"Are you all right? What happened?"

"I'm fine," she mumbled.

Cate watched as Matt crossed the room. He stepped over her husband's lifeless body. Once he got to her, he grabbed her and then pulled her in close to his tight chest. He didn't let go, and she didn't want him to. She inhaled the hint of his deep sandalwood scent. Cate could have breathed him in forever.

He pulled back, but just long enough to bend down and kiss her. His soft lips touched hers, and, for a moment, Cate forgot where she was and what had just happened.

Then he was holding her again. His big arms were wrapped around her, briefly shielding her from the ugly outside world. It was just the two of them.

She was loved.

She was protected.

She was *saved*.

"What happened?" he repeated. "Tell me everything."

"It's like I told you on the phone," she spoke into his body, her voice muffled. "He attacked me. Joshua attacked me. He was the killer. And I-I-I shot him."

He pulled back again, but she was relieved he still kept a firm grasp on her hands. "Did you call 9-1-1? Sheriff Sutton?"

"No, not yet." She shook her head. "I was scared, and I didn't want to be alone. I only called you."

"Okay," he nodded. Then he frowned. He looked down.

"What's wrong?"

"I should have been here," he said. "I should have protected you. I told you yesterday that I'd never let O.J. hurt you again."

"Shh," Cate whispered. "Don't do that to yourself. I told you: I'm fine. Joshua didn't hurt me too badly."

"You're bleeding." His thumb grazed the side of her mouth. "What if you hadn't gotten the gun in time? O.J. could have…"

"But, he didn't. I lived, not him. That's all that matters now."

Matt nodded. "I guess you're right. So, how did this all go down? What set him off?"

She thought for a moment. Cate wanted to choose her words wisely. She let go of Matt's hands and took a seat on the bed. She exhaled slowly.

"Everything kind of happened so fast," she began. "I found the earrings in the drawer of Joshua's nightstand. As soon as I saw them, I knew. I knew what they were, and I knew what he was. I had proof.

"Then I just started screaming at him. I was so angry and scared. I confronted him. That's when he smacked me. We started fighting. He threatened to kill me."

"Is that when you got a hold of the gun?" Matt asked.

"Yes. I grabbed the gun, but he still charged me. And, I shot him. I couldn't stop shooting him." Cate didn't cry. She wouldn't cry over Joshua ever again.

Be strong.

Matt sat on the bed beside her. The mattress dipped down under his weight. He put his arm around her, and she leaned into him. He began rubbing her back up and down. The gentle friction calmed her.

As much as she wanted out of the room, and out of the house, Cate didn't feel like moving her body. Not yet. She still ached from Joshua's earlier blows.

She looked up at the wall in front of her. A framed photograph of her and Joshua stared back at her, almost taunting her. It was the only picture that hung on the otherwise bare, white walls. As much as Cate wanted to rip it down and break it in half, she didn't. She managed to contain herself because she knew that, ultimately, she'd won, and Joshua had lost.

Matt sighed. "So, when you saw the earrings, you knew O.J. was the killer?"

"Yes."

He stopped rubbing her back and folded his hands in his lap. "But, how could you have known that?"

"From the earrings," she answered. Her voice grew louder. "It's like I said: I found the earrings and…"

"But, the fact that the killer stole the victims' jewelry wasn't in the paper. That detail was never released to the public."

"Oh." Cate's eyes darted around the room. "I guess Joshua must have told me about it, then."

Matt stood up. His back was to her. "Except he didn't tell you about it."

"What?"

"O.J. and I discussed the earring angle of the case, Cate. A lot. And, he told me he never mentioned it to you. Actually, he'd made it a point not to tell you. O.J. didn't want to scare you."

Cate felt the pace of her heartbeat starting to pick up speed. She jumped up. "I-I-I don't know, then. Maybe I heard it from—"

Matt spun around. He faced her, finally. "Only the police and the killer knew about the earrings. And, you're not part of the Perry's Creek Police Department, Cate."

She thrust her hands onto her hips. "What are you implying exactly, Matt?"

"I think you know, Cate. Are you the killer? Did you strangle those four girls?"

"Matt! How can you even ask me that? After everything I've been through, do you really think I would…?"

"Don't lie to me, Cate. Not after yesterday, not after we made—"

"I love you, Matt, and you love me. Why are we even having this conversation? Joshua's dead. He got what he deserved. We can be together, finally."

"Oh, my God! It *is* you. You're the killer!" Tears filled his eyes.

"No!" Cate argued. "I-I-I...Matt!" She bit her lower lip. Her plan was veering off track. It wasn't supposed to go this way, and now she felt herself being backed into a tight, dark corner. She was stuck.

"Just admit it!"

"Fine!" she screamed. "I'm the killer, okay? I did it! I strangled all of those girls. I stole their earrings, and I set up Joshua to take the fall. Are you happy now?"

"Happy? I just found out that the girl I'm in love with is a cold-blooded killer. How in hell can I be happy?"

Cate threw her hands up. "What was I supposed to do, Matt? My husband was beating me. He would have killed me eventually. You certainly weren't going to do anything about it."

"Fuck you! No, Cate, you don't get to blame me for this!"

"I don't! I know that...I-I-I blame..." She shook her head. Her tears came, finally. "I didn't want to hurt those girls. I tried to—"

"Why?" Matt interrupted. His voice was hollow. "Why'd you do it?"

"You know why," she muttered. Cate couldn't look at Matt. Not yet. Instead, she stared down at the floor.

"Because you wanted out of your marriage?"

"It's so much more than that," she sobbed. "Let me paint you a picture of Orlin Joshua Abbott. The *real* Orlin Joshua Abbott.

"Joshua was a man who wined and dined me for two months. He made me fall in love with him. And then, he got me pregnant and forced me to marry him. He wanted to protect his name and his religious image. But, he always blamed me for that baby, for trapping him. In his twisted mind, he felt like it was me who had forced him into marriage.

"Then he started beating me on our honeymoon. Was it a power thing? A control thing? I'm not sure. I've asked myself those questions every single day for the past ten months. But, truthfully, I think he just hated me.

"He beat me so badly, I lost the baby."

"Cate..."

"No, Matt," she argued. "You wanted to hear this. You wanted to know how I was capable of murder."

"But..."

"So, I lost the baby," Cate continued. "Naturally, Joshua blamed me. But, we were already married. He wouldn't divorce me. He didn't believe in divorce. But, he sure as shit believed in abusing his wife.

"Joshua went on hitting me, controlling me, doing whatever he wanted to me. Until, one day, he decided he wanted a baby. Specifically, he wanted a baby boy to carry on the Abbott name. I guess he figured that since we were stuck together, we might as well be a family."

"Maybe a baby would have helped," Matt suggested. "Maybe..."

Cate rolled her eyes. "You can't be serious. I refused to have a baby with that man. I refused to bring a poor, defenseless child into our toxic relationship."

"So, then what? Instead, you decided to start killing for sport?"

"I couldn't go to the police and report Joshua's abuse because he *was* the police. And, I couldn't kill him in self-defense because there was no evidence that he'd been hurting me. No one would have believed that the great and powerful Orlin Joshua Abbott was a wife-beater. Hell, you didn't even believe me. Not at first."

"You still had other options, Cate. You didn't have to—"

"My hands were tied. Joshua was forcing me to have a baby with him, yet still hitting me whenever he felt the urge. I snapped. I needed a way out, so I created one."

"How? How did you sneak out of the house without O.J. knowing it?"

"The Ambien," she admitted. "It was never for me. I drugged Joshua so he would sleep. It worked out nicely, too. It cut back on the times I had to sleep with him.

"But, I had to somehow connect him to those girls. Those poor girls..." She sighed. "I chose blondes with blue eyes because of my own features. If you remember, I tried to sell you on the idea that Joshua was killing women who looked like me because he hated me."

"I remember," Matt mumbled.

"But, I needed more than that. I needed physical evidence. That's where the idea for the earrings came in. I figured if the killer took a trophy from each victim, and if Joshua was later found with those trophies, that..."

"Everyone would automatically assume he was the killer."

"Yes." Cate nodded.

"And, what about the first three victims, huh? They all had me in common. Did you plan that, too? Did you want me to be a suspect? Go down for—"

"No, Matt! Of course not!" Cate frowned. "I thought Joshua was the one who was connected to all of those girls. He was always bragging, taking credit for your work. I didn't know you were the one who was involved in all of their traffic violations until you told me. But, I tried to fix the mistake."

"What?" Matt's forehead creased. "What are you talking about?"

"The murder last night," she said. "I only killed that girl to clear your name."

"Oh, my God! That's why you were so persistent about me going out last night, letting off some steam. You wanted to make sure I had an alibi."

Cate nodded. "I wasn't lying, Matt. I do love you. I want to be with you."

He looked across the bed at her, and his eyes grew wider. "What?"

"Why not? Why can't Joshua be the fall guy just like I planned? He was a bad person, Matt. He…"

"That doesn't mean he deserved to die or take the blame for what you did. And, all of those girls! They didn't deserve to die, either."

"I know," she agreed. "And, I feel horrible about what I did. I'll have to live with the guilt every day for the rest of my life. But, with time—"

"Then, why did you do it? Why did you *keep* on doing it?"

"I-I-I don't know!" she cried. "I'm sorry. I'm so sorry for what I did. But, I kept telling myself to wait. I thought that if I waited just a little bit longer, maybe you would change, come around. I-I-I wanted someone to save me. But, no one ever did. Instead, I ended up saving myself."

"No, Cate," he argued. "You ruined yourself."

She nodded. "I've been ruined for a long time, more than fourteen years. You'd be surprised how damaged and messed up a person can truly be—and what they'll do to survive. What they'll do when they feel like they've been backed into a corner."

"You ruined us, Cate, our future, what we could have been."

"What does that mean? You're just going to turn me in? Act like you don't love me?"

"I can't act like I don't love you, Cate. Believe me, this is breaking my heart."

"We can be together!"

"No." He shook his head. "We can't. I have to turn you in. It's the only thing to do. It's the *right* thing to do."

"Love isn't always about doing what's right, Matt. We can figure this out. We just—"

"Stop!" he ordered. He reached into his pocket. "I'm calling Sheriff Sutton."

"No! You can't!" she demanded. "I'll do it."

"What?"

"I'll do it. I'll turn myself in. It's only fair. You shouldn't have to do it, Matt. I've hurt you enough."

Cate didn't give him a chance to argue. She had her cell phone out, and she scrolled through her contacts. She found the one she needed and hit Send.

Again, she waited.

"Hello?"

"Sheriff Sutton?" she asked through a heavy breath.

"Yes, this is Sheriff Sutton. Who's this?"

"This is Cate Abbott. I'm Joshua's wife. I'm at home, and I need you to get over here immediately."

"Is everything okay?"

"No! I w-w-was just attacked! Joshua and Matt did it together. They strangled all of those girls. They're *both* the killer!"

"What?"

"They attacked me," she repeated. "I shot them. They're dead. But, still, please hurry!" Cate ended the call. She dropped her phone.

"What the hell was that, Cate?"

She fell to the floor, her hands roaming the hardwood, and then she was back up on her feet again.

His face went white. "What are you doing, Cate? Put the gun down."

"I'm not spending the rest of my life in prison, Matt. I can't!"

He raised his hands. They were shaking. "Just calm down. Don't—"

"I have to be strong. I have to save myself. No one else will."

"You said you loved me, Cate."

"I do, Matt," she whispered. "That's why this is going to hurt so damned much."

Cate pulled the trigger. She watched as the bullet raced from the barrel and ripped into the center of Matt's chest. He went down.

Cate crossed to the other side of the room. She dodged her husband's body and stepped up to where Matt lay struggling on the floor. A thick, red stain was already soaking through his white T-shirt. Blood was starting to leak from the corners of his mouth. He wouldn't stop shaking.

"Cate..." Her name barely escaped his quivering lips.

More tears flooded her eyes. They fell down her raw cheeks. A sharp pain erupted in her gut. She thought she might be sick. Although her legs were becoming wobbly and she wanted to sit down, she knew she couldn't.

Cate couldn't go back now. She'd come this far. She had to keep moving.

Be strong.

"I'm sorry, Matt. I love you." Cate raised the gun again. She pulled the trigger one last time, and, just like before, the bullet entered Matt's chest.

He quit moving. He was dead.

The metallic stench of blood mixed with the dense smell of gunpowder and invaded her nostrils. Her head became heavy. She needed out of the bedroom. She wanted to go someplace else, someplace she could mourn.

However, that would have to wait, she knew. Right now, she needed to finish what she'd started. She didn't have much time.

Cate dropped the gun and ran to the wide oak credenza in the corner of the room. That's where she kept her jewelry box. She opened the first drawer and removed the small velvet holder. She lifted the lid and took out her favorite earrings: a dainty pair of pearls. Her mother had given them to her last Christmas.

She tiptoed back to Matt and placed one of the earrings in the palm of his hand.

Cate noticed now that her surroundings had suddenly filled with an odd, peaceful quiet. She liked it.

Next, she stepped out of the room and into the hallway. She stopped when she reached the round mirror that hung on the wall.

Cate peered into it. She didn't smile, and she didn't cry...she didn't even scream. She didn't do anything. She just looked at herself.

Maybe she was a cold-blooded killer. Maybe she was even a little crazy, somewhat broken, and damaged.

But, above all, she was a survivor.

About the Author

Cutter Slagle is the published author of several horror, suspense, and crime fiction works, including the novel *The Next Victim*. He currently lives in San Diego, California, where is working on his next novel. Discover more by visiting www.cutterslagle.com.

Made in the USA
Las Vegas, NV
06 February 2024

85368604R00146